SECRET UNDER PITTSBURGH

A THRILLER

JON KLEIN

SECRET UNDER PITTSBURGH

ISBN 978-1-7327141-1-3

For Conner Klein

ACKNOWLEDGMENTS

I wish to offer my heartfelt thanks:

To my son Conner Klein, for his unflagging love and belief in me, and for being the inspiration in writing this book. To Lisa Cheney, for helping me to see, and her guidance, love, and brilliant artistry. To Angela Klein for her friendship and patient proofreading. To K. A. Hunt LTC (USA Retired), for his incisive military expertise. To Lorelei Logsden, for her expert copy editing. To Jim Reidenbaugh for the crisp, professional photo. To friends Walden Hughes and Monica Hughes. And finally, to my parents Dr. Sanford Klein and Barbara Klein, for inspiring me to learn and achieve.

FOREWORD

If I told you a fantastic story, would you believe me? A story that could shake and rattle your definition of reality? Can I ask you a question? Have you ever experienced something truly bizarre, something that really scared you? Did you reason yourself out of the experience? Or did you confide it to a friend or family member, and then what happened? Did they laugh, give you that sideways "I think you're crazy" look, or did they believe you? Either way, you probably gained a hard-earned wisdom. You learned that most people don't want to deal with things that are beyond their comfort zone. If you have experienced something out of the ordinary, or at the very least, entertain the possibility of the unexplained, then you've joined a very exclusive club: a club whose only membership fee is that you keep an open mind. If we sat around the campfire and told our tales one by one, I think we'd find that many of us have traveled down the same strange, ethereal road. So my fellow traveler, hopefully you'll find some solace in what you are about to read.

This story never made it to the newspapers or the television nightly news. There's no use trying to Google it. You see, our government suppressed every bit of it. In fact, the world could easily dismiss this account of what happened in East Pittsburgh that fall of 1975, if it weren't for the seven mini-cassette tapes sitting in my office safe. It all started when my employer, the *Pittsburgh Press,* sent me to interview legendary industrialist Cecil Stewart. What began as an interview with him about his upcoming experimental artificial heart transplant, turned into a hospital-bed confession of a long-held secret. For reasons unexplained, Cecil Stewart trusted me—no, *picked me*— to share his tale. That lengthy interview and further interviews with those involved make up the material for the book I present here.

Honestly, I've gone against the wishes of my friends and family in writing this book, but it's going to take more than anonymous threatening phone calls to stop me. The public deserves to know what really happened in those woods, and this reporter refuses to be intimidated. Maybe by writing it down, I thought I could exorcise what has become my obsession, but yet it still haunts me. Sometimes, I wake up in the middle of the night drenched in a cold sweat, with an indomitable urge to head to those woods, and dig.

J ohnny Hawn was working hard and sweating under his faded Levi's jean jacket as he lifted another shovelful of semi-frozen Frick Park dirt. His arms ached, growing numb from the effort. Johnny's mind drifted as he thought about his dad's trips to Morocco. He pictured him caravanning across the parched, desolate African land, braving Morocco's jagged mountain ranges in the relentless pursuit of a rare, prehistoric fossil. East of Marrakesh, Morocco's southern mountains hold a treasure trove of dinosaur fossils, and it was there his dad had finally found his Mosasaur. Mosasaurs were giant meateating sea reptiles that roamed Earth's oceans sixty million years ago. Scientists believe the larger Mosasaurs were the most ferocious creatures that ever existed on the planet—a fifty-foot long behemoth that even the mighty Tyrannosaurus Rex would have feared.

Johnny closed his eyes for a second and pictured the two-inch long, sharp, amber-colored Mosasaur tooth his dad wore as a pendant. Thinking about his dad always put a smile on his face, and now it was helping to make the time fly. Then, without warning, *crack!* Johnny's shovel hit something solid.

"What'd ya hit?" Darren asked.

"Not sure, bro." Johnny looked up. "Maybe a rock or something. Ow! It stung my hands pretty good. Dang this cold!" Johnny jumped out of the hole he was digging and threw his shovel aside.

"Well, hold on, let me look," Darren said. "Maybe you got something."

The woods in Frick Park were damp and bitter cold this mid-October afternoon. The sun refused any temptation to come out from the smothering gray blanket it was hiding behind. The frigid air was starting to seep into Johnny's bones.

"I don't know how you can wear just a tee..." Johnny started to say as he watched his younger brother jump into the hole.

Boom, boom, boom . . .

"I wouldn't do that," Johnny warned.

Darren kicked his Timberland boot down. "Don't worry. Hey, it sounds hollow. Do you hear that? Hollow!" He flashed a grin as he continued stomping.

"Take it easy. Seriously, get out of there!" Johnny pleaded.

"Let me see!" Crayfish said. Mike Crawforth was the brothers' next-door neighbor and their on-and-off-again friend. Neither brother knew exactly who gave Mike the moniker *Crayfish*, but the nickname stuck. Crayfish was big for a seventh-grader, rotund, with an acne-scarred face. He had a natural aptitude for pissing people off, as he was always putting down somebody's mother, or trying to steal a skateboard. In fact, Darren's skateboard mysteriously ended up in Crayfish's garage, but that's a whole other story. Fortunately, Crayfish did have one great redeeming quality: he could play football. See, Crayfish had the speed of Hermes in those fat legs of his, and it never failed to astonish the neighborhood gang to see such a chubby kid move so fast. Crayfish's swiftness had rightfully earned him the reputation as one of the best street football players in Squirrel Hill. So the boys forgave his corpulence, penchant for theft, and his constant lying, just to keep Crayfish on their team.

"Yeah, check it out," Darren continued. "This whole thing's made out of wood. Looks ancient, man."

"Maybe it's a coffin?" Crayfish said.

"Ooh, that's freaking me out," Darren said. "What's it doing here?"

"Could be," Johnny said. "Wait. No, it's not a coffin. See? It's perfectly round."

Tap, tap, tap . . .

The Hawn boys loved dinosaurs, and they had a genuine obsession with discovering a fossil. They began by digging in their back yard, hoping to find a fragment of a petrified tree or at least a brachiopod. But the six-foot-deep trench they dug only yielded chunks of coal, a few bits of old brick, roots, and the occasional indignant earthworm. They dug during the summer and everyday after school, but after four months and a grave-sized hole, the boys realized they'd wasted their time. When their back yard proved barren, they decided to relocate their efforts. They decided to pay a visit to Frick Park.

It was Thursday, after school, and the boys coughed up a quarter each to ride the city bus from the corner of Forbes Avenue and Murray in Squirrel Hill, to the corner of Forbes and Braddock St. in Regent Square. It was two-and-a-half miles away as the crow flies, but the bus was way quicker than walking. They decided to enter the park's dense woods on the Regent Square side.

As they passed empty tennis courts and two vacant baseball fields, the boys took turns holding the heavy garden shovel they brought. They followed the Kensington Trail under the Forbes Avenue Bridge for a good twenty minutes, until Johnny led them to a small box canyon that cut into a hill on the right side of the trail. Two large boulders deposited by the last Ice Age, and a stand of massive maple trees obscured the canyon's entrance. If you weren't looking real hard, you'd walk right by it. A few years before, Johnny's father had pointed out the canyon on one of their hikes. Now, Johnny saw signs that the park's creek had recently flooded and eroded a section of hillside next to one of the boulders. Johnny's dad liked to say, "Look for erosion, where the water is or was, and that's where you'll find fossils."

"Hand me the shovel, Johnny," Darren said.

"Okay, here."

"I'm glad it's not a coffin," Crayfish said.

"It's not a coffin, guys, but it's definitely weird. We wouldn't have even found it if the creek hadn't flooded and washed off a foot of topsoil," Johnny said.

Just then they heard two sharp noises.

Crack! Crack!!

"Oh, shit! Get out of there!" Johnny yelled. "The wood's breaking!"

Darren grabbed his brother's hands just as the boards beneath his feet started to collapse.

Crack! Whoosh!

Darren dangled on the edge of the hole, holding on to his brother's wrists, as a giant black abyss opened up beneath him.

"Crayfish, help me!" Johnny screamed. "Holy shit! I got you, Darren! I got you!" But even as the words left his mouth, Johnny could feel his brother's wrists starting to slide in his grip. "Crayfish, now!" Johnny yelled.

Darren kicked his legs out and made a "Y" with them, helping to support his weight. "Johnny!" he screamed.

"That's it, Darren, hold on! Use your legs, dammit! You hold on!" Johnny was crying now, feeling his brother's arms slowly slip through his hands. He was losing him!

Crayfish dived to the edge of the hole and grabbed the collar of Darren's T-shirt.

"Fuck!" Crayfish screamed.

"Pull, Crayfish! Shit, pull!"

In a sprawl of arms and legs, the boys were fighting for Darren's life. Suddenly, they moved him up an inch, then two.

"That's it!" Johnny screamed. "That's it! Come on! Come on! We got you. Kick!"

"Ahhhhh!" Darren yelled. Then in one motion, the two boys managed to yank him past the rim of the muddy hole. They kept pulling until they'd all slithered a few feet away from it. Crayfish and Johnny released their grips, and the boys collapsed onto their backs.

"Dude, that was close!" Crayfish heaved, sucking in his breath.

"No lie," wheezed Johnny.

Darren didn't move.

"You okay?" Johnny asked.

"Holy shit," Darren said. "Holy shit!"

"Hey, Casper! I swear you should see how white your face is," Crayfish said.

"Shut up, whale-ass…" Darren said, speaking between gasps. "But thanks anyway for grabbing me. I think you tore my shirt." He smiled and gave Crayfish the finger.

"Anytime, butthead!" Crayfish returned the salute.

The three boys stood up and wiped the caked mud and leaves off their blue jeans. They gathered, pale-faced, around a hole that was slightly wider than a manhole cover. They felt a steady rush of warm air coming out of the void.

"Well, I guess we found something," Crayfish said.

"We sure did, knucklehead," Darren said. "We really found something. Boy, that was messed up."

"It smells," Johnny said. And it did smell—kind of like that sickly-sweet mothball scent in his father's closet. But something else caused the skin on his arms to pop goose bumps. He tried to focus on what was gnawing at the edge of his perception.

"You guys feel that?" Johnny said.

"Feel what, bro?"

"I don't know. There's something weird about this place. I can't put my finger on it."

"Oh, no," Crayfish interrupted, "Johnny's getting weird vibes! We'd better get a Ouija board!"

"Listen, *Crayfish,* thanks for saving my butt and all, but maybe you should listen to my brother!"

"Whatever, man. All I'm saying is, it's just a hole. Listen, guys, how about we throw a rock down there and see how deep it is? What do you say?"

"I don't think that's such a good idea," Johnny said.

"No, it's okay. Let him do it," Darren said. "Maybe Crayfish will piss off the dragon living down there, and then we can sit back and watch him get barbecued."

"Very funny," Crayfish said. "But I think you might wanna stop living in your fantasy world. Dungeons and Dragons is rotting your brain. There's about as much chance of a fire-breathing dragon down there as me catching a winning pass in the Super Bowl. It's probably just a sinkhole or something."

"A sinkhole?" Darren said. "Yeah, I read something about that in the *Encyclopedia Britannica*. They've got sinkholes in this place in Australia. These massive holes in the earth just appear all of a sudden. Scientists aren't sure why."

"That post sticking out there,"—Johnny pointed his finger—"that looks manmade. And by the way, we're not in Australia. This is Pittsburgh, Pennsylvania."

The two boys looked to where Johnny was pointing and, sure enough, sticking out from the mud and rock was a thick, heavy post set into the wall of the hole, about ten feet down.

"Yup, look at that." Darren nodded his head. "You're right. I guess this isn't a sinkhole. Man, I sure wish we had brought the flashlights."

"This should work." Crayfish held a cantaloupe-sized rock, encrusted with mud, over the center of the hole. "I bet this thing is way deep, so how about we find out?

Bombs away!" Before the boys could stop him, Crayfish's hand sprang open, and they watched the rock fall out of sight.

Johnny started counting. "One one-thousand, two one-thousand, three."

"Oh, man!" Crayfish yelled.

"I heard it hit bottom," Darren said.

"Me too," Johnny said. Let's see, it took just over two seconds." He winced. "I think I can do the math." He tried to remember the lecture that Mr. Hughes, his seventh-grade science teacher, had given the class a few weeks ago. It was all about how everything falls at the same rate of speed, independent of mass. Mr. Hughes spent an entire class on Galileo and Sir Isaac Newton, and though he was in the gifted program at Reizenstein Middle School, he couldn't remember the equation for rate of fall.

The first rumble of thunder startled the boys into looking up. Dark gray clouds swirled above them, and heavy raindrops began to pelt down from the darkening sky.

"Hey, I'll do the calculations at home," Johnny said sheepishly. "But I'm pretty sure that just over two seconds means the hole is somewhere between seventy to eighty-feet deep."

"Listen, guys, that's wicked thunder," Darren said. "It's gonna be a big storm."

"Okay, Einstein, you can figure out how deep this thing is after we split," Crayfish said. "I think we should leave now. You guys know I don't like lightning!" Crayfish glanced down at his shoes and then at the trail. His eyes filled with a nervous terror.

Johnny was still contemplating the physics of rate of fall, when a loud *clap-bang* of thunder broke his concentration. "Wow, okay, listen up. We're gonna need to find a board or tarp, something like that. Let's look around. We've got to cover this thing so nobody falls in, and so nobody finds it."

The boys fanned out through the trees in the woods, searching. Johnny and Darren stuck together and went up a hillside, while Crayfish headed down toward the creek. Pretty soon, Crayfish hollered, "Over here, guys!" Darren and Johnny ran down to see what he'd found, their sneakers kicking up leaves, and the brothers yelling in unison, "Crayfish!"

Sure enough, Crayfish found the perfect object to cover the hole. It was a large piece of plywood lying next to a miniature stone footbridge that spanned the Frick Park creek. Only problem was, the six-foot plywood plank was nearly fifty yards away.

"Okay, we're going to have to use some muscle to move this thing," Johnny said.

The autumnal forest was dense with sticker bushes, rocks, slippery black mud and an ankle-deep blanket of red, orange and yellow leaves; moving the board wasn't going to be a cakewalk.

"Pull, you lazy butt!" Darren said to Crayfish as they both struggled with the couch-sized piece of plywood.

"I am pulling, butt-munch!" Crayfish replied, evening up their insult score. Crayfish took the lead with, "At least I got pubes, girlie-boy!"

"Yeah, on your head, Crayfish," Johnny said, kicking a freebie in for his brother. "Now, shut up, you girls, and pull."

The three boys hoisted the board over their heads, looking like giant ants trying to move a mammoth chocolate bar. Their sneakers slipped and slid in the mud, but they avoided toppling over. Finally they passed the two boulders guarding the threshold of the box canyon. "We're almost there!" Johnny yelled. With a final burst of energy, they shoved it the last few feet up the trail and right over the hole. Pretty as you please.

"Okay, good work, guys," Johnny said. "Now we've got to find some camouflage. You know, I saw this movie last week, on channel four, where these three miners went digging up in the mountains in Mexico. After searching and digging, they finally found a mine that was chock-full of gold. The only problem was, the place was surrounded by bandits who'd do anything to get their hands on the gold. So, anyway, the three miners—and Humphrey Bogart was one of them—used camouflage to cover up the entrance to their mine. You guys know what camouflage is, right?" Johnny was talking excitedly, his hands moving.

"I know, it's when you make something blend in with its surroundings," Crayfish said.

"That's right. Anyway, the miners went around and gathered dead trees, bushes and rocks, whatever they could find," Johnny continued. "I think the movie's called *The Treasure of the Sierra Madre*."

"Hey!" Darren interrupted, "There's a big log over there, see it? Uh…maybe we could use it to put over the board. That would camouflage it, right?"

"Good eye!" Johnny said. "That'll work perfect. Okay, let's get it. If we hurry, we might make it out of here before we get drenched."

The boys ran down to the log, and made like ants again as they pulled it up the embankment, past the two boulders and over to the hole. They slid the rotted-out tree trunk over the plywood board, and covered the log with leaves to complete the disguise.

"Man, what were those white things under the log? Caterpillars? They looked gross!" Darren said.

"Those are grubs, man. Good eating." Crayfish smirked.

"Yeah, right," Darren said. "Let's see you eat one, then."

"Alright, you guys, settle down," Johnny said. "Cool it." He put his hands out, palms down.

"Can we go now?" Crayfish asked with a scowl on his face. "You know I have stormaphobia, and besides, my mom is going to kill me if I'm late for dinner!"

"Okay, we'll go. But one last thing: I think we should take the pledge," Johnny said.

"Ah, man! The pledge?" Crayfish complained.

"Yes, the pledge," Johnny said. "We have to keep this place a secret. We don't know what we'll find down there. Could be fossils, treasure, or who knows what. But if we tell just one person, then pretty soon everybody in Squirrel Hill will want to see it. We don't want that, right?" Johnny pointed at Crayfish. "So that's why we're going to take the pledge."

"Okay, whatever. I just wanna go home," Crayfish whined.

"It won't take that long, guys. Let's do it," Johnny said.

The three boys stood in a strangely intimate circle, their hands piled one on top of the other, as they quietly recited in unison: "I pledge allegiance to my friends and the United States of America. One nation, under God, indivisible, with liberty and justice for all." After it was all said, the three boys looked at each other and nodded. That was it. That was the simple oath that guaranteed their silence, and they only used the pledge for "major secrets," as they called them. What the boys didn't know, was that sixty years ago, three young men had stood in the very same spot and made a similar vow.

2

D octor Peter Hawn was spending his Thursday afternoon in the Rare Documents Conservation Laboratory at Charles Masters University, or CMU as everyone called it. His cafeteria coffee had turned cold in the regulated 64.4-degree temperature of the lab, and his cup was crying out for a microwave warm-up. Peter got up and exited the hermetically sealed door, happy to have a break from the unnatural environment of the "clean room."

Besides the low temperatures, there was the constant forty-percent humidity maintained in the room. Humidity levels were kept high, to prevent any shrinking or cracking of bookbindings or parchment. Lighting was kept movie-theatre low, because excessive light levels increased the physical degradation of paper, causing cracking and embrittlement. The low light was a real strain on the eyes. Peter had earned his fair share of aspirin-resistant, head-splitting migraines from sojourns spent in the lab, and he was trying hard to avoid one today.

As he set the microwave's timer to 45 seconds, Peter's thoughts wandered to his two amazing boys, and how his career had finally, truly established a steady course. Then his mind drifted to the sad fact that he and his wife were down to having sex only once a month or so.

Once a month! He thought. *How many times a day does the average man think about sex? Let alone in a whole month?* He was certain that he was at least average in that regard. Okay, if he was being honest, maybe quite a bit higher than average. As he approached his forty-eighth birthday, he still felt good, he still felt *horny.* But Laura had changed. She had gone through an early menopause, and though only five years Peter's senior, she had lost interest in their lovemaking. *Okay, stop it*, he thought. That's when he heard a knock on the window and saw it was one of his favorite graduate students, Amy Lee. Amy was twenty-four. *Very pretty and very young*, he thought. She was in the archeology master's program at CMU, though she could have easily pursued a career in modeling. She was beyond your normal attractive girl. She was the spitting image of supermodel Cheryl Tiegs, with a killer combination of an incredible figure, a sunny smile, and piercing blue eyes that never failed to turn heads whenever she walked across campus. She was simply gorgeous.

Amy opened the door. "Oh, hi, Dr. Hawn. Hey, I really enjoyed the last class about cartography." She nodded. "And I see we have the same fine taste in coffee." She laughed as she held up her own cafeteria paper cup, and then Peter laughed. He couldn't help but notice that Amy's shirt was unbuttoned, maybe one button too many. He got a good glimpse of the lacy white bra underneath her pale yellow camisole. Lately, he'd been paying more and more attention to this kind of thing. He thought even a mild breeze could give him an erection nowadays. On top of all that, he felt guilty that one of his students was the impetus for his hard-on. Was he becoming the stereotypical dirty old professor? That was a disturbing thought, he mused, but quickly decided it probably wasn't enough to deter his recently acquired perverted mind. He began to mentally undress Amy, and soon he had a steamy vision of her standing there stark naked.

"I'm glad you liked the class, Amy. There's so much to learn about cartography. I still feel like the perpetual student when it comes to that part of archeology. No matter how much I know, I realize there's so much more to learn. Don't tell the other students I feel like a novice sometimes." While Peter talked, he felt his penis start to deflate. Thank God, he had somehow managed to stop thinking about Amy in her skivvies.

"I won't tell. Yes, I know what you mean, Dr. Hawn.

Though I think I have a lot more to learn about archeology than you do," she said.

Amy loved the way Dr. Hawn was so self-deprecating. She thought he was very modest, especially for a man who had graduated from Princeton and had gone on to assist in some of the biggest archeological finds of the late sixties and early seventies. Dr. Hawn was fairly famous in archeological circles. His discoveries had been featured in issues of *National Geographic* and *Archaeology* magazines. He was one of the main reasons why Amy had enrolled in the master's program at CMU. She truly felt lucky to have him as a teacher, because Dr. Hawn had a wealth of hands-on archeological experience. She sometimes heard the other students gossiping about him. Mostly they were just envious, she thought. He had achieved so much at such a young age. She was sure he had his reasons for moving back to Pittsburgh and taking a teaching position at CMU.

"So why did you decide to settle down here, Doc?" Amy blurted out. She blushed a little at her forwardness.

"Well, that's a long story. Don't you believe what the students say about me? That I've lost my touch? Or, that I couldn't find an ancient needle in a haystack? Take your pick."

Wow, Dr. Hawn was being especially playful, Amy thought.

"Well, yes, I've heard the gossip, but I like to make up my own mind. I imagined you tired of all the traveling, or you'd had enough of the goat cheese in sub-Sahara Africa."

"Yes, it was something like that. It's a long story." He didn't want to get into the multitude of reasons why he went for the "meal ticket," as he'd described the job to Laura. "And to change the subject, what brings you down here?" Peter said.

"I didn't mean to pry, Dr. Hawn. Me? Well, you know my thesis is on Indian sites in Western Pennsylvania? I'm proposing that some of the old mining sites around Pittsburgh could have originally been tool sources for the cultures I'm studying. My hypothesis is that the Colonials needed flint for their flintlock weapons. They found out where the Indians were sourcing their flint, and eventually seized those sites for themselves. That would have increased tensions between the Colonials and the local Indian tribes, adding to their disputes over land and the fur trade. I believe flint was the straw that broke the chief's back, so to speak," Amy said.

"Flint, huh? That's interesting," Peter said. He thought she had the grounds for a great thesis. CMU's rare documents lab provided a unique opportunity to obtain that kind of information, especially in light of the previous year's donation of scores of boxes of seventeenth- and eighteenth-century documents from the Shafer Institute. Peter knew the magnitude of the treasure that Mr. Shafer had graciously given the school, because he was the first faculty member to review it.

"You know I started cataloguing the Shafer collection?" Peter said.

"I heard, and that's why I think we should get together and talk about it. That's exciting!"

He felt a stirring in his pants and realized she was turning him on again! Of course Amy was very attractive, but he was married. Married with a conscience. Married with two kids and a great career. He pushed the thumb of his left hand down, feeling his gold wedding band. He pushed down on it until it dug into his skin and hurt.

"Well, it was great seeing you, but I think it's time to get back in that refrigerator and finish up," Peter said with a tight grin.

"Okay, Dr. Hawn, it was really nice talking with you. I love your class, and I'll see you on Monday," she said to him as she played with her long, blonde hair. She turned and started out the door.

"Bye, take care," Peter said. He wondered as he watched her walk away, *Was she flirting with me? No, couldn't be. Even if she were flirting, I'd be the last to know. Wait, she did say she wanted to get together?* Peter always seemed to be the last to know when a woman had the hots for him. In high school, he had no clue that one of the most popular girls, Jamie Davis, had wanted to date him. Only at his twentieth high school reunion did Peter learn the truth about Jamie's crush. So did Amy like him? He thought it was possible. He had read a book on body language once, and he noticed that Amy always faced him directly. *That's one of the signs*, he thought. The way she played with her hair, that was further proof, wasn't it? *Well, if she likes me, then I'm flattered,* he thought. It didn't feel too bad. *It's certainly good for my ego. This girl could have any guy on campus in her back pocket, yet she's hot for me? Well, it doesn't do any harm if I just look,* he thought to himself. *Right? I mean, it doesn't matter where you get your appetite, as long as you eat at home.* He thought that sounded logical, if a bit cheesy. *Then why do I feel so guilty?* That was the twenty-thousand dollar question, he thought.

The answer was that he was still crazy-in-love with his wife, Laura. He had never stopped being hot for her. That fact alone really amazed him. It also was driving him nuts. For, in the past year, he practically had to beg Laura to touch him. And she used to touch him all the time. He remembered when they stained the seats in that rental car in Florida. How he couldn't help himself around her. But that was over ten years ago. That was a menopause ago. He pondered that depressing thought for a minute as he pulled his semi-hot coffee from the microwave. Whatever happened between him and Laura, at least he had two great boys to show for it. He loved Johnny and Darren so much, that sometimes it made his heart hurt. And then there was his work. He could always disappear into his research, anytime he wanted to. Those two thoughts comforted Peter as he re-entered the special documents lab, and began to forget all about Amy Lee.

3

"Man, I hate stuffed cabbage," Johnny said as he sat at the dinner table.

"Polish hand grenades!" Darren joked. Johnny laughed.

"Makes me fart," Darren added. They both giggled as their mom returned from the kitchen with another plateful in her hands.

"Here you go, guys. I know you love my stuffed cabbage and mashed potatoes! Be careful, it's hot!" She placed the steaming plate of food on a folded dishtowel.

Johnny thought, *Well, Mom, you got one part right.* He did LOVE her mashed potatoes, especially when she smothered them in homemade brown gravy.

Johnny had to admit that his mom was a good cook, a fact he came to appreciate from eating dinner over at his friend Dave Lample's house. Johnny helped Dave with his

Sunday paper route, and he often spent the whole day and night over there. He liked hanging out at Dave's house, but he grew to fear Mrs. Lample's cooking. She burned the eggs. She burned the macaroni and cheese. She used so much salt that it made Johnny gag. Yuck! Eating Mrs. Lample's gruel helped foster a real appreciation for his mom's cooking. When he told his mom that she was a way better cook than Mrs. Lample, it brought a huge smile to her face. Johnny learned something right then and there. *Women are competitive about their cooking.* Kind of like how boys were about playing football. His mom took just as much pride in making a killer omelet as he took in catching a touchdown pass.

The boys went upstairs after they had finished eating. In fact, they couldn't wait to get upstairs so they could talk about what they'd found. Johnny was particularly excited because he believed that they had stumbled onto an abandoned coal mine. All through dinner, he had been thinking about the hole. He was forming a hypothesis, because of what his grandfather had once told him.

Johnny and Darren loved listening to Grandpa Lou's stories about his growing up in turn-of-the-century Pittsburgh. He told them how each neighborhood in the city had its own gang. Pittsburgh's hills and rivers served to separate the neighborhoods and their respective ethnicities. Hardly anybody owned a car back then. Automobiles were a novelty at the dawn of the twentieth century. If you wanted to get around Pittsburgh then, you had three choices: you walked, rode your bicycle or took a trolley.

Grandpa spent the majority of his youth in the predominately Irish South Side. He managed to survive the gang fights and even served a stretch in juvenile hall. Once he graduated high school, he enrolled in a trade school downtown to learn carpentry. He worked construction all over the city, eventually saving up enough money to start his own building company. He worked hard to make his business a success, and soon Grandpa had the means to build his own apartment building. He named the place Dithridge Towers. Two buildings, each eight stories tall, but they might as well have been eighty stories tall to the boys. Johnny and Darren loved to visit Grandpa at The Towers. As soon as they got there, they would politely ask to see the incinerator in the basement. Grandpa always put on a heck of a show with that thing. He'd throw garbage and old newspapers in there, and sometimes on a good day, something bigger, like a chair or coffee table. The boys got swept up in pyromania, and they'd spend hours down in the basement, just watching things burn. When they got bored with that, they'd ride the old wood-and-iron freight elevator up to Grandpa's penthouse apartment, then back down again to the basement. It was one of those Otis switched-gear elevators, and it soon became the boy's amusement park ride.

Grandpa loved to spoil his grandsons, giving each of

them a pack of red licorice or a chocolate bar whenever they visited. Then they would sit down cross-legged on the carpet in front of his recliner and listen intently as Grandpa told them one of his elaborate stories. Tales about how he dealt with the Mafia in order to get the cement he needed to lay a foundation. How the unions were riddled with corruption and political derring-do. Grandpa Lou knew this guy and that guy, and his extensive group of cronies helped him get things done. "Time is money, boys," he would say. Sometimes his voice got quiet and sometimes he'd roar with laughter, and the boys could only shake their heads in wonder at how he survived each amazing twist of fate.

Johnny clearly remembered the most fantastic story that Grandpa Lou ever told, and it all took place right where Johnny and Darren's house stood today. The story went like this: The year was 1880. A man named David Clark started selling chocolates and confectionaries from a horse-drawn wagon on the North Side of Pittsburgh. Clark's business grew steadily over the years, until he introduced his masterpiece to the American public. The "Clark Bar" was an instant success when it debuted in 1886. It became the nation's new favorite candy bar treat, featuring an intoxicating blend of peanut butter, crunchy wafers, and chocolate. The "Clark Bar" earned David Clark a fortune. With money pouring in, Clark decided in 1888 to build a mansion in the fashionable suburb of Squirrel Hill. Situated on the East Side of Pittsburgh, 19th century Squirrel Hill was a scenic wonder of rambling woods and picturesque farmland.

As Pittsburgh's steel industry grew, many of its wealthiest families wanted to move out of the city proper. A majority of them headed east to Squirrel Hill. It was far enough away from the smoky steel mills that lined Pittsburgh's three rivers, yet close enough for an easy commute to the corporate offices downtown. Families like the Carnegies, Mellons, Fricks, Schenleys, and David Clark, chose East Pittsburgh to build their sprawling mansions. These families thrived in Squirrel Hill for the first half of the twentieth century, but by 1960, many of these large estates in Squirrel Hill were sold off, or in desperate need of repair. David Clark passed away in 1955, and the once great red brick Clark mansion on Beechwood Boulevard stood unloved and abandoned on its two-acre lot. The bank eventually foreclosed on the property, and Grandpa Lou bought it at auction. In 1963, he decided to demolish the Clark mansion, subdivide the lot, and build two modern homes on the properties. Lou's men brought in a wrecking ball to smash the upper part of the towering red brick manor. With the upper part of the house gone, they proceeded to dynamite the foundation. The boys listened in fascination as Grandpa told them how he personally set the charges. But he made a mistake and used too much dynamite. It blew a far deeper hole than he or his crew had planned.

When the dust cleared, they found they'd exposed an

abandoned mineshaft, six-feet in diameter and sloping downward at an angle of fifty degrees. Grandpa and his men stood there slack-jawed, as none of them had ever seen anything like this before. Grandpa told the boys that whenever a contractor wanted to excavate within the city limits, it was standard procedure to contact the Pittsburgh City and Allegheny County planners. Old blueprints and property maps were checked and double-checked to make sure that any natural gas, water and electrical lines were cleared. The mine Grandpa found predated the City's maps, and thus was uncharted.

Grandpa said Pittsburgh was built upon a series of rich deposits of bituminous coal, the kind used in the making of iron and steel. After the Civil War ended in 1865, there was an intense need for wrought iron and steel in this country and abroad. New technology such as the blast furnace, made steel production easier, faster and of higher quality than before. Pittsburgh became the leading supplier of steel for the nation's bridges, train tracks, ships, construction and more. Pittsburgh's steel industry flourished, aided by waves of cheap immigrant labor, easy transportation via the three rivers surrounding the city, and plentiful local coal and iron ore. Mining became a key industry in the area as the steel industry boomed, with coal and iron ore mines springing up all over Allegheny County.

As Pittsburgh grew outward, often these mines were casually abandoned. They simply dynamited the entrance, and then walked away. This left the inner structures of the mine intact. Grandpa Lou had been unlucky enough to run into one of those abandoned mineshafts that day in 1963.

"Hey, Darren," Johnny said as soon as the two of them entered the bedroom they shared, "I think I know what we found."

"Yeah? What is it?"

"I think it's an abandoned coal mine." Johnny's eyes lit up. "Remember the story Grandpa told us? About all the uncharted coal mines under the east side of Pittsburgh? Well, I think we found one—smack dab in the middle of Frick Park."

"Really? A mine? C'mon. It's probably just an old well or something."

"No, I'm pretty sure it's a mine. Remember the wooden post in the inside of the hole? They used timbers like that to reinforce mine tunnels. See, it's right here in the encyclopedia." Johnny had the 'L to M' volume of the *Encyclopedia Britannica* opened to the article on mining. They stared at the pictures together.

"See! That looks like what we found today. Our house even sits right next to a mine tunnel, so maybe there's more of them around here?"

"Coal? Like what we found out back?" Darren said as he reached in his nightstand and retrieved a fist-sized lump of bituminous coal.

"Yeah! Cool, you saved it. Smart!" Johnny said. Darren smiled and tossed it up and down in one hand, then handed it to Johnny.

"It's heavy, huh?

"Yeah. It's way heavier than it looks. Wouldn't exactly work in your slingshot, now would it?" Johnny laughed. "Imagine miles of that stuff! In the encyclopedia it says that coal is found in veins. Just like gold or silver. It says here that coal is used nowadays to fuel electrical plants, so our house could be powered by coal." Johnny was pacing around their bedroom now.

"Here, look. Here's some pictures of coal miners, and the machines they use," Johnny said, holding the encyclopedia. Darren nodded and reached again into his nightstand and pulled out a large stack of yellowed photos.

"Like this machine?" He was pointing to the top picture in the stack he held in his hands.

"Yeah, kinda like that," Johnny said while looking over his brother's shoulder.

"Hard to believe that this is right under our house!" He handed his brother the photos of the mineshaft that Grandpa had found. The boys pored over the pictures.

"Grandpa was cool," Johnny said.

"Yeah, check out his hardhat and that crazy machine he's on!" There was Grandpa, a younger, more serious looking and skinnier version, operating a giant bulldozer.

"Remember he told us it took them four weeks to fill

in that hole?" Johnny said. He added, "He doesn't look very happy in the picture."

"Why don't we tell him about what we've found?" Darren said.

"Hmm, hmm. That's a toughie. Well, I think we should wait. I don't think we should tell anybody just yet. For sure they'd stop us from doing anything, thinking we're just kids. We need a chance to check it out on our own."

Darren nodded in agreement, but he wasn't smiling. "What's wrong?" Johnny asked.

"I almost went down that thing today, Johnny. I almost got killed. That was a really close call. Do you think maybe that place has some kind of jinx on it or something? Like what we found was buried for a reason? Like a lamp with a genie stuck in it?" He paused. "What do you think?"

"I think you're being superstitious, but I'm not going to rag on you for it, because I'm the same way. Yeah, I got a funny feeling there too, but think about what we might find! You know, I read in last week's paper about Seattle and the Seattle Underground. There was this great fire in Seattle in 1889, and the entire downtown was destroyed. They ended up building a new downtown, right on top of the old fire-damaged buildings. Now there's this underground city in Seattle. What if we just discovered the Pittsburgh Underground?"

"Wow, that would be crazy! Okay, I guess you're right. We should keep it a secret."

"Good." Johnny nodded his head. "So I was thinking that we should get some rope and flashlights. Heavy rope, the kind they have in Murphy's Hardware. You know, the yellow stuff in the back, on that big spool?"

"Yeah, good idea." Darren said. "We'll need rope and stuff. But I don't want to go down there, okay?"

Johnny thought, *Boy, he really is scared.* But how could he blame him for that? Darren nearly fell down that hole today. He would've been hurt bad or killed in the fall. *Maybe we shouldn't go down there,* he thought. He had to admit he was more frightened of what they'd found than he was letting on.

"Well, it's our hole," Johnny said. Just you, me, and Crayfish are in on it. I'm not even going to tell Dave, because he's got a big mouth. Don't worry, I'll go down first, or Crayfish can go first if he wants. We're not going to play around with this thing, okay? We'll make it like one of Dad's expeditions. We'll be prepared. I've got seventy bucks saved up. That should be enough to buy everything we need."

So the brothers sat down and made a list of supplies to purchase at the hardware store. Before going to bed, they called Crayfish and told him of their plan.

4

D ave Rondinelli was in the middle of his seventh year working as a park ranger for the Pittsburgh Park Service. His cousin Vince had gotten him the job when Dave's musical career was cut short by an accident. Dave had been a pretty good bass player in the late 1960s. He worked in several tri-state area bands, and had even cut some tracks on a few local records. But it all came to an end one night after about a dozen bottles of Fink's Ale. See, Dave liked his alcohol a bit more than the next guy. And he was having a really good time at this one party, when this cute blonde girl in cutoffs, walked up and asked him if he was the owner of the pretty blue motorcycle outside. It didn't take long before they were flying down Forbes Avenue, his twin-cylinder Triumph hurtling them along at twice the speed limit, with the girl's arms wrapped tightly around his waist. Dave didn't know it, but fickle fate had decided to hitch a ride with them that night. Ten minutes later they were lying in a ditch, with the bike, Dave and the blonde girl whose name he didn't know, upside down in wet leaves and mud. Dave had tried to take a shortcut through the golf course next to Schenley Park. In the dark, he'd failed to see the 'road closed' sign and the thick steel chain stretched taut across their path. The chain cut through his motorcycle's front forks like a knife going through butter. The girl got a concussion, the bike was totaled, and Dave broke his wrist so bad that the doctors at Shadyside Hospital told him they'd have to fuse the bones or amputate. Dave kept his hand, but that was the end of his bass playing, the end of his motorcycle riding, and the start of his career working as a park ranger.

Dave was out in Frick Park that Friday morning, walking the trails and taking care of his morning chores—checking the fountains, picking up trash, and making mental notes of the seemingly perpetual maintenance projects he was in charge of. Dave loved working in the park, loved most things about his job, except his asshole boss. Tim Bruno was his name, and he was a narcissistic, elitist jerk. Bruno had taken his job description of general manager and turned it into a fiefdom, with him the self-appointed king. Physical labor was reserved for his loyal subjects—ahem, employees. That's why Dave received all the truly back-breaking projects: clearing trails, building cement bridges and lots and lots of painting. Bruno, on the other hand, almost never left the office. He was a pencil-pusher of the highest order. Dave loved that phrase, *pencil-pusher*. He first heard it in the Lynyrd Skynyrd song "Gimme Back My Bullets," and he thought the term described his boss perfectly. Bruno had been transferred to the parks department years ago from the city zoning office, but nobody seemed to know the reason for the switch. *Probably because the guy doesn't like to actually work,* Dave was thinking to himself. Anyway, when Tim Bruno wasn't jerking off in his office, he liked to frequent the Schenley Park Golf Club. It irked Dave to think about Bruno parading around in a golf cart, while the other park employees were up to their eyeballs in mud and sweat. *Pencil-pusher!* Dave thought.

So Dave was out on the trails today, walking the miles of dirt and gravel paths that wound their way through Frick Park, right in the heart of the city of Pittsburgh. Frick Park was three-quarters the size of Central Park, spanning several neighborhoods, from Regent Square and Edgewood, to Swissvale, and back up to Squirrel Hill. Six hundred and forty-four acres was a lot of territory to cover, but Dave enjoyed his walks. He got some good exercise while at the same time keeping Tim Bruno off his back.

Dave could see his breath "smoke" as he huffed his way down the path. The forest inside the park had already dropped half its foliage, the copper-colored leaves forming a thick, undulating carpet that lay neatly between the sugar maple, oak, elm and black cherry trees.

This morning, Dave was thinking hard about *her*. He had just begun working at the park when it happened. She was only thirteen years old when Dave found her lifeless body. The tune "Autumn Leaves" used to be his favorite song. Now, he hated to hear it because it reminded him of her. The thought *dead leaves* crossed his mind. *She was found dead, in the dead autumn leaves.* He thought about how old she'd be today, and shook his head at the thought of the bastard who'd snuffed out her life. Dave never told anyone that she didn't look real, folded up there in the gully. At first, he'd hoped it was a mannequin, an upside-down mannequin wearing a torn red dress. But what would a mannequin be doing in the middle of Frick Park, lying in a ditch? It's funny how the mind works, because while he'd hoped it was somebody's idea of a practical joke, Dave felt horror's cold, clammy claw reaching for his heart the moment he spied her. It *was* a dead girl lying there. When he touched her arm, her flesh was stone cold. He saw a crazy roadmap of blue and purple bruises covering her neck. He saw her yellow little-girl panties with the white panda bear print, torn and hanging off of her left foot. He felt dirty somehow, by being the one that found her.

But it didn't end there. During the following weeks and months, his coworkers teased him about it. They'd call her 'his girlfriend.' It took an almost superhuman self-control to stop himself from turning around and throwing fists and elbows. Some things will never be joke material, and a strangled thirteen-year-old girl was certainly one. Some people had no class, no clue, he thought. *Those are the kinds of people who need their asses kicked, them and those stupid reporters.*

Sure enough, news reporters were all over the park those first couple of days. But after she was buried and the police had run out of leads, the reporters stopped sniffing around. Thank God, he thought, because all he wanted to do was forget about it. But then he'd see her again, occasionally in a feverish nightmare, when he'd see her broken body ambling towards him with her arms outstretched. He'd wake up in a sweat, with his heart thudding in his chest. That terrible autumn morning would come flashing back like it happened yesterday. What an awful thing to wake up to. After one of those episodes, Dave would shake it off and remind himself to remember her as the happy-looking girl in the pictures on the TV news—the girl with the red hair, freckles and all-American smile.

5

D ave had 'exceptional vision,' as his optometrist liked to say. It was 20/15 in both eyes, and age hadn't diminished that one iota. *Eagle eyes*, he thought. He would have made a good hunter, except for the fact that he didn't like to kill anything. Even squashing a spider in the bathroom made him feel sad. He'd gladly spend five minutes carefully catching a house spider under a drinking glass, and then gleefully releasing it on his back porch. The Buddhist beliefs in karma and rein-carnation had really made sense to Dave. Every animal has the capacity for suffering, and humans are no more or less special in the eyes of God. Every animal had the right to live, just as much as a human.

Dave's enlightened philosophy dovetailed nicely with his job. He counted himself lucky to get paid to spend so much time in Frick Park, this wilderness within a city.

On this day, he did his usual once-a-week ritual of walking the trails, just looking around. "Damn litterbugs," he said as he bent over to pick up a crushed-flat Iron City beer can. And that's when he noticed the fallen tree in the box canyon. He damn well had the park memorized, and his memory told him that this particular fallen tree used to be next to the rock with the graffiti on it. The one with "Joe and Ellen 1968" scrawled in red paint on the side. Anyway, the rotting tree log had moved, he was sure of it.

"Well, it didn't move itself," Dave muttered out loud.

This was his favorite part of Frick Park, because it was the most remote and always full of wildlife. Dave had seen everything from white-tailed deer to giant garter snakes in the canyon. *Well, time to investigate*, Dave thought.

He hiked to the end of the canyon, and as he got closer to the felled tree, he couldn't believe his eyes. The old tree was neatly resting upon a piece of plywood that Dave had purchased at Monroeville Lumber Supply last week. He knew it was the same one, because he could make out the word "Property" of the "Property of Pittsburgh Parks & Recreation," and the department's unique logo. He'd spray-painted the stencil himself in Krylon's Hunter Orange paint. *Wait a minute*, he thought. *I know I used that board for the footbridge across the creek*. He could feel the blood rising in his cheeks as he thought about faceless vandals messing with his work. "That bridge is a real pain in my ass!" he said to himself. *First they steal a couple of my bags of concrete, and now they're moving boards around.*

"Freaking drug addicts! Juvenile delinquents!" he yelled to a startled squirrel watching him from an oak tree.

He inhaled deeply. *Okay, calm down, champ. No big deal, just move the tree, move the board back, order some more concrete and let the city pick up the tab.* He relaxed and felt his heart rate slow down. It wasn't his money, after all. Maybe he was getting wise in his old age. *You gotta let the little stuff slide, Dave.*

"Okay, I'll just move this bad boy off to the side," he said quietly as he lifted one end of the log and heaved it ninety degrees so it cleared the piece of plywood. "And you, Mr. Board, you are coming with me!" As he picked the board up and placed it over his head, Dave should have looked down. Instead, he rushed forward. And if someone had been watching, they would've seen the large hole reveal itself from under the board. Nobody but maybe the chattering squirrels saw Dave fall straight down, abruptly stopped by his arms getting pinned under the board as it re-covered the hole.

"Owwwwww!" he screamed. He was instantly in darkness. "What the hell?" he grunted. "Oh, shit!"

Dave looked up and saw sunlight leaking around the edges of the plywood. As he took in the darkness and realized he was dangling in an empty void, he thought, *a well?* His mind searched for an explanation, running through dozens of scenarios in a single second. Then the realization hit him over the head like the board he was clinging to. He remembered the legend that one of the senior park rangers had recounted while he was in training--a wild story about a lost coal mine in the park, forgotten after Henry Frick donated the land to the city. And he knew then that he was in deep shit. "Fuckin' mineshaft!" he screamed.

"HELP! HELP!" he yelled. But no one was going to hear Dave's frantic pleas today.

"Ohhhhhh," he moaned as he felt his arms getting crushed by the plywood board.

"SOMEBODY HELP ME! HURRY!" Dave screamed.

And somebody might have heard him, if he weren't stuck under a piece of plywood at the top of a secret abandoned mine tunnel in the most remote part of Frick Park on a quiet Friday morning. Nope, Dave was in real trouble, and down deep he knew it. His fused wrist started to burn as he desperately held on to the board. His mind flashed to the motorcycle accident and how he'd flipped over the handlebars, how his body went weightless as he'd flown with his arms outstretched like Superman until the brutal landing.

With morbid curiosity and frantic disbelief, Dave watched, bug-eyed, as his now completely numb hands slipped from under the board. The bits of light were extinguished as he finally let go, and Dave was swallowed from the surface of planet Earth, swearing like a sailor.

Dave awoke and groaned as he lifted his head. His

forehead was wet with sweat, his eyes burned. His whole body *hurt. Do you hurt in Heaven?* he wondered. *Could this be Hell?* As he struggled to open his eyes, he saw towering walls illuminated by a faint glow.

What is this place? he thought. A sharp pain in his right leg grabbed his attention away from the room, and Dave tilted his head down to look. He passed his glance down over his chest, past his nametag and the gold-and-blue Parks and Recreation badge, and to his groin, which to his relief seemed perfectly intact. He giggled at the thought: *Thank you, God, for not taking my nuts!* Dave looked lower to his legs, and saw something sticking out of his right thigh.

A jagged tree branch was somehow growing out of his leg. *I'm impaled on a tree branch!* he thought. Then he ran his hand over it, and he felt something slimey.

That's not a branch, ol' Davey, that's your leg bone! his mind screamed.

Compound fracture of the… he thought, and then he felt his breakfast start to rise up.

Don't barf, Rondinelli! His stomach inched back down.

Stay cool, idiot! Think!

"*FEMUR!*" A nausea tidal wave crashed over his brain. *I'm holding my femur in my hand!* He moved his fingers over the jagged edges of the bone, down his own thick ossein to the torn flesh surrounding the violent puncture.

"What the fuck!" he yelled.

"Damn it!" he screamed louder.

"Amit, amit, amit," his voice returned in a soft echo.

Some kind of underground chamber? he thought.

He swiveled his head to look behind him, and he saw what looked like a glowing, black *pyramid? What the heck? No, not a pyramid,* he decided.

His mind searched for the right word. *The Washington Monument is one. They're from Ancient Egypt...wait...I know this. Obelisk!"* It didn't make any sense, a glowing obelisk underneath Frick Park? What was this place?

"Why me, God?" he screamed to the ceiling.

Then Dave remembered. He reached into his coat pocket, the inside one, closed his fingers around the cool metal. *At least I didn't forget my trusty Zippo."* He took a deep breath.

Now, calm down, Rondinelli, you're freaking out. You're hurt, but try to think. He brought the lighter up and held it in front of his face.

Flick, flick. It wouldn't catch.

Flick, flick, flick, flick. It's not catching!

Flick, flick...vroom! "Ahh!" he said.

The sudden, two-inch flame blinded him. His pupils reflexively closed tight, then dilated back to reveal a view he wasn't expecting. His trusty lighter illuminated an immense hall! He guessed the room was as long and wide as a football field and several stories high. Shadows jumped up and down but Dave could see the roof was arched and smooth, with a perfectly circular hole near the middle, directly above his head.

That's the hole I fell through, he realized.

"This is impossible. This room shouldn't be here," Dave said to himself.

He struggled to lift himself up. "Owwww!!!!" he screamed as he turned over. He moved the lighter down over his leg, and the sight of his own bleach-white femur sent his head spinning on a merry-go-round. He closed the lighter's lid as he slipped into unconsciousness.

6

D ave awoke in what he thought was a dream. He was standing on a street on the South Side of Pittsburgh. He knew that because there in front of him was a giant electronic billboard that read, "Welcome to the South Side of Pittsburgh...home of Carnegie Robotics." He looked around and guessed he was on Carson Street, though the place seemed subtly different from the stomping grounds of his youth.

Suddenly, Dave heard a faint whir, and a car came zooming down the street. It had to be doing over a hundred miles per hour. The silver metallic car was sleek. Dave watched it approach like a little missile, and then *whoosh*! It was gone. *What the hell?* he thought. It was a perfectly sunny day, and Carson Street was usually jammed with cars. Jammed with people. But the street was completely empty of both. *Where is everybody?* he wondered. Dave thought back to the time in high school, when he got a part as an extra in George Romero's *Night of the Living Dead*. The Pittsburgh director had arranged for the South Side's streets to be closed down for certain scenes they were shooting. He thought, *What next? Zombies?*

Dave laughed. "C'mon," he said to himself as he started walking. He'd walked about a block when it hit him that whatever this was, it wasn't a dream. For one thing, he could smell the air. It smelled sweet, like if you could make purple into a scent. A silly grin pulled at the corners of his mouth. *I smell colors!* The air smelled so good! He couldn't ever recall smelling in his dreams.

He noticed he was sweating, and he could feel drops of perspiration trickle down his armpits. As he rounded a corner, Dave clamped a hand over his mouth. There, parked in front of him, sat one of those spaceship-looking silver cars! It looked even wilder than the futur-istic show car he'd seen at the car show last month at the Civic Arena. Walking up to it, Dave was slack-jawed as he studied it. For one, the wheels were humongous, about the size of manhole covers. They looked like over-sized chrome-plated dinner plates. They carried giant chartreuse-colored tires that appeared to be painted on the rims. The paint seemed to glow and change color from silver to light blue as he moved around it. "Toyota" was embossed on the rear bumper. *Maybe it is a show car or something,* he thought. He looked in the side window but couldn't see a thing. *Very weird glass*, he thought. Not tinted, but completely black, like a television turned off. All of a sudden he was blinded by a message flashing on the side window of the strange car. "Good afternoon, David Rondinelli...this is not your car. But it could be! Owner is asking $95,000 worldwide currency. Please touch the side glass to begin your purchase process." Holy smokes! *This car talks and knows my name*. Dave touched the side glass, and after a second, a message flashed on the television set-like car window. "You have $35,000,000 in your account, Dave. Please press your hand anywhere on the glass for finger-print verification." $35,000,000! Dave fell backward and looked down. Was he dreaming? Maybe it was some kind of acid trip, but again, it felt real. Where in blazes did that money come from? If you subtracted three zeroes from that number, that was exactly his yearly salary from the Park Service. Things were getting weirder by the minute.

He noticed a man approaching. *Maybe this guy can help me*. The guy was looking straight ahead as he walked. He seemed to be having a conversation with an invisible someone. *Oh*, Dave thought. *He's got a two-way radio*.

"Excuse me, mister." The man slowed his walk.

"I don't mean to interrupt your radio call..." Dave said.

The man replied, "Hold on, Bernard, I've got someone

in my reality talking about radios. This might be funny, do you want to hear it?"

"Can you tell me what day it is?"

The man laughed. "Did you hear that, Bernard? This guy is great! A real net comedian."

"No, really, I'm serious. Can you tell me where's the nearest gas station?"

"Gas station? This guy's so 2018," the man said out loud.

The man spoke in between bouts of laughter. "Listen to this, Bernard. Ah, sir, the nearest 'gas station' is in Monroeville. In fact, unless you've been living under a rock for the past twenty years, you'd know it's the ONLY gas station left in the tri-state area. You might want to 'fill up' there. Is your net down?" He laughed again. "Do you think you're immune from the emissions laws, sir?" Then the strange man tilted his head back and roared with laughter. Afterward, he walked away, still chuckling.

Dave turned and yelled at the guy, "I'd just like to know where a stupid gas station is, you jerk." But as the word "jerk" rolled off his lips, he heard a female voice in his head say, "10999 Washington Drive, Monroeville, Pennsylvania. Tram leaving from tram station number seven in five minutes for Monroeville, point-two miles or point-three kilometers southeast of this location."

Whoa, what was that? Dave thought. *There's a voice inside my head giving me directions? Hmm, I'm having the weirdest dream of my life, but alright, let's run with it.*

"Find the nearest McDonald's restaurant," he said.

The voice came again. "The nearest McDonald's is point-five miles or point-eight kilometers northeast of your location, Dave." The female voice was soothing, bordering on sexy.

Dave shook his head. The voice was clear and coming into his ears in stereo! He ran his hands over his ears, expecting to feel wires or something, some kind of headset. Instead, just behind both ears, he felt two match-head-sized bumps. They reminded him of the warts he contracted when he was a kid. He felt one of the bumps vibrate under his fingertips.

The voice said, "You have located your internal interface unit, do you want to run a diagnostic?"

"Okay, this is some very weird shit," Dave said to nobody. *What kind of dream is this?* he wondered.

"No, I don't want to run a diagnostic," he said loudly.

The sultry female voice responded, "Diagnostic aborted."

Dave kept walking until he saw a strange contraption that looked like a shiny shoebox that was sitting on a translucent four-foot pole. The box was made out of a shiny metal that gleamed with rainbow iridescence. He reached out with his right hand and touched the box. Suddenly a door on the box popped open, causing him to jump back.

"Wow, weird," he said.

Inside, he could see there were about two dozen

pancake-flat pieces of smoked glass, stacked one upon the other. He removed one of the glass sheets to get a better look at it. *No, not glass*, he thought as he flipped it over in his hand. *Plastic*, he decided, and then a voice rang out from the silver box.

"Thank you, Dave Rondinelli, for purchasing the *Pittsburgh Post-Gazette*, weekday edition. Ten dollars has been deducted from your net account. Good day." Then the box's lid closed automatically and the piece of plastic he was holding lit up like a movie screen. He watched in fascination as a date scrolled across the top of the small screen. Dave read the date, and a shiver ran down his spine. *October 26, 2045*. 2045!

7

A my Lee drove her Mercedes 280SL convertible along Fox Chapel Road, paying little attention to how fast she was going. The chilly October air whipped her cheeks a rosy red, but Amy didn't care. She loved driving her convertible, and she'd put the top down anytime it wasn't raining or snowing. The tires howled in protest as she met the apex, then accelerated out of each turn. She had a rhythm going, and she was enjoying stringing the turns together as her long blonde hair flew about. She passed a group of men playing football in Fox Chapel Park; they turned and stared, dumbfounded, as she rocketed by. She beeped her horn and waved. Then she noticed an Irwin County police car parked up ahead on the right side of the road. Amy pushed the accelerator down, and her Mercedes jumped forward.

"Hello, Fox Chapel PD!" she yelled as she passed the

police cruiser. She watched in her rearview mirror as the patrol car sat there.

Oh, the perks of being a Stewart, she thought. There were definite advantages to being who she was, and the ability to speed along Fox Chapel Road unhindered was certainly one of them. Her grandfather was one of the richest men in the world, and most people opted to stay on his good side, including the local police department. She pressed the gas pedal down until it touched bottom. She was running late to Grandpa's house, and he hated it when she showed up late. The inline six-cylinder of her "Merc" growled as the speedometer needle climbed.

Like most families, affection often skipped a generation. Amy noticed this in her friends' families, and it was certainly true of her own parents. The workaholic talented surgeon married to the beautiful blonde rich heiress. Rita and Jay Lee presented themselves bright and shiny to the public, throwing lavish parties instead of providing the supportive love that Amy desperately craved. Amy felt closer to her grandparents (at least on her mother's side) than her own parents. When she heard her mother tell stories about Grandpa and his cruel tirades, Amy ignored her. Mom criticized him for his ruthlessness in the corporate world and said Grandpa had taken control of the unions by using "dirty tactics." Again, Amy just ignored her, because to Amy, Grandpa was encouraging and gentle. When she was a child, Grandpa's visits were always full of laughter, gifts and candy. He never ceased to give Amy his full attention, which sparked a green jealousy in her mother. When Amy graduated high school from prestigious Linden Hall boarding school in Lititz, Pennsylvania, she returned home that spring to find a sparkling baby blue 1971 Mercedes 280SL waiting in the driveway. It even had a bow on it! That one really blew her mind. She had casually mentioned to Grandpa about wanting a nice car, and he went out and bought her dream car! That was over six years ago, but Amy never forgot how special she felt that day. Her Grandpa Cecil loved her, and that she was sure of.

Grandpa's eighty-fifth birthday was today, and there was going to be a big gathering at his house in Fox Chapel. The "house" was more like a castle, a huge sprawling complex spread out over ten acres. The best parts to Amy were the tennis courts and heated, indoor pool. Amy loved to swim there year round.

As she pulled past the gate at the bottom of the hill, security guard Tom Daley gave her a wave and shout.

"Looking sharp as ever, Ms. Lee. And, ah, if you get bored up there, I'll be right down here. You haven't forgotten about ol' Tom, have you?"

Amy thought, *Yeah, okay, Tom, not even if you were the last man on planet Earth.* During her early teens, Tom's attentions towards her began to step over into creepy. He began to follow her around, pretending to do odd jobs that just happened to be within ogling distance of young Amy. He'd appear at her side, drape one of his hairy arms over her shoulder and squeeze. One time she told him, "Move your arm or lose it!" Her outburst surprised her, and she happily remembered the shocked look on old Tom Daley's face. Right then, Daley's wide smirk transmogrified into a snarl, and she glimpsed the monster within. *You might fool everyone else, Tom, but you don't fool me!* She thought. She often wondered if she could get him fired. She fantasized about tossing a steaming hot cup of coffee at his crotch, or jabbing him with the sharp tip of an umbrella. Rich fantasies, but she had grown to hate Tom Daley. She knew her Grandpa and what would happen if he caught Tom harassing her. He'd fire the scumbag in two seconds. She thought, *Wouldn't that be a kicker? Justice served!* Oh yes, Amy had a very wicked imagination. But deep down, she was too full of 'nice' to pull off a stunt like that. Her mom's WASP etiquette brainwashing had produced the desired effect. Amy could produce on-demand a thin, taut smile, when every nerve in her body wanted to scream "No!" How she had wanted to scream, "You're the world's biggest jerk!" to Tom, and yet what came out was, "Oh, hi, Tom." Yes, she covered her anger with civility, but she didn't like it one bit. *Well, one day I'll just say it,* she thought. Wouldn't that cause mouths to drop and tongues to wag at the Fox Chapel Country Club? *Why do I care what they think?* Amy thought as she drove her convertible up the neatly paved driveway.

Amy had gone shopping in downtown Pittsburgh the day before, to her grandfather's favorite clothing store, Larrimor's. Fine men's clothing, indeed! She could always count on the owner, Harry Slesinger, to help her choose the perfect gift for the man who literally had everything. Harry and Grandpa had known each other for over thirty years, and Grandpa's elegant wardrobe consisted mostly of clothes purchased at Larrimor's. Amy ran up and hugged Harry, and they stood and shared anecdotes about Cecil for a while. Then she followed Harry as he showed her the finest clothes in the store. She walked out of Larrimor's carrying a gift-wrapped package containing one forest green merino wool sweater, a white cotton button-down dress shirt and a scarlet red silk tie.

Amy grabbed the birthday present from the passenger seat, careful not to disturb the big, shiny blue bow gracing the gold foil covered box. She stood in the driveway for a moment, and steeled herself for this gathering of her extended family. We don't choose the family that we're born into, and Amy certainly wouldn't have chosen the cast of characters she was obliged to call 'her family.' What irked her the most was their constant gossiping. They were a backstabbing, brutal bunch that waited until family get-togethers and the requisite gourmet hors d'oeuvres and expensive libations to unleash their verbal bile. Amy didn't trust them as far as she could throw them, and she knew that distance would be measured in mere inches due to their shared corpulence. *Blue-blooded brown-nosers, but brown-nosers all the same,* she thought. *At least Joe will be here*, she remembered. Joe was her wild-child cousin, who lived the jet-set lifestyle to the fullest. His passion was racing. Cars, motorcycles and boats, Joe and Amy shared a fascination with speed. He often called her from a Grand Prix car or motorcycle race, and his globetrotting had Amy struggling to keep up with his whereabouts. But Amy trusted Joe, because he respected her, and he was always real with her. He was her constant conspirator in a rebellion against their superficial family. She had a memory of Joe leaning over at one Christmas dinner and saying, "This sucks, doesn't it? Do you want to get out of here?" And they did. Joe took her to his friend's private Christmas party downtown at Lamont Restaurant, on top of Mount Washington. She was an awkward fifteen-year-old gangly girl then, yet she felt like a movie star walking into that gala, arm-in-arm with her tall and handsome twenty-one-year-old cousin.

Amy switched the package from one hand to the other to get her key in her purse, when suddenly the front door opened.

"Hi, Amy!" Joe greeted her with a big smile. "I saw

you drive up." They hugged, and Amy was relieved to see him. "So what'd you get him?"

"Oh, I went to Larrimor's and found this great green wool sweater, plus a shirt and a tie."

"Well, we know he likes anything that has to do with green, right?" Joe winked at her.

"Very funny. I got it to keep him warm. Winter is just around the corner. Somebody has to look out for him. He doesn't have many years left, you know."

"He's eighty-five today, but I swear he's the healthiest octogenarian alive! C'mon, you know I care as much about him as you do! Don't worry, he's going to be around for awhile."

"I know, I know, but I still worry."

"I understand. I guess I just try not to think about it. You know, he's got the biggest soft spot for you. The vultures that showed up today are jealous of you. You do know that, right? They're NOT members of your fan club."

"Yeah, well, just let them be jealous. Umm, where is he anyway?"

"He's in his office. Where else?" Joe laughed.

"Listen, I'll catch up with you out on the patio. I really want to have a few minutes alone with him on his birthday. Before the vultures swoop in." Amy flapped her arms.

"Right, see you out back."

Amy walked down the hallway to Grandpa's office

and knocked on the door.

"Grandpa, it's Amy." She listened. A few seconds passed.

"Oh, come in, child, come right in."

She pushed the antique wood door open, and there was her Grandpa Cecil Stewart. He sat in his wheelchair behind that huge desk of his, looking down at some papers. He was intently holding a magnifying glass under the Tiffany lamp's pale yellow light.

"Someone asked me tonight why I don't just retire. Isn't that the silliest idea, darling? Retire! Balderdash! I'm going to work until I die! As long as this old body keeps ticking along, that is. I like to work, unlike those good-for-nothings sitting out on my patio. Excuse my French. I don't work half as long as I used to, but I can still work harder than the bunch of them. They're waiting for me to die so they can get their inheritance—well, all of them besides you and Joseph. And you and I both know Joseph has only two things on his mind: fast cars and women!" Grandpa laughed. "I love Joe, and I guess I can't blame him, but he doesn't apply himself like you do. You are the joy in my life. Anyway, get over here and give me a kiss!" Amy walked over and put one of her arms around her aged grandfather.

"I love you, Grandpa," she said softly into his ear. "What would I do without you?" She turned away, her whole body heaving.

"Hey, hey now. Why the tears? You know I love you

too. You're my favorite! And look at you, my budding archeologist! Tell me about graduate school, dear," he said. "Any young suitors I should know about?"

"Oh, Grandpa! I don't want to talk about that stuff. It's your birthday!" Amy pulled her arm out from behind her back. "Happy birthday, Grandpa!" She squealed as she placed the gift-wrapped box in his lap. She watched his wrinkled hands fall on the box, his head bowed down, quietly looking at the present. Without saying a word, but muttering a few "hmms" and "ahhs," Cecil began to unwrap the package. Holding up the sweater, he said, "Oh, child, it's absolutely beautiful. And this tie is splendid!"

"I think about you all the time, Grandpa, our talks, and everything. I've learned so much from you."

The old man held on to the box and the sweater, while a poignant silence drifted between them.

"Well, you were the one who truly listened to me, even when you had to watch *Washington Week In Review* for the fortieth time, you listened! But, it turned out you didn't have a passion for business and politics. You fell in love with science. I always marveled at the perfect scores you brought home on your chemistry and math tests. You were a resplendent student when you were younger, and from what I hear, you are making a name for yourself at graduate school. Tell me all about your research, darling, please."

Amy frowned.

"What's the matter?" he asked. She continued frowning as she stared at the floor.

"You promised that you wouldn't spy on me anymore, remember?" There was quiet sadness in her voice.

"Well, I care about you, dear. I just want to protect you; that is all. I am not spying on you! Do not get paranoid, darling. I just care about you," he said.

"Who is keeping tabs on me at CMU, Grandpa?" Amy asked.

"Well, the president there is a good friend of mine. We had lunch a few days ago at Kaufman's. You realize I fund several large research projects at the school, and I like to know how my money is being spent. During lunch, I suppose I did ask a few questions about you and your progress. And yes, I did phone your department chair. Dr. Peter Hawn, is it? He said you are a rising star in the archeology program. He seems like a very nice fellow. Now is that so bad? Just to ask?"

Amy smiled. "No, I guess not. I'm not upset. I just get overwhelmed with it all sometimes. People think I have it so easy because…" She trailed off.

"Because you are a Stewart," he said flatly.

"Yes, of course." Amy shook her head.

"It's a blessing and a curse, child. Money is. Most people think if they attain wealth, then their problems are over. They can't imagine that along with wealth comes complications. Money opens doors, creates opportunity, but it can act as a kiln to forge the toughest enemies. It took me a lifetime to learn this, and now it is your turn. But you are proving yourself, and you will make your own way. I am so proud of you. So proud."

"Thanks, Grandpa. Thank you for always supporting me. I just wanted a few minutes alone with you, to wish you a happy birthday, to give you your presents, and to tell you thanks...thanks for everything."

"It's my pleasure, dear. My curiosity for life lives on in you. I can see that. Now, please, tell me all about your work."

"Well, right now I'm researching the source locations for Indian flint production. I have a theory that Colonial settlers commandeered these sites from the Native American population, and that exacerbated tensions between the two groups."

"That sounds plausible. Please continue." He watched her intently.

"Well, actually, Grandpa, you might be able to help me with a portion of my work."

"Sweetheart, what could I possibly do to help you in that regard?" he asked, looking surprised.

"Well, after doing some research, I discovered that our family owned several flint production sites in the eighteenth and nineteenth centuries. Is that true, Grandpa?"

"Yes, that is true. My great-grandfather, your great-great-great-grandfather, made his fortune through firearm production and flint supply, mainly supplying the Colonial Army under George Washington. Later on we diversified, of course, but the Stewart fortune started there."

"Grandpa, do you know if the company still has maps that show the locations of those flint sites? I'd love to find those charts and surveys."

"There was a time in my youth when I relished the fieldwork. In those days, I could have escorted you to every coal mine, steel mill and quarry that Stewart Company owned. But, the years have distanced me more and more from such things, and this failing body isn't helping any. As far as cartography, it's possible that some of the old survey maps have survived. I would venture to guess they are now over at Carnegie's museum. You see, a few years ago we donated pallets of old books and materials being stored in the warehouse on the North Side. I would recommend starting there, darling. Just be sure to tell the museum curator you are my granddaughter. I was an acquaintance of Andrew Carnegie's, and I'm a benefactor to the museum."

"Oh, thank you, Grandpa. I never thought I'd be asking you for help with my research. But I just did, didn't I?" She laughed. "What would I do without you?"

"Anytime, child. I am here to help you in any way that I can. Well, let's make our appearance, shall we? Are you ready?"

"I should be asking you that. Do you need a hand?" She pointed to the wheelchair.

"No, I have several year's experience in this motorized contraption, ever since your Grandmother Janet left us, god bless her. She was a saint, and a part of me died when she passed. But I've carried on. I've survived just about everything, now haven't I? But what is left of me—what remains—is still feisty!" he barked. "Don't you agree?" he whispered.

"You know what I think, Grandpa."

"Yes, I do. Well, let's go see that pack of wolves, shall we?" And with that, Amy escorted her grandfather to the patio.

8

The three boys walked side by side after they got off the noisy school bus. "Ring-around-the-rosies," Johnny sang, trying to break the tension.

They'd usually be tripping feet, elbowing ribs and shoving each other around. Today, though...today was discernibly different. Today they were on a mission to explore the strange hole in Frick Park. First, though, they needed their supplies.

"Hey, how much does rope cost?" Crayfish asked.

"They sell it by the foot, and it depends on the kind of rope you're buying. My dad bought some last year for our swing when it broke. Remember that?" Johnny asked.

"Yeah, I remember because I broke it."

"That's what happens when the thirteenth planet tries to ride a swing," Darren said.

"Hey, lay off him, Darren."

"Yeah, lay off or I'm gonna sit on you…wimp," Crayfish said.

"You're right. I'd get squished for sure."

A pause. "Well, I brought money, guys," Crayfish said. "I emptied my piggy bank. Thirty dollars and seventy-eight cents."

"Good, let me have it," Johnny said. He added, "I figure we're going to need serious cash for what we need. Last night I looked through my dad's books. I learned a bunch of stuff. One of the things was, 'You should always bring more rope than you think you'll need, because most likely, you'll end up using it anyway.'"

"How much rope?" Crayfish asked.

"I worked the math last night," Johnny said confidently. "That rock fell for just over two seconds. That comes out to twenty-five meters or about seventy-five feet. I figure ninety feet of rope should do it."

"Man, that's a lot of rope!" Crayfish said.

"Well, we can't take any chances," Johnny said.

"Can we carry that much?" Crayfish asked.

"The three of us can carry it; don't worry," Johnny said.

"What are you going to tell Murphy?" Darren asked.

"What?" Johnny said.

"What are you gonna tell old Murph?" He knows Dad, you know."

"That's right! I didn't even think about it. Hmm. Let me think."

"Oh, man, it's starting to rain again," Darren said.

"Tug of war," Crayfish blurted out. "Tell him we need the rope for a tug of war." The boys looked at each other and smiled. Johnny shoved Crayfish and he tripped on a crack in the sidewalk, his backpack coming off his shoulder and hitting the ground.

"Hey! What was that for?" He growled.

"That was for coming up with a great idea, dork." Johnny laughed. "That's what that was for! Sometimes you are such a dork, Crayfish, and sometimes you're like a little Einstein," Johnny said incredulously and with a smile.

"Really?" Crayfish said, swinging his red backpack over his shoulder.

"Yeah, but don't go getting a big head over it. Tug of war it is. That's the plan, and I think it's going to work."

"Yeah," said Darren and Crayfish in unison.

"Okay, listen up," Johnny said. "We don't go in the store together. I'll go in first, get the rope, and then I'm out. Darren, you go in and buy the flashlights and batteries. Umm, Crayfish, you'll go last and get whatever's left on the list. Cool?"

"Cool," Crayfish said.

"Murph won't figure it out if we go in separately. As long as you guys didn't tell anybody, then we're in the clear." Johnny looked at the other two. "You guys didn't tell anyone, right?"

"Of course not," Crayfish said.

"C'mon, get real," Darren said.

"Cool guys, just checking."

The boys finally made it to the hardware store. The rain was falling heavily now.

"We'll be next door at Baskin-Robbins. It's pouring out, and I need some ice cream," Crayfish said with a grin.

"Alright you two. I'll be over to get you." All of a sudden Johnny was pretty hungry for one of their banana splits. The whipped cream was his favorite part. But he had work to do, so he walked into the hardware store.

9

"Ummm, Cahah," Johnny coughed.

"I'd like to buy something," Johnny spoke as he stood by the fertilizer display.

"Can I help you?" old man Murphy asked as he walked out from behind a stack of paint pails.

"Ah, yeah. I need to buy some rope. Pretty good stuff, if you have it."

"What length do you need?"

"Ninety feet of yellow nylon rope should do it," Johnny said a bit weakly.

"Ninety feet—that's a lot of rope, son. I don't know if we even have that much in stock. What's it for? Hey, you're Dr. Hawn's kid, right?"

"Yeah, my dad's always in here. Anyway, I need ninety feet of rope. It's for a tug-of-war game that we're having up at Hunt's Field," He blushed, wishing he hadn't added the last part.

"Hunt's Field, eh? I used to play there when I was your age. I suppose you went to Whiteman Elementary, huh? Well, that sounds like good clean fun. You sure you need that much for a tug of war? You're not walking there, are you? Ninety feet of that nylon rope is going to be awful heavy. Is your father picking you up?"

"Well, he's at work, so I just walked. I'm pretty strong, you know. I started working out, Mr. Murphy. Look at this muscle!" Johnny flexed his bicep.

"That's quite the arm you have. Going to be the next Charles Atlas? Okay, hold on a sec."

Old Murphy walked to the back of the store and studied the spools of rope lining against the wall. There were six different types, starting with the thin tan-colored stuff and going up to the heaviest he carried, the bright yellow nylon rope that Johnny wanted.

"Tell you what, it looks like I have exactly ninety feet of that yellow nylon rope," he shouted. "It's your lucky day."

"I'll take it."

Murphy pressed the eraser side of a pencil to his temple.

"Let's see, ninety feet of heavy rope, at thirty cents a foot. That comes to twenty-seven dollars plus the governor's share, and the tax is one dollar and sixty-two cents.

Twenty-eight sixty-two is the total. Do you need a hand with that?" Murphy looked concerned.

"Ah, nah. I can manage," Johnny handed over a wad of crumpled cash. Murphy rang him up, and Johnny stuffed the change and receipt in his pocket and slung the oversized coil of rope over his head. "Thanks again."

"See you soon, son."

Johnny walked next door to the Baskin-Robbins and peered through the store's window. Darren and Crayfish were sitting in the back, laughing and stuffing their faces with banana splits. Johnny stuck his head through the door and yelled, "Hey, c'mon. It's your turn." He raised his voice and yelled again, "Hey, c'mon, guys, let's go," before they stopped chomping on their sundaes.

It was Darren and Crayfish's turn, and Johnny hoped that they'd stay cool and not say too much to Mr. Murphy. After all, things were going as planned. After fifteen anxious minutes, Darren strolled out of the hardware store holding a large paper bag. Inside were three waterproof heavy-duty flashlights with three big 6V batteries with the springy-things on top. Next it was Crayfish's turn. After a short while, he came out, holding his own shopping bag and wearing a big grin.

As they walked down Forbes Avenue toward the park, they agreed to stop at Crayfish's house. After all, it was on the way. They needed to empty their backpacks of school stuff and refill them with the newly bought supplies. They switched out their backpacks, then headed into Crayfish's garage. They grabbed two large shovels that Crayfish's dad had bought the year before. They had sturdy, white oak handles and looked brand new. Then they set off to raid Crayfish's kitchen. Twinkies, Ho Ho's, Keebler cookies and cans of V8 juice were pilfered and placed into their backpacks. Then they filled up the canteens in the kitchen sink. The boys were ready. Their next stop: Frick Park.

"We got plenty of food in case something happens, like a cave-in," Johnny said matter-of-factly.

"What?!" Crayfish gasped.

"Don't spaz!" Johnny shot back. "Just in case. You know how Charlton Heston had that gun in *Planet of the Apes*, the first one?"

"Yeah, that was cool," Darren said.

"See, he didn't go into the Forbidden Zone unprepared. And guess what, we're not either. See, that's what I'm talking about."

"You think there's a Forbidden Zone down there?" Crayfish asked.

"Better not be," Darren said, his face clearly worried.

"Of course there's no Forbidden Zone! There's nobody down there with the tops of their skulls missing, people with ESP that worship a giant nuclear bomb. Now, that would be crazy, wouldn't it?" Johnny laughed. "But we're prepared. We got rope, food, water and shovels, and just in case, just in case, we brought a secret weapon. Just like my hero, Charlton Heston," Johnny said with a wink.

"Yeah, we brought the Wrist Rocket!" Darren said proudly.

"That thing's wicked. Can I see it?" Crayfish squealed.

"No way," Johnny said. "You can't handle it. Remember the cherries?"

"How could we forget?" Darren said.

The boys had been playing in Crayfish's front yard last summer, lobbing cherries at passing cars, when Crayfish had thrown one at one of their "off limit" cars—a white Chevrolet Caprice Classic. They had deduced by trial and error, and the many foot chases that ensued, that only borderline psychos or undercover cops drove white Chevrolet Caprices. Crayfish had ignored all this hard-won common sense when he hit the driver's side window of an off-duty policeman's white Chevrolet Caprice! The boys watched incredulously as the guy slammed on his brakes, jumped out of his car and started hoofing it after them. Darren, being the youngest and slowest, was the one who got caught. Johnny and Crayfish watched from a hiding spot below the Smiths' front porch as the cop dragged poor Darren down the sidewalk.

"Let me go! Let me go! I'm just a kid!" Darren screamed.

Incredibly, the crazed cop released his grip on Darren's shirt. He did a lot of finger-pointing and yelling, then he calmly got in his car and drove away. Johnny and Crayfish couldn't believe it: Darren had successfully played the little kid pity card! Ever since, the event had become a sore spot with Darren, as he never forgave Crayfish for being so reckless with those damn cherries.

"I'm not going to fire it, I just wanna see it. Okay? I promise." Crayfish persisted.

"Okay, here it is. I don't even know why I'm being nice to you." Darren pulled the slingshot out of his bag and held it up for a second, pulling back the little leather pouch. "Don't mess with the best," he exclaimed. Then he handed it over.

"Wow, thanks, guys. You know, I had a slingshot once. I won it when my uncle took me to Kennywood. It was made out of balsa wood. It broke the first time I used it. It sucked," Crayfish said while examining the Wrist Rocket. "But this...this is cool! This is a genuine weapon! This thing could hurt someone!" he shouted. "Okay, I feel better now. The bottom of Frick, sometimes it gives me the creeps."

"Well, we're here," Johnny said. The three boys stood under the large brownstone arch that framed the west entrance to the park.

"I wonder who built the gate?" Johnny added, pointing to the "Frick Park 1885" emblazoned in cast-iron letters above them.

"Who knows?" Darren said as he ran under the arch. "It sure is old." Turning around, he said, "Hey, what do you think we'll find down there?" Do you think there's treasure?"

"Could be anything down there. Probably nobody's been down there for a hundred years. Sounds like a Hardy Boys mystery, huh? I'm the one going down that hole today," Johnny said, staring stone-faced at the other two. "I'm not kidding."

"Okay, I'm coming along, but your brother is crazy, Darren. I wouldn't go down that hole for all the Klondike Bars at Islays."

"How about I buy you a Klondike Bar at Islays, when we're done?" Johnny said.

"Deal," Crayfish said

"I want one too!" Darren shouted

"Alright, one for you too!" Johnny said.

The three boys still stood under the stone arch at the park's entrance. "Careful with the shovels, guys. My dad will get sore if he finds out we used them."

"Well, of course we're gonna use them. I think what you're trying to say is don't throw them on the ground like this." Darren threw his shovel down.

"Son of a biscuit! Seriously! Be cool," Crayfish pleaded.

"Darren, don't start up with him, okay?"

"I haven't forgotten about the cherries," Darren said sharply.

"Enough with the cherries! I said I was sorry about forty times!"

"Okay, you two. Cool it!" Johnny ordered.

"Hey, guys, did you hear the one about the constipated mathematician?" Crayfish asked. "He worked it out with a pencil!" They all laughed.

"Awww, man, that's nasty!" Darren said.

"Gross," Johnny joined in. "That was foul!" The boys shook their heads and giggled. The humor helped push back the fear, helped take their minds off the "what if"s. Chitchat seemed to work, too, so the boys debated the Steelers' current player roster, relived scenes from the movie *Earthquake*, and argued whether or not Bruce Lee could kick Muhammad Ali's ass. They started walking down the pea gravel trail, shovels slung over their shoulders, their overloaded orange, red and yellow backpacks swinging. If they broke into song, they would have looked like three of the Seven Dwarfs. Instead, they just kept talking as they finally disappeared into the canopy of trees.

10

YEAR 1914

"I'm glad to be rid of it!" Cecil Stewart said to his two friends. "Glad and relieved!"

"How can you say that? You know what it's done for us. Sacrifices have to be made in any venture that's worth a damn!" Charles said, almost shouting.

Cecil respected Charles Shafer, even if he was irritated by his friend's obvious cold-hearted ruthlessness.

"I agree with Cecil," echoed William "Bill" Nollem. "While it has given us gifts, it's become too dangerous. Let's not forget the side effects." Bill unwound the wire from the spool as he walked backward, straightening the plain silver wire as he went. He was eighty yards from the entrance of the mine when he turned and spoke, "Does everyone have their wax in? This one is going to make some noise."

"Sometimes I have nightmares," Charles said. "Does that sound familiar, Cecil?"

"I did not see what you saw, Charles. You know that. For reasons unknown, it has affected each of us differently."

Charles looked at his friend and wondered, *Is that the whole truth?*

"I'm going to go check the charges one last time. I won't be long," Bill said. Cecil watched him enter the mine tunnel.

"I was waiting to tell you this, Charles. Bill confessed to me a dream where he witnessed the deaths of his children. He is convinced that what he saw was real, and he is haunted by what The Pulpit showed him." He paused. "Maybe there are things we were never meant to know," he said with a hushed voice. "We have managed to reach into God's palm, and I fear the information we have snatched from it."

Charles stood there and considered Cecil.

"Like Eve in the biblical garden, we lost our innocence through our quest for knowledge. This serpent is a very seductive beast. How far has the snake led you out of the garden, Charles?"

"Far enough that I cannot smell its flowers nor the sweet scent of its apple tree."

"Enough! We are going to bury this dragon today, by God!" Cecil said. "It will no longer tempt us with its glimpses of the future. May the good lord help us forget we ever found this horrid place."

Bill returned, "Okay, all the charges are set. A case of nitroglycerin should do nicely. I've got the blasting box located behind that large boulder. We tried to destroy it, but having failed that, let us bury this place like an unmarked grave!" Bill shook his fist in the air. "Have ye want for one last look? Remember, though, gentlemen, to keep your distance. See that white chalk line? Stay behind it!"

"The Pulpit's powers we will never partake of again!" Cecil shouted.

"It is somewhat a shame. Are you not the least bit curious how The Pulpit induces narcolepsy, how it heals the body, or our time-traveling dreams? Perhaps it is capable of even more? Our highly paid *geniuses* couldn't decipher the symbols. I would think that you, above all else, would want to continue our investigations."

"No, I am resolute on my decision, Charles. It is true, I have seen much, but I fear at what cost? Look at what it's done to Bill." Cecil spat on the ground.

11

The three young men stood in the giant cavern, staring in awe at The Pulpit. A fitting description for the towering obelisk standing on the far side of the room, with its perfectly symmetrical dimensions, made out of an indestructible glass-like material. It was October 13, 1913, when it was discovered by accident. Charles's men were drilling, exploring a coal seam, when it happened; the foreman and his crew of soot-faced miners were shocked when their steam-driven hammer punched through into a strange cavern. At first, they thought it was just a cave, perhaps one chamber in a rambling, limestone cave system that might've stretched for miles. They instead found a strange, glowing obelisk standing defiant in a single, symmetrical domed room. It nearly caused a mass panic among the superstitious, predominately Irish, miners. They gave it the nickname "The Devil's Lantern," and refused to tread near it. That's when the worried foreman decided to call his boss, Charles Shafer. When the young industrialist arrived, he too was flabbergasted by their discovery. Charles gathered his men, and promised double overtime pay to those who would remain and work. A small contingent agreed to stay and install wooden posts to reinforce the access tunnel, though they all made the sign of the cross and warily kept their distance from the glowing device.

Charles was instantly fascinated by the grandeur of the underground room, and of course the mysterious obelisk. It reminded him of an Egyptian burial chamber. Since his youth, he had devoured books on Egyptology, and had successfully petitioned his parents for a trip to Cairo for his sixteenth birthday. Once he landed in that capital city, he set off to explore the Great Pyramids. Viewing pictures of the structures in textbooks was one thing, but witnessing the pyramids' magnificence in person was quite another. Charles found the pyramids were mostly unattended and unguarded. He didn't squander his chance, visiting them every day of his vacation, writing and sketching in his leather-bound notebook.

Soon Charles met and befriended a young British Egyptologist named Edward Matthew Petrie. Charles had lucked into meeting a worthy mentor, and Petrie in turn had found a wealthy benefactor. In return for arranging a meeting with Charles' parents, Petrie allowed him to accompany him on his excavations. The most fantastic of which was the giant burial chamber of King Ramses II. He and Petrie spent several days underground, studying every inch of the fifty-yard-long royal chamber. He marveled at the painted reliefs that wrapped around the room, their vivid blues, reds and greens born from the minerals azurite, iron oxide and malachite.

Incredibly, the room containing The Pulpit dwarfed King Ramses' burial chamber. The workers measured it close to an acre, and two-stories high. But this enormous hall was devoid of murals; instead, it seemed to function solely as a vessel for the monolith. The glowing obelisk stood twelve feet tall at one end of the room. It radiated a soft, kaleidoscope of light. Made from a strange material that resembled smoked glass, most of the surface was perfectly smooth, except for strips along the sides with tiny, raised symbols. Charles brought in engineers, metallurgists and chemists, and they performed various tests, yet after a fortnight of work, they could only report, "It's harder than diamond and impervious to our attempts to dismantle it."

Charles hoped the strange pictographs on the obelisk could be translated. He made charcoal rubbings of the markings and sent copies via transatlantic cable to his old friend Edward Petrie in Hampstead, England. "Shocking to say the least, and pre-Sumerian at best," came his reply. "What source?" Petrie asked in his cable. Charles never sent a reply.

12

A fter the first feverish dream that came the night after the discovery, Charles telephoned Cecil and Bill, and informed them of what he'd found. He attempted to describe the room and the obelisk in great detail, but found his voice rising and cracking, his adjectives too small and weak to adequately convey the enormity of his find. Then he told them all about his dream. Charles described the experience as feeling incredibly real, more like a "trip to the future than a dream," he'd said. He consciously slowed the metronome of his voice as he recalled seeing the U.S. stock market values plummet on October 29, 1929. He told Cecil and Bill that he had held the newspapers of that day in his hand, that there would be a "Black Thursday" and a "Black Tuesday." He saw downtown Pittsburgh clogged with haggard-looking men standing in mile-long unemployment lines, and a stock market on a downward slide for *years!* Charles was shocked that his two friends withheld their skepticism; instead, they both listened intently, then demanded to see firsthand this "obelisk." *Ah, good old Bill Nollem and Cecil Stewart*, Charles thought. *They actually listened, embracing the news without cynicism.* Charles gladly invited both of them to the chamber the following day, and that's when his friends joined in Charles's slack-jawed incredulity.

He and his friends spent that entire day in the chamber, and it was then and there that Bill had christened it "The Pulpit." It was true that the obelisk had a platform at its base that seemed to function as a type of gangway, and when the men stood there with their hands outstretched, touching the monolith, one could say they looked like they were praying to it. The epithet stuck, and they called it that ever after.

Later that same day was when the strangeness began. All three friends started experiencing an intense lethargy, but it was Bill who fell sound asleep while crouched on The Pulpit. Charles and Cecil carried him through the access tunnel to the outside woods.

"The fresh air will rouse him," Charles said, but it did not.

They tried to wake him by means of shaking and then even splashing cold water on his face, but he stayed frozen in slumber for several hours. When he awoke at nightfall, on his own accord, he reported having a futuristic dream much like Charles's. He described seeing a tiny movie screen that was dubbed "television." He witnessed a sleek craft flying overhead that was called a "jet airplane." Bill and Charles sat outside the mineshaft, excitedly comparing notes. They concluded their similar surrealistic journeys went far beyond the typical nighttime dream. They were convinced they'd been time traveling to the future. Cecil stood and listened to his friends as they elucidated on every single detail of their "trips." Cecil was both fascinated and secretly jealous of his friends' experiences. He wanted to see what they had seen. He needn't have worried, because that very night after Cecil returned home, he took his own "trip." While sitting in his office, warmed by the steady blaze in his fireplace, Cecil succumbed to The Pulpit's narcoleptic effect. He was transported into the future, just as his two friends had been. Cecil saw a great war not too distant in the future (he saw bolt-action rifles of familiar design), and then he, too, saw the stock market's decline, just as Charles had. He saw the advanced airplane with no propellers, just as Bill had seen. His fantastic voyage concluded with Cecil standing in the midst of a political rally. He watched, transfixed, surrounded by tens of thousands of Germans with outstretched right arms, as they cheered a diminutive, dark-haired, mustached man who was giving a particularly fevered speech. He listened as the man on the podium shouted for "German expansion." Cecil woke up in his armchair, drenched in sweat, the sunrise's reddish light glaring into his wooly eyes. A feeling of dread crept through his body as he remembered the terrible events he'd witnessed, and then, in turn, an opposite state of wonder overcame him as Cecil recalled the airplane with no propellers. He focused on the telephone that had been recently installed in his office. *This is just the beginning*, he thought. *Is this a curse, or a gift?* he wondered. Cecil stood up and poured himself half a tumbler of single malt scotch. He swallowed a mouthful and felt the comforting burn of the peaty scotch shoot down from his throat into his stomach. The alcohol did little to comfort him, so he went to the telephone. He didn't care what time it was, he needed to speak with Bill and Charles. Cecil thought with some satisfaction that at least he wasn't alone in this. Together with his two friends, he was sure they would devise a logical plan of action and proceed forthwith. He took a deep breath as he picked up the black telephone handset and got a very sleepy-sounding switchboard operator. Cecil waited to be connected to Bill.

The two friends listened to Cecil's retelling of his dream, and they agreed to meet that morning. It was there that Charles first proposed the idea of using The Pulpit's strange powers for economic gain. "What if...?" Charles began his speech about their glimpses into the future, and how they should record the details of their experiences. In particular, they would try to gather as much information as they could about this upcoming Great War. Charles reminded them that tensions were high in Europe at the moment, and if they knew particular logistics of this upcoming conflict, then they would invest their monies appropriately. Charles expanded on the stock market crash they'd seen. That was a longer-term proposition, but one he was convinced would bring them even greater wealth. Charles, Cecil and Bill agreed to the plan. The following months went by in a blur as the three friends took turns slumbering, notating and exploring the future.

At first, it was fun. They'd meet at the mine's entrance in the morning carrying picnic baskets loaded full of gourmet food. They brought folding chairs and small writing tables, which they carried into the chamber and placed around The Pulpit. They brought lanterns and note-books and writing pens, and even pillows. They saw it all as an adventure, as a golden opportunity. They each fell into sleep at different rates, but when they awoke, they each duly went to their writing desks and recorded what they saw.

They cataloged the events leading up to this war, which they found historians named "World War I." They recorded what companies profited from the war, their stock market prices before, during, and after. They paid particular attention to the Pittsburgh companies that bene-fited the most. Often they'd fall asleep on or near The

Pulpit, but eventually they'd stumble out of the mine tunnel into daylight or night. Their notebooks soon grew full of facts, full of details of a future that was both horrible and wondrous. They should have been happy, as they achieved what they set out to do. But as their mind travels progressed, Cecil and Bill both witnessed events that left them anything but. Cecil attended the future funeral of his newlywed wife. He experienced what it felt like to be in love, and then the horror of losing this incredible woman to influenza.

Bill experienced his future family, a gorgeous wife and three kids. He came to know the unexpected joys of marriage and fatherhood, only to be laid waste when his wife and adorable children perished in a house fire. Cecil and Bill suffered a rapid, rancid insomnia that slowly ate into their sanity. They soon began to want to rid themselves of The Pulpit, but Charles objected. He stated his case like a clever trial attorney: he was immune to the troubling visions, so perhaps he alone should continue their work. Besides, he argued, The Pulpit was an archeological treasure like the Great Pyramids of Giza, a gift to mankind that had deserved to be examined by experts like William Petrie. Bill and Cecil confronted Charles and waved their heavy notebooks filled with future facts in front of his face.

"There is enough information contained in these three books to make a hundred men richer than Rockefeller. Forget Petrie!" Cecil said.

"He's right, Charles. We achieved our goal; we have what we came for. We've spent the last ten months gathering our precious information. This...thing... It's too powerful for men of our time. The world should be protected from it. I don't know what it is, but it's somehow infected Cecil and me. You seem immune at the moment, but that might not last. I vote to destroy it!"

There was nothing Charles could do; his determined friends neatly outvoted him. He reluctantly went along as they devised a plan to destroy The Pulpit.

At first they tried to burn it with gasoline, yet it remained shiny and unaffected. They brought in acetylene torches that could slice through armored steel plate like a hot knife through butter, yet they failed to even scratch the obelisk. They tried moving it using chains and a giant steam engine, but it sat unmovable. They decided on explosives next, and Bill ringed The Pulpit with nitroglycerin. The blast sent a massive shockwave down the mine tunnel, and they thought, *Nothing could survive that*! They waited for the dust to settle, then shook their heads when they saw The Pulpit standing there unscathed, and its chamber undamaged! It was as if the charges had never detonated; only the lingering smell of nitrate gave proof of the blast. Bill suggested if they couldn't destroy it, then they could at least bury it by blowing the access tunnel to the chamber. Afterward, they'd landscape the area and hide their secret forever. They all agreed; if they couldn't destroy The Pulpit, then by God they'd bury it.

Ah, the secrets that will be buried in this place—theirs and ours, thought Cecil. *Theirs and ours!*

"Alright gentlemen, let's move and take cover," Cecil said.

The three men crouched down behind one of the two large granite boulders that sat fifty yards from the mine-shaft's entrance. Cecil and Charles sat crouched five feet behind Bill's lanky frame. They watched as his hand lifted and twisted the lever on the blast box in one fluid motion.

"She's primed," he said. Cecil and Charles kept their hands over their ears, waiting for Bill to lower the lever and close the contacts. The closed circuit would send a jolt of electricity hurtling down the wire to the blasting caps, and they would ignite a long series of mason jars filled with nitroglycerin.

"Fire in the hole!" Bill barked. All three men ducked as their friend drove the lever down. A second passed, and just when Charles was going to lift his head, *BOOM!* A huge explosion rocked them. All three men were pelted and peppered with rocks, dust and debris, and each of them struggled not to fall over as they felt the earth shake beneath them. *BOOM!* A second larger explosion knocked them off their feet, and a searing wave of heat passed over the men. The mine tunnels were collapsing, sending out violent tremors. After a few minutes, they rose from their crouches, patted their jackets and pulled the clumps of dirt and rocks from their hair. After the dust had cleared, they realized they had successfully destroyed the access tunnel to The Pulpit.

Cecil spoke first. "It is over now. I want us all to promise that we will never speak of it to anyone, and that none of us will ever attempt to visit this place again. Friends, can I count on you to keep our secret?"

"A secret it shall remain," Charles said. "I will never speak of it."

"I can keep a secret," Bill added.

"Thank God for nitroglycerin," Cecil said. "Gentlemen, we are rid of this scourge at last. This secret under Pittsburgh shall remain just that."

13

P eter came home and the house seemed empty. That wasn't unusual for three o'clock on a Friday afternoon. The kids were usually out playing, and Laura was probably grocery shopping for dinner. Well, in that case, he'd help himself to an extra-large slice of lemon meringue pie. Peter's love for lemon meringue bordered on obsession, and today he'd have no competition for his favorite treat. As he carefully cut out the wiggling piece of pie, the phone rang. One ring, two rings. As he reached for the phone, it stopped ringing. *That's weird*, he thought. He gently picked up the phone and surprisingly heard Laura's voice on the upstairs line. He listened as she told her friend Judy that she was busy. Laura sounded out of breath, then she hung up. Placing the phone back in its cradle, Peter began mustering up his courage. *This could be a good time for us to talk*, he thought as he maneuvered the pie slice from metal spatula to plate, then grabbed a fork out of the drawer. Yes, it was time to have a real heart-to-heart about their nonexistent sex life. He wanted to tell Laura what he'd read in the latest *Newsweek*, how doctors had recently began using synthetic estrogen to treat menopause. *But then again*, he thought, *it could piss her off and start another fight. She'd probably say he was trying to control her*. His brain took off on the subject. *I just want some intimacy in this marriage. Another argument is worth it, just as long as I get Laura back!* As he climbed the stairs, he readied himself. *Okay, I'm going to just say it. I'm going to say,* "I think we should try hormone replacement therapy." *No, no, no, that sounds too clinical*, he thought, chiding himself. *She'll get mad and turned off. Okay, I'll tell her I miss being with her physically*. When Peter opened the bedroom door, the first thing he saw was the profile of his wife crouched naked on the bed, her ass in the air, her head bent down. The second thing he saw was a very sweaty and naked Monica Greenberg playing quarterback to Laura's center.

"Oh," was the only thing Peter managed to say, and it came out "Aooah," because his mouth was stuffed full of lemon meringue pie.

"God, Peter!" Laura screamed.

Peter almost dropped the plate of lemon meringue.

"Laura?" Peter just stood there. His mind was freeze-framed on the word "lesbian." Hair, boobs and arms went flying as he watched, dumbfounded, as the women untangled themselves.

"Umm, excuse me?" Monica said as she jumped off the bed and quickly ran past Peter and down the stairs. Peter leaned over the balcony and watched naked Monica Greenberg grab her overcoat, slip it on, then bolt out the front door.

"Gay?" Peter was down to one-word questions at this point.

"I don't know. It's been going on for a while. Oh, God, I'm so sorry." Laura sat down on the bed and started to cry. Peter felt really dumb as he stood there holding the plate with the giant, wiggling, half-eaten piece of pie. Laura kept on crying, her boobs jiggling back and forth, keeping time with the pie. Peter thought about metronomes, then started to giggle.

"Oh, great, laugh about it!" Laura shouted.

"I'm sorry," Peter said in between giggles. "It's just that your boobs, and the pie…they're jiggling. I'm sorry."

"Oh, Peter. You are so immature sometimes!"

Peter's thoughts drifted to a funeral where he had been one of the pallbearers. One of the other guys tripped, and they'd almost dropped the casket. He'd almost laughed then, a giggle born from pure nervousness.

"It's just that I can't believe that you're having an affair! My wife is having an affair. A lesbian affair!"

"Peter, can you keep it down? Your voice carries. What if the kids come home and hear you?"

"Oh, yeah, our kids. Well, what if the boys had found you with Monica, what then?"

"I know, I know. I'm sorry. I've tried to be careful, so nobody would get hurt."

"Well, not careful enough, obviously!" Peter yelled. "I saw the whole thing!" He paused. "Honestly, how long has this been going on?"

"We've been seeing each other for about six months. I swear I was going to end it. I just didn't know how!" Laura said in a whine, still sobbing, her nose running.

"I don't know what to think. My mind is just shattered right now. I'm just shattered, okay? How could you do this? Where does this leave us?"

"I know you're not going to believe a word I say right now, but I do love you. I don't know what it was. Something happened when I went through menopause. You felt it, and I felt it. I don't know, and then Monica made a pass at me, and I was curious, and now I'm sorry!" Laura said with tears in her eyes. "Can I have a Kleenex please?"

"Yeah, here." Peter handed her the box of tissues sitting on their French armoire.

"I'm afraid 'sorry' doesn't cut it right now." He grimaced. "I don't know what to think. You really caught me off guard. My brain is spinning and my pride is hurt. I think I'm going to need some time alone with this." Peter shook his head in disbelief. "You could have at least talked to me about it. You didn't have to cheat. Remember that grad student who had a crush on me? I told you about it. It's okay to feel attraction to others, but I trusted you. What happened?"

"Yes, you're absolutely right, Peter. You're so right. I'm an asshole. I'm sorry. There's no excuse for what I've done." Laura's head dropped, then it heaved up and down as she continued to cry.

"Just let me think about it. I can't believe this. I'm just pissed off right now." Peter put the plate of half-eaten lemon meringue pie on their bedroom dresser and turned to leave. "And I just lost my appetite."

"Peter, I love you," Laura called out to him as she heard the front door slam.

14

"Okay, I got the rope tied off, Johnny," Crayfish said.

"Good, we're just about ready. Okay, hand me the flashlight. I'm going to clip it on my belt," Johnny said.

"Okay, here ya go," Crayfish said.

"Thanks," Johnny said.

"You want the Wrist Rocket?" Darren asked.

"No, it's cool. You hang on to it for now. If I need it, you guys can drop it down."

"I'm just checking to be sure we have everything. Did you put the new batteries in the walkie-talkies, Darren?" Johnny asked.

"Yup, they're fresh. Crayfish and I checked 'em. They're working good," Darren said. Crayfish reached over and tried to hand Johnny a second canteen.

"No, I don't have any more room. Thanks, man, I got

one. Okay, I'm ready. Is the knot tight?" Johnny looked over at Crayfish.

"Oh, yeah. I tied it with a fisherman's slipknot. My dad taught me how to make it when we used to fish up at Donegal Springs. It'll hold," Crayfish stated proudly.

"Cool, thanks, man," Johnny said. Crayfish smiled and nodded his head.

"Here, put this on." Darren said, taking his ball cap off his head and putting it on his brother's.

"Good idea. That'll help protect my head."

"Well, you got a hard head, bro." Darren laughed.

"Yeah, yeah. I know," Johnny admitted, then asked, "Okay, if there's any trouble, tell me again what you guys are gonna do?"

"Just like you said, Johnny, if something happens, we'll go and get Dad. We'll call him from the phones near the baseball field. I've got enough dimes on me, and we can get there pretty fast if we run."

"Right. Okay. Just checking. Sounds like you know the plan. Hopefully we won't have to use it."

"Good luck, dummy!" Crayfish said with a smile across his face.

"Yeah, that figures." Johnny shook his head. "Alright, I'm going to start the repel down, like Dad taught me. Keep your ears open, 'cause I'll yell up if there's any problem."

"Good luck, Johnny," Darren said.

"Thanks."

Johnny had the rope wrapped around his waist and was holding it out in front of him as he lowered himself into the hole. He reached down and clicked on the flashlight as it swung from the clip on his belt.

"Man, it sure is dark down here." Just the top of his ball cap was visible above the rim of the hole. His voice echoed a little bit. "So far so good."

The boys watched as Johnny disappeared. They kept their eyes fixed on the yellow rope; it was twisting and making creaking noises but seemed to be holding fine. Crayfish had tied it off to a big oak tree behind them.

"Good knot, dude," Darren said.

Crayfish's face beamed. "Thanks."

About ten minutes had gone by when Johnny's faint voice came up from the hole.

"I'm pretty far down, and I see some kind of light below me. Can you guys hear me?"

"Yeah, we hear you, Johnny!" Darren yelled down.

"What?!"

"We can HEAR YOU!" Darren yelled louder this time.

"Well, I can barely hear you!" Johnny yelled back. "I don't want to use the walkie-talkie. I'm afraid I'll drop it. I'll use it when I reach bottom, okay?"

"Okay, Johnny," Crayfish yelled down the hole.

"Aw crap, we forgot the candles and matches!" Darren said.

"He's got the flashlight. He'll be okay," Crayfish said.

Another few minutes went by, then they heard Johnny's faint yell.

"Did he say what I think he said?" Crayfish asked.

"I think he said somebody's down there," Darren said.

"That's impossible," Crayfish stated flatly. "There can't be anybody down there. Maybe he found a skeleton or something. Try the walkie-talkie. He's gotta be near bottom by now."

The boys turned on their Murphy's Mart walkie-talkies. The brothers had gotten the five-watt walkie-talkies for Christmas last year. They were the second-best one that Murphy's Mart offered, but they shared the legal limit five-watt, high-power rating with the top-of-the-line unit. The boys had wasted no time in going outside and finding out if they truly had a five-mile range. While Darren stood in their front yard on Beechwood Boulevard, Johnny stood at the corner of Wilkens Avenue and Murray Avenue, and they were amazed they could hear each other crystal clear.

"Those things have a good range?" Crayfish asked.

"Oh yeah, they're awesome…We got 'em last Christmas, remember? I just put fresh batteries in there. Umm, he doesn't have his turned on yet. Let's wait a second."

The two boys stood at the edge of the hole. Darren held the walkie-talkie, both of them listening to the white-noise static. Crayfish was lifting his legs and walking in place, trying to keep warm. Darren stood, unbothered.

"C'mon, Johnny," Darren said out loud. "I'm getting worried."

"Oh, he's alright, Darren; the rope's still got tension on it, see?"

Sure enough, the rope was still tight, making its creaking noises.

"I hope he's got enough rope."

"Me too," Crayfish said. "Ninety feet should be enough, but I don't know. I had to use some of it for a tie-off around the tree."

"C'mon, bro, are you there?" Darren said as he keyed the walkie-talkie. "Come in, Johnny, what's going on?"

"Darren, I'm at the bottom. Over."

"JOHNNY!" Darren yelled into his walkie-talkie.

"Hey, you won't believe this. There's a park ranger down here. He's unconscious and hurt pretty bad. This place is weird. It's huge! Unbelievable! Over."

"What? A park ranger?" Darren asked.

"Roger that, a park ranger. Call in a 10-200." Johnny loved to use the CB talk whenever he was on the walkie-talkies. He even memorized some of the 10 codes and would say stuff like, "My 10-20 is about two blocks past Linden School." A 10-20 was citizens band code for location.

"What's a 10-200? Over," Darren asked. His brother may have memorized a bunch of the 10 codes, but Darren only knew two of them.

"This guy's hurt bad. A 10-200 means police or ambulance. Over."

"Why don't we call Dad?" Darren asked.

"Good idea. Over. Wait a minute. I think he's waking up. Hold on a sec. Over."

"Do you believe this?" Darren asked Crayfish.

"What's up? What's that guy doing down there? What if he found our hole and fell in? I bet he's pretty jacked up. We could get in trouble." Crayfish was obviously worried. "I really don't want you to call your dad, because if you call him, then he's gonna call my mom. Oh, she'll tan my hide if she finds out I've been digging with you guys down here in Frick Park."

"Well, hold on, Crayfish. If that guy's hurt, I don't think anyone is going to be mad at us for helping him. And your mom's not going to paddle you for saving some guy's life. Right?"

"Yeah, I guess you're right. Okay, yeah, that sounds better. That sounds better," Crayfish nervously repeated.

"Listen, we should call my dad. He'll know what to do. He's an expert climber, you know. He could get that guy out of there, just by himself. He's been on expeditions into Central America, the Himalayas, even Egypt. He's been inside pyramids and found all kinds of cool stuff. My dad will know what to do, trust me," Darren reassured him.

"Guys, the ranger's name is Dave Rondinelli. He's got

a broken leg and other injuries too. Over," Johnny said. "Send down the blanket, would ya? He's shivering."

"Blanket coming down," Darren said.

Darren went over to their backpacks and pulled out the red-and-blue Indian blanket that his dad bought him in New Mexico. It was one hundred percent wool and had a design of a coyote howling at the moon on it.

"Coming down. Ready?"

"Ready, over."

Darren dropped the blanket down the hole and waited.

"Got it. Good shot. Okay, thanks. This guy keeps saying something about dreams. He must've hit his head pretty good. He's talking crazy. Over."

"Roger that, Johnny. What do you want me to do?" Darren asked.

"Okay, here's the plan. I'm fine. I've got to help this guy right now. You two go to the phones by the baseball field. Call Dad at work, and if he's not there, call Grandpa. Over."

"Got it, Johnny. We're gonna call Dad or Grandpa. It'll take a few minutes, especially since I got chubby with me."

"Very funny, goofus," Crayfish said, shooting him the finger.

"Okay, Darren, don't worry about me. Just get Dad here. Over."

"On our way, bro. Sit tight. We'll be right back."

"Roger that, Jabberjaw here, 10-10, 10-8 on the side," Johnny said.

"Cool handle," Crayfish said.

"Yeah, he's Jabberjaw on his CB."

"10-4, Johnny—I mean, Jabberjaw." Darren switched off the walkie-talkie and clipped it to his belt. Then he and Crayfish took off running full-speed down the gravel trail before veering up the hill to the pay telephones.

15

Amy was sitting inside the rare documents laboratory, her latex-gloved hands holding a treaty, dated 1701, signed between the Delaware Indian tribe chiefs and none other than William Penn himself. This was the earliest treaty that she had seen completely intact, and the last agreement negotiated by Penn himself. William Penn died in England in 1718, taken down by a debilitating stroke. Amy marveled at the pun. She was looking at William Penn's penmanship! Ha ha! She had to admit she had a corny sense of humor. Still, the document she held was in staggering, pristine condition. The 270-some-year-old parchment was faintly yellowed, the edges smooth and unfrayed, and the indigo ink and red wax seal of William Penn lay perfectly preserved. The Shafer institute collection was absolutely incredible, she thought. Perhaps here she could find the written proof that she was looking for, documents that proved that white Colonial settlers had taken lands from the Delaware and Iroquois tribes in order to pilfer their lead and flint mines. Amy realized the exact treaty she was hoping to find wouldn't resemble this seminal document. Still, she was thrilled at her discovery and immediately thought to call Grandpa and tell him all about it.

She got up to exit the room and headed towards the special airlock. It would do her some good to get warm, she thought. Amy had worn her wool sweater and wool socks today, yet the rare documents room had still managed to freeze her. Her eyes itched too. *Damn low light levels. You need endurance just to study this stuff,* she thought to herself. And she was right. The university's priority was in preserving rare documents, not coddling the scientists who studied them. *Oh well, that won't stop me,* she thought. *It's going to take a whole lot more than a 40-watt light bulb and a room you can hang meat in to keep me from completing my thesis.*

"Hi, Amy, funny seeing you here again!"

Dr. Peter Hawn was standing in the doorway, tall, pale-complected and ruggedly handsome. His hair was sandy brown, and he wore a button-down shirt, blue jeans and new-looking white Adidas running shoes. "Hi, Dr. Hawn! Yeah, if this keeps happening, people are going to talk," she said with a big smile on her face.

"Yes, they might. Are you doing more research this Friday afternoon?"

"Yeah, I think I'm on the right track, but I haven't found my Holy Grail, so to speak. It's time-consuming, sifting through all these treaties in the Shafer collection."

"I can relate to that."

Honestly, Doc, most of what I've read so far is very confusing; each document references yet another arcane document. And most of those are either missing or incomplete. And, it feels like Antarctica in there."

"Oh, the room? Sixty-four degrees sure chills the blood, doesn't it? I guess there's no way around the temperature thing, short of wearing long johns. I usually bring a jacket. You look prepared, though. That sweater looks nice and warm."

"I'm never warm enough in there, Doc. A hot cup of coffee helps, but I'm pretty skinny. Next time I'm going to wear double ski socks, and bring my down parka. That should do the trick." She laughed.

"Maybe we ought to donate some cold-weather clothing to the school? We could store it in the lockers next to the lab, and staff and students could 'suit up' to do their research."

"That's an excellent idea, Dr. Hawn."

"Call me Peter."

"Okay, Peter it is. Are you sure?"

"I'm sure. Dr. Hawn sounds way too formal for my tastes."

"Hey, the intercom's buzzing," she said, turning her head.

"Yes, it is. Hold on a sec."

Peter went to the far wall, near the door. He pushed the intercom button, but he was standing far enough away that she couldn't hear what he was saying. He returned, looking concerned.

"That was Betty over in the office," he said, referring to the secretary of the archeology department. "One of my kids is on the phone and it's urgent, I've got to hurry over there. Do you want to accompany me?"

"Sure, Doc—I mean, Peter. Sure, Peter, let's go."

"Great. Well, it's a good thing it's just three buildings down." Peter said.

She and Peter exited the library complex and started quickly walking over to the archeology building. Peter was worried. The boys didn't usually call the school, and if they did, it was always Johnny on the phone. He was the oldest and usually took the lead between his boys. Peter thought about how stressed out he was lately, and how the distance between him and Laura wasn't helping.

"So how's your wife?" Amy asked, interrupting his private reverie and causing him to wonder if she could read his thoughts. "I've seen her on campus. She's tall, and very pretty."

"Umm, she's fine," Peter said. "Yes, she is very pretty. We have two boys, you know, Johnny and Darren, ages twelve and ten. Darren's the one who called."

"So what's the secret to a happy marriage?"

"I'm afraid I don't have a clue. In fact, I'm not sure

my marriage is even working. I found out something terrible today."

"Oh, I'm sorry, Peter. What's going on, if you don't mind me asking? Wait. No, don't answer that. I'm just being nosey, that's all."

"It's funny how life leads us down these twists and turns. I guess we never really know anybody."

They were almost at the archeology building and just starting up the concrete stairway toward the Doric columns that framed the front doors.

Peter turned to face Amy. "I don't know why I'm telling you this. But here goes. I found out today that my wife is having an affair."

"Oh no, I'm so sorry! Wow, that is terrible news." She reached out to touch his hand. He felt her warm fingers close over his.

"She must be crazy, because you are an incredible man. Why would your wife do that? You guys have kids and everything."

"Well, my wife is somewhat older than me, and menopause is more than hot flashes," Peter said. "It changed our relationship. We've grown apart. It's complicated. But, um, can we continue this another time?"

"Oh, sure. Hey, I can wait in the lobby so you can have your privacy."

"No, come on in. It's okay, Amy. Thank you, Betty. I'll take that in my office. Come in, and please, sit down. Betty's great, isn't she? I don't know what I'd do without her. She keeps me organized." Peter went over and sat down behind his desk and picked up the receiver.

"Darren, this is Dad. Uh-huh. You're where? You what! A Park Ranger? Oh, my God! How deep? Okay, okay, calm down, honey. I'm coming down. I have to get my gear, but I'll be there soon. Where are you exactly? By the baseball field? Yes, I know where it is. Okay, just wait for me. Don't go anywhere! No, I'm not mad. Listen, it'll take me about twenty minutes to grab my gear. Wait, okay? Okay. I love you, too." Peter hung up the phone, a stunned look on his face.

"You won't believe this."

"I heard some of it."

"I'm not sure I believe it. My boys went digging in Frick Park this afternoon, and they found an abandoned mineshaft or maybe a well. My oldest boy, Johnny, rappelled down, and at the bottom he found an injured man, a park ranger. The guy's got a fractured leg; he's badly hurt. My son also said something about a giant underground chamber. How in God's name could there be a giant underground chamber under Frick Park? I don't get it. And my neighbor's son is involved, Mike Craw-forth. That boy's always getting my boys into some kind of trouble."

"Listen, maybe I can help. I went spelunking three times last summer, at Colossal Caves in Tucson, Arizona. I'm pretty handy with a rope."

"Well, it's good you have some caving experience, but you know this is going to be dangerous, right?"

"I know, and I'm okay with that. I want to help."

"Good, then follow me. I keep some climbing gear in my locker."

"Actually, Peter, maybe it's not so unbelievable. As part of my research, I've located several undocumented, abandoned coal mines under parts of Pittsburgh."

"Really?"

"Yes, and my grandfather's company used to own many of them. I just asked him the other day if he'd kept any of his old maps."

"What did he say?" Peter asked as they walked quickly down to the locker area.

"He told me he donated most of the company's maps, the old ones anyway, to the Carnegie museum. But what are the odds that your boys could have found one of my grandfather's mines?"

"I'd say pretty steep odds, but it is possible. Here, take this." Peter handed Amy a cord of military-grade manila climbing rope, along with a ball and tackle set. "It's heavy, be careful," Peter added.

"You're not kidding," Amy said, rocking back on her heels. "Are we going to need all this stuff?"

"Yeah, we are. I only hope we've got everything we'll need. As you know, raising someone up from a cave is always tricky, and doubly so if they're injured."

"Well, let's take my car. It has a phone in it."

"You've got a telephone in your car?" Peter asked incredulously.

"I know; it's brand new technology. See, my grandfather bought me a Mercedes for my high school graduation. And last year he put a telephone in, saying it would help keep me safe. I guess there are benefits to being a Stewart."

"Listen, I'm not a fan of university politics, but is it true your grandfather donated the lion's share of the money for the new Stewart Business Center?"

"Yes, it's true. This school is one of his pet causes." She opened the trunk, and tossed the rope and tackle into it. "Here, you drive."

"Really? I'm probably going to break a few speed limits getting us there."

Amy laughed. "I doubt that you're going to scare me. I like speed. In fact, I have one of the fastest speedboats on the Ohio River. Drive as fast as you want."

"You're brave, aren't you? You know, that might come in handy today. If my boys did find a coal mine, it's got to be a hundred years old, and probably falling apart." Peter heaved a sigh.

"You have every right to be worried. I can tell you're a great father."

"I could've been a better dad, actually. I spent too much time away from home in pursuit of my doctorate, my expeditions. I was obsessed with being the best archeologist in the world. I've tried to make it up to them these past few years. That's the reason why I took the teaching position at Charles Masters, despite all the inane rumors floating around. I honestly got tired of being away from my family, and my kids were growing up without me. I feel tremendously guilty about it."

Amy just looked at him, listening.

"Now my wife is having an affair. We grew apart for a lot of reasons, but my jet-setting around the world didn't help our marriage."

"Don't be so hard on yourself. I've never been married, but I did live with my college boyfriend for two years until I found out he cheated on me with one of my best friends. We were engaged too, the bastard! You know, I threw his ring into the Ohio River." Amy laughed. "Remember, you didn't cheat on your wife, she cheated on you! I'm sure you had plenty of opportunities to stray, but you didn't. Right?" Her eyebrows were raised. "Am I right?"

"I don't know. I took our wedding vows seriously." Peter took one hand off the steering wheel and turned his palm up. "Well, I guess you're right. There was this one research assistant once. I met her while working in Utah. She was Mormon, I think." He laughed. "She was coming on to me pretty heavily, but I ended it before anything ever happened. I think I was having some kind of mid-life crisis. I told Laura about it, and we worked it out. I don't know what changed, but we used to be able to talk it out."

"What happened, I think, is that your wife isn't like

you." Amy sighed. "I hope you don't mind me saying this, but I think she's an idiot. Oh, left turn here, this road is a shortcut to Regent Square and the park." She paused. "Oh yeah, back to your wife. She's an idiot."

"Thank you for saying that. You know, I forgot about this shortcut. I'm feeling pretty distracted."

"Don't worry, Doc, you're in good hands."

"Well, I guess at least we're getting to know each other, huh? Just tell me if I'm giving out too much information. Sometimes I wear my heart on my sleeve. Jeez, my life sounds pretty crazy right now. Am I boring you?" Peter asked.

"No, you're not. But you've got to make a right here. A RIGHT HERE! Whew! That was close. You almost missed the entrance. Listen. Just try and relax, okay?"

"You're right. I guess I'm under more stress than I realized. Oh good, there's my son." Peter parked the convertible.

"Dad!"

"Darren! Son, are you okay?"

"Yeah, I'm okay. I'm so glad you're here!"

"Come here, honey," Peter said as he hugged his son. "Listen, we have to hurry. This is one of my students—Amy Lee. She's going to help us."

"Hi, I'm Darren." Darren stuck out his hand while still hugging his dad.

"Hi, Darren." Amy shook his hand. "Hey, would you do me a favor?"

"Sure."

"You look pretty strong. Do you think you could give me a hand with some of this equipment? It's back in the trunk."

"Sure," Darren said while blushing.

"Does Johnny have his walkie-talkie on him?" Peter asked.

"Yeah. Here, I don't know if it'll reach this far from the hole." Darren handed his dad the radio and then ran over to the car to help Amy. Peter turned the walkie-talkie on, adjusted the squelch, and checked that it was on channel 9.

"Johnny, come in. Are you there? This is Dad, over. Johnny, come in." He waited, but heard only static.

"I'm not getting anything!" Peter yelled.

"We're too far, Dad!" Darren hollered back.

"Damn." Peter shook his head and shut the radio off. *Better conserve the batteries*, he thought.

"Okay, let's go," Peter said.

"Wait a minute, Dad. Crayfish is in the bathroom." He opened the bathroom door. "HEY, CRAWDAD, HURRY UP! MY DAD'S HERE!"

Amy, Peter and Darren continued to grab gear out of the Mercedes' trunk.

"Alright, I'm comin'." Crayfish straggled out of the bathroom.

"Took you long enough," Darren said.

"Hey, Mike, can you give me a hand with this?" Peter

asked, holding up the heavy ball and tackle set. "Oh, and this too." He held up a bucket.

"Sure, Dr. Hawn."

"The bucket's in case you gotta pee again," Darren joked.

"Ha. Very funny chucklehead," Crayfish said.

"Hey, you two! Cool it, please!" Peter shouted. "We don't have time for fooling around. Let's go."

"Okay, Dad." Darren and Crayfish started walking, carrying some of the equipment. Peter and Amy followed as the four of them made their way down the dirt trail and disappeared into the dense Frick Park forest.

16

J ohnny was talking with the park ranger when the man fell asleep in the middle of his sentence. At least the ranger had managed to gulp down Johnny's peanut butter and jelly sandwich, and wash it down with swig of water. *That should help him*, Johnny thought. He noticed one leg of the man's green work pants, from top to bottom, was stained a dark brown. Johnny realized it wasn't dirt, but dried blood. *How did he survive the fall,, the broken leg, and losing all that blood?* he wondered.

Johnny remembered his descent into the mine. Even though he'd used everything his dad had taught him about rappelling, it was still a nerve-wracking trip down. When he finally reached bottom, he was astonished at what he found. He stood in an enormous room, as big as the football field at Three Rivers Stadium. Perfectly smooth walls arched upward to form a hemispherical dome. The space was featureless, except for three things: A small stream neatly bisecting the dirt floor, the hole that Johnny came through, and a tall, dark, glowing object at the far end of the chamber. The glowing device looked like a monstrous Pong arcade machine built for a giant. Johnny wanted to go get a closer look, but he reconsidered after looking down at the injured park ranger. *What if I have to perform mouth-to-mouth resuscitation?* he thought. *That would be so gross*! But, he knew he'd have to do it, if it meant saving the man's life. The ranger was sound asleep, lightly snoring on his back on the ground. Strangely, Johnny realized that he, too, felt tired. *I better grab my chance now, before this guy wakes up!* He dropped his backpack down and stretched out, leaning his head against the pack. *That's weird*, he thought. *I slept okay last night.* His eyelids grew heavy. *I'll just rest for a minute. Ah, that's feels good.* Johnny relaxed and gently drifted into the strangest dream of his life.

17

"Dad, I'm home!" Johnny shouted. But no one was there.

"Darren, Mom, Dad, where are you?" He walked up the stairs. "Darren?"

Nobody was home. Johnny noticed things were different as he walked from room to room. "Hey, when'd you guys decide to take out the shag carpet?" he yelled. "Why'd you change the wallpaper?" Practically everything in the house had been changed.

"You guys bought a grand piano?" Johnny said, amazed.

"Oh, hi, Johnny," a strange woman's voice called out.

"Who are you?" Johnny said to the beautiful young blonde woman standing in the front doorway.

"Can you help me with these? I've got quite a few bags in the car," she said.

"I said, who are you, lady?" Johnny said with a bit of a tone in his voice.

"Umm, last time I checked, I was your stepmother—Amy. Are you feeling okay? Please stop kidding around, I've got all these groceries, and I could use your help. Tell you what, help me get the rest of these bags in, and then I'll be happy to play your game of 'I don't know you,' okay?"

"I'm not playing, lady, and for your information, I don't have a stepmother. I have a mother, and her name is Laura Hawn! What are you doing in my house?" His voice sounded tight.

"Of course you love your mom. I didn't mean to upset you. Listen. I'm sorry. I thought we'd gotten past all that, but it's okay if we need another session with the counselor. Don't worry about it. I'll unload the groceries myself. Um, your dad called, and we're all going out to dinner in about an hour. Your blue dress shirt would look nice," she called out to him as she moved into the kitchen. That's when he noticed the picture on the kitchen table. The photograph was of him, Darren, his dad, and this strange lady. *That's weird*, he thought. Then he noticed a stack of mail on the kitchen countertop. A couple of the letters were addressed to his dad, and as he picked up the stack, he saw that four of the letters were addressed to "Amy Hawn." *Amy Hawn?*

"We have the same last name?" Johnny asked as the woman was putting another bag down.

"Okay, you're acting delirious, you must be getting sick," she said. "I'll call your dad. Sit down, Johnny. I'll take your temperature."

He was about to scream. *Who's this lady? Am I dreaming? Am I dead? Is Mom dead, and Dad remarried?* Johnny started to cry. *Mom...dead? This can't be right. Mom's too young to die! What happened to Mom?*

Johnny woke with a fright.

What the hell was that? he asked himself. *Was that a dream? That was scary!* Johnny stood up and shivered, trying to shake off the terrible, lifelike nightmare.

"Johnny, are you there? Come in," came his dad's voice over the walkie-talkie. "Are you alright? Come in, Johnny. I'm coming down to get you out of there. Do you read me?"

"Dad! DAD! Yes, I hear you!" Johnny's voice was strained. "I'm okay, Dad, but there's a guy down here; he's hurt real bad."

"I know, honey, just sit tight. I'm coming down."

"Okay, please hurry, Dad. The guy's not doing too good, over."

"I'm coming down there, Johnny. I love you."

"I love you too, Dad."

18

P eter couldn't believe it. His boys had actually found a mineshaft, right in the heart of Frick Park. An hour before he was at his office, and everything was fine. Now, everything seemed to be happening at light-speed, and he wished he could somehow slow it down. They were losing daylight, and he wondered how long the flashlights would last. He checked his watch. 4:30 p.m. Would he be able to make the descent and get Johnny and the injured man out by nightfall? Peter doubted he could get both, but maybe at least he'd get Johnny up to the surface if everything went smoothly.

"Maybe we should call the authorities?" Amy asked.

"You know, I'm thinking that's a pretty good idea right about now. I'm worried about the structural integrity of that hole. Those wooden posts there, they look to be a century old. What do you think?"

Amy was surprised and flattered that Dr. Hawn wanted her opinion.

"Yeah, they look pretty rotted. I think calling in the fire department isn't such a bad idea."

"But how are they gonna get a ladder down here, Dad?" Darren asked.

"They're going to have a tough time with it, I imagine. This is a remote part of the park. Hold on a second, I'm going to call Johnny again."

"Johnny, come in. I need to know more about that injured man. Can you tell me how tall and how heavy is the man?"

The radio was silent.

"Johnny, come in. Are you there?" Peter said loudly. "Darren, how old are the batteries in this radio?"

"They're brand new. I just put them in."

"Then something's not right," Peter said.

He turned down the squelch and turned up the volume on the walkie-talkie. It seemed to be working perfectly.

"Peter, tug on the rope. It might still be attached to him," Amy said.

"Good idea. No, great idea." Peter went over to the edge of the hole and pulled up the yellow rope. He was able to pull up about 10 feet of slack, and then the rope went taught. He tugged on the rope. Once. Twice. Nothing. "C'mon, Johnny. Pull back on the rope!" he pleaded.

"Let me try," Amy said, taking the rope from Peter's hand. She tugged on the rope just like Peter had. "Your son is still on the rope. That's good. We could pull him up if we had to."

"No, it's too risky. He might be hurt. If he's unconscious, pulling him up in that condition could make things worse. Something's wrong," Peter stated flatly. "The radio is working fine. Something is wrong down there."

"I agree," Amy said.

"What're we gonna do, Dad?"

"I'm going down there," Peter said, grabbing a rope in one hand. "Darren, I'm going to send you and Mike to the payphones, to call the fire department. Amy, I'll need you to stay here."

"Of course. I'm not going anywhere." She smiled at him.

"A 10-200?" Darren said.

"What?" Peter asked.

"CB talk, Dad. It means police or fire department. Dad, do you have some more dimes? I'm out."

"Let me check. Yes, I got four. Here." Peter handed Darren the change.

"Okay, let's go, Crayfish. Bye, Dad. I love you." Darren and Crayfish took off running.

I love you, too, Peter thought.

"This is bad, Amy. Let's get the ropes set up."

"I know it is, but we're going to get your son and that guy out of there." She continued after a pause. "Listen, we just take it step by step. We're going to run a safety line for you. This looks like good solid rope."

"It does look like good rope. Listen, thank you."

"It's okay. I'd be worried sick too if it was my son down there. Let's just concentrate, okay?"

"Okay, Amy." Peter drew in a breath. "Darren told me that Johnny said the hole is seventy-five feet deep. We've got enough rope, thank God. Of course, you're going to double-check my rig once I'm done?"

"Definitely. No way you're going down there with an unlocked 'biner.'"

"No, that wouldn't work out so well," Peter said. "This is vertical caving; it's dangerous enough." He attached his rappelling device to the main rope that Amy had tied off to the same tree that his boys had used. He noticed Amy had laid down a safety rope and had tied a figure-eight loop at the end. That would stop him from zipping off the end of the line.

"You know, I'm really glad you're here," Peter said.

"I told you I'm not going anywhere. I'm just glad I can help."

"We're starting to lose the light. Damn! I brought some flashlights, but I'm really wishing I'd brought my generator and some klieg lights as well," Peter said.

"We're all set to go. Listen to me. You have to stay focused on your descent. Okay?"

"Okay. I'm okay," Peter said gently.

"Ready when you are," Amy said. Peter tied on to the

rope, using four bars in his rappelling device to compensate for the long drop. *Is it really 75 feet?* he thought. *That's like falling off of the Liberty Bridge! How did the park ranger survive that fall?* he asked himself.

"We'd better test the two-way radios. They're better than what the boys used, but I have no idea how they'll perform in that mineshaft," Peter said.

"Okay. How does this sound?"

"Loud and clear. They're working fine, at least here above ground. Well, I'm going in." Peter donned his climbing helmet.

"Good luck. I'll be right here."

"Thanks, I might need that luck." Peter started his descent backward down the hole, in classic rappelling technique. In a few minutes, his orange helmet disappeared in the dark.

All she could do now was wait. The gray Pittsburgh sky was growing darker by degrees, making the subtle change into night. The wind picked up and began howling through the trees. The mournful sound wasn't comforting to Amy. She zipped up her down vest and raised the collar to protect her neck. She felt desolate all of a sudden. The wolf-howling wind and approaching night conspired together to wash away her usual optimism. She pulled black leather deerskin gloves out of her coat pocket and slipped them on. The act of slipping on her gloves was as much about her need to keep busy as it was to relieve the numbing chill in her hands.

Holding the radio, she played with the volume knob. *What a strange day*, she thought. What began as a trip to do research at school had evolved into a bizarre and dangerous rescue operation in Frick Park. *Everything is going to be fine,* she thought to herself. But honestly, she was losing faith, and there were just so many unanswered questions. Like how did that guy survive that fall? Why did Johnny stop responding? That one really got her worried. Did he pass out from carbon monoxide? An underground mine fire would explain it. A mine fire produces huge quantities of carbon monoxide or CO gas, which can render someone unconsciousness very quickly. Amy thought about an article she had read in *Newsweek* about the Centralia mine fire. It started in 1962, in a garbage dump in Centralia, Pennsylvania. The dump sat right on top of an exposed coal seam. The fire started in the garbage and soon ignited the coal lying underneath. CO gas started seeping from underground, up into people's homes, making them sick. The last she had read, the government was buying up the homes and quarantining the town. Supposedly there was enough coal under Centralia to keep the fire burning for decades. *Is that what's happening here?*

"Amy, come in. I've reached bottom." The sudden crackle from the two-way radio made her jump.

"Peter, I'm here. Is your son okay?" Amy's voice was anxious as she turned the volume down a bit.

"He's breathing fine, but I can't wake him. The park ranger is alive, but he's also out cold. They're both unconscious, and I'm not sure why. There are some amyl nitrite capsules in the first-aid kit. I'll need you to drop that kit down."

"What if it's carbon monoxide? A mine fire? Over."

"That could be, but Johnny's color is fine. Let me check his pulse, hold on. Okay, his pulse is fine and his breathing is strong. His skin color is good. It's not CO poisoning, over."

"Those are good signs. Do you think we can pull him up?"

"Yes, I think so. I'm going to get my son ready so we can lift him out of here. I'd still like you to send that kit down, because if I can use those amyl capsules to wake him up first, it'll make this whole thing easier. And I might need one myself, because I'm starting to feel tired. Just give me a few minutes to set up the ropes, then I'll give you a call back, over."

"Okay, I'll wait until you give the signal, Peter, over."

Silence.

"I said, I'll wait for your signal, over." Only static was coming over Amy's radio now.

"Peter, come in. Are you there, over?" Amy gripped the radio tighter in her hand.

"Peter, come in!" she shouted into the radio. But there was no response. "Peter!" Amy screamed.

Amy's thoughts started racing. *Peter's unconscious. Maybe he was wrong about the carbon monoxide. If it's CO poisoning, then they need oxygen immediately.* She glanced at the gear they'd brought from CMU. She'd looked in all the containers, except one, the beat up, gray metal toolbox that Peter had carried in.

Oh, come on! Be in there! Amy hoped. She ran to the toolbox, worked the latch, and flipped the lid open. *Come on! Yes!* She yelped when she saw the toolbox held a medium-sized O2 cylinder. Pure oxygen! Complete with mask! She knew what had to be done. She grabbed the oxygen bottle and shoved it down inside her vest.

"Peter, I'm coming down." Amy gripped the call button furiously. "I'm not waiting for the stupid fire department. Peter! Can you hear me? I found your O2 bottle. Hold on!"

Amy's hands became palsy. She tried to calm herself. She knew that trying to rescue them solo was a risk, but a risk she had to take. They might be dying down there. If Peter was wrong, and it was CO, she could save their lives with the oxygen. She grabbed a carabineer and a rappelling device, and hooked herself on to the main rope. She made sure that the rappelling device was right side up. She added four brake bars to slow her down and positioned herself at the lip of the hole. Her foot came loose, and a bit of the edge gave way. Clods of dirt and pebbles rained down the hole. *Great!* she thought. She heard the echoes of falling debris. With steely resolve, Amy grabbed an orange climbing helmet and began lowering herself into the hole.

20

Darren and Crayfish ran in a mad dash to the telephones. Darren struggled to catch his breath as he spoke to an unbelieving dispatcher, until Crayfish got on the phone and corroborated his story. Darren shouted, "Yes!" when he heard trucks would be sent from old station number 6 on Northumberland Street. That was only a few blocks from his house on Beechwood Boulevard.

"I want to call my mom," Darren said.

"Man, you're braver than me. What my mom doesn't know won't hurt her."

Darren dialed his own number. The phone rang and rang.

"Your mom's not there?"

"No answer." Darren hung up. "Hey, Crayfish, what if I call my grandpa?"

"Yeah, do it! Your grandpa's cool. You know, my mom met him the day they found the mine in your back yard. My mom and dad still talk about that."

"Okay, I'll call him." Darren dialed the only number he had memorized besides his own and Crayfish's.

"Hello? Grandpa…"

21

Amy made good progress in her descent. She checked her watch. It was 6:15 p.m., and she guessed she had dropped fifty feet. She checked her own lucidity by counting backwards from 100. She made it to zero with no problems. If there was CO, it hadn't affected her yet.

Boink!

A tennis-ball sized clump of dirt hit her hardhat.

Boink, Boink!

Amy kept her eyes down and increased her rate of fall. "This can't be happening," she said out loud. But she knew exactly what was happening. The hole was collapsing on top of her. She slid faster, pushing off with her feet, getting big drops of five feet in between touches. It was hailing dirt and rocks now, her hardhat taking a lot of abuse. She hit the side of the rock wall, hard enough to scrape her arm through her sweater.

How much farther! Shit!

Something hit her hard and shoved her head back, and she screamed, "Ahhhhhhh!"

There was a maelstrom of stones pelting her whole body now. They stung her neck, arms and chest like angry wasps. Amy pushed off, trying not to go too fast, but desperate to escape. *Not much farther now!* So much dust, she was choking on it! Her arm was knocked off the rope. She started to freefall. *Boom!*

She was down. Amy scampered away from the falling rocks. She could move! She was okay. She brought her flashlight out and clicked it on.

"Peter? Where are you?" Through the dust, Amy saw three bodies lying about fifteen feet away.

"Peter!" She shook him by his jacket. He was fast asleep, snoring loudly. She thought, *What the hell?* She firmly slapped Peter's handsome face. He didn't even flinch! More desperate now, Amy pointed her flashlight at the first-aid kit and quickly removed an amyl nitrite capsule. She cracked the cloth-covered glass capsule under his nose.

"Hey. Hey!" Peter shouted. "What gives?"

"Get up and help me move them. Peter, wake up now! The hole is collapsing!" Amy screamed.

"Oh, my God!" Peter shouted. He quickly grabbed under the ranger's shoulders, while Amy was already pulling Johnny toward safety. Together they dragged the unconscious duo away from the falling rocks and debris.

"Over there. We can hide behind that thing way over there!" Peter yelled.

Peter and Amy pulled as hard and fast as they could. They got Johnny and the ranger behind what looked like a large, thin pyramid standing on end. Peter's arms ached from the strenuous effort.

"Keep your head down!" Peter yelled. "Put this over your mouth and theirs!" He handed Amy a couple of handkerchiefs.

There was a strong rumble, and then a huge *KABOOM*! A tremendous blast of silt-strewn air hit them. Peter covered Johnny, and Amy fell on top of the sleeping ranger's face as the rocks and choking dust continued. After what seemed an eternity, the cacophony ceased.

"Johnny. Johnny! Wake up. Amy, can you hand me one of those capsules?"

"I hope this works," He said as he cracked the capsule under his son's nose. Johnny's eyes fluttered open.

"Dad? Dad? What happened?"

"Johnny, that hole you found has just collapsed, and it looks like we're trapped down here. Are you okay?"

"Yeah, I guess so, Dad. But, Dad, I just had the weirdest dream. I mean, in my dream, it was our house, but this strange, blonde lady was living with us." He was trying to find the right words. Then his eyes widened. "It was her!" Johnny pointed at Amy. "That lady was living in our house! She asked me to help her with the groceries!"

"Johnny, relax. It was just a dream. That woman you're pointing at is one of my grad students, Amy Lee. She's been helping me in our failed rescue."

"Nice to meet you, Johnny," Amy said.

"Nice to meet you, too. And um, thanks for helping my dad."

"No problem. I'm just glad you're okay. Peter, here—I brought the oxygen from the toolbox."

"You're as amazing as you are reckless. You know you shouldn't have come down here," Peter said as he took the oxygen bottle from Amy's hand.

"Well, I didn't want you guys to get lonely," she quipped.

Peter and Johnny laughed.

"It seems you're stuck with us now," Peter said.

"That's not such a bad thing, Dr. Hawn—I mean, Peter. It's still weird to call you Peter, you know?"

"Yes, but really, it's okay."

"Okay, Peter. Hey, are you sure it's not carbon monoxide, that's affecting us?"

"I don't think it is. None of us feel nauseous, and besides being dirty, our skin color is fine. There's another factor at play, although I'm not sure what it is."

"His leg looks pretty bad," Amy said, pointing to the park ranger. She let out a big yawn.

"His nametag reads Dave Rondinelli, and he shouldn't

be among the living. I think he fell straight down," Peter proclaimed. "With his injuries, I think we should let Mr. Rondinelli sleep. If he wakes up, he could go into shock."

"How are you holding up? Amy?"

"Peter? I feel so, so tired." Amy's eyelids began to flutter just as Peter cracked an amyl nitrite capsule underneath her nose.

"Whew! Those things are strong. Wow! Thank you, I think. This wave of exhaustion swept over me."

"Yeah, I thought that might help." he paused. "How many of those capsules do we have left?"

"Let me count…um…fifteen." She held up the first-aid kit so he could see.

"I have a feeling we're going to need every one of them. Not to change the subject, but what about the fire department?"

"They should be here soon. Darren didn't come back, so I don't know for sure. When you went incommunicado, that's when I decided to drop in."

"We're going to need another way out. That way's not an option anymore." Peter pointed his flashlight to illuminate the huge mound of debris, a mass of rubble stretching from the floor to the ceiling.

"What do you make of this?" She said, shining her flashlight on the tall, black object.

"It's an obelisk. The question is, what the hell's it doing down here?" Peter said as he ran his hands along the sides. *Hieroglyphics? No, definitely not hieroglyphics,* he thought. *Sumerian*? Peter had a doubtful look on his face.

"To be honest, I've never seen anything like it, guys. It's definitely an organized form of writing. Not hieroglyphics, but closer to cuneiform or pictograph writing. Hey, look here."

"It's raised unevenly," Amy said.

"It's like a sophisticated cuneiform, but with three dimensional differentiation. See this symbol? This one over here is the same, but it's half the height. Tell me this, why would someone write anything in three dimensions, unless they were blind?"

"I don't know. It's very odd. Hey, look around. This is strange too." They both shone their flashlights around the room, their crisscrossing beams resembling Hollywood searchlights.

"The ceiling is perfectly smooth!" Amy said.

"I saw that too, guys," Johnny said. "It kind of freaked me out. I feel like we're in a huge church with no windows."

"This place wasn't formed by nature," Amy said flatly. "I wasn't expecting this at all. It's nothing like any cave or coal mine I've ever seen."

"Hey, give me a lift?" Peter asked.

Amy put her hands together, fingers interlaced, and Peter stepped one foot into her palm. She lifted, and he used his arms to pull his chest over the top of the structure.

"Okay, now this is really getting interesting."

"What do you see, Dad?" Johnny was standing by his dad's dangling boots.

"The top of this thing is illuminated. It's glowing. It looks a bit like a television screen, only the resolution is much, much higher. There are more of those symbols on the screen here."

"I want to see," Amy said.

"Me, too," Johnny said.

"Alright, let's switch. Here, you go first." Peter hoisted Amy up with his hands under her tennis shoes.

"Well?" Peter asked.

"This is incredible! A triangular shaped screen that's almost three feet wide! It's completely flat, and it's like staring at a painting because the resolution is off the charts. I wish my home TV looked this good! Who made this? Us? The Russians? Aliens?"

"You're not serious," Peter said.

"I know, I know, it sounds crazy, but hear me out. This isn't something Native Americans or pre-Columbian civilizations could've made. And if they didn't make it, and we didn't make it, then who?" Amy climbed down and looked at Johnny and Peter. "That writing looks pictographic," Amy added. "Not hieroglyphics though."

"Aliens! Hey, I wanna see!" Johnny squealed.

"Dad, what do you think?" Amy asked. Peter nodded his approval. "Alright, kiddo, here you go. Just don't touch the screen," Amy said as she lifted Johnny up.

"Wow, it's really cool! I think it looks like a giant Pong!" Johnny's face was lit up by the blue-green glow of the screen. "Wow, wait until Darren hears about this!"

"This thing could be the source of the physiological effects that we've been experiencing, guys," Peter said. "What if this machine is emitting radiation? Ah, hold on. Hey, Johnny, get down from there. I've changed my mind, I don't want you near that thing until we figure out what it is."

"Oh, alright. It's really neat though. I wish I'd brought my camera." Johnny climbed off.

"Alien technology. Hmm. An advanced civilization's technology would likely operate from a power source beyond our understanding. It would be akin to a dog trying to learn the principles of alternating current. It just wouldn't happen. Maybe the obelisk's power is affecting us. Like a dog that gets shocked by an electric fence, it might be wise to put some distance between this thing and us. We also need to look for another way out of here. There might be another way out besides the way we came in." Peter yawned. "How are you guys holding up?"

"I'm okay, Dad, but I'm starting to feel sleepy again."

"I am too, Peter. Now that you mention it."

"Alright then. How long has it been since you used the amyl nitrite on me?"

"I would say twenty minutes, Peter."

"Well, there's our starting point. Every twenty minutes, we'll each need to breathe in some of those fumes to stay awake. We can conserve the capsules by sharing them."

"Good idea," Amy said

"That's smart, Dad."

"Let's crack one, and breathe deep, guys. Better sit down. Amyl nitrite can get your head spinning," Peter warned.

All three of them sat down and shared a capsule under their noses, quickly passing it around. They breathed in the pungent vapor until their eyes watered.

"Oh yeah, and nobody strike a match," Amy said. "Amyl nitrite is highly flammable." Peter laughed.

"Well, I guess I'd better put my cigarettes away," Peter joked. Amy and Johnny started giggling.

"Dad, you've never smoked!" Johnny said between giggles.

"No, I never did. I'm just kidding around. A little humor can't hurt right now, can it? I hope you two know some good jokes, because we might be here a while. But don't worry, we'll get out of here eventually."

Amy smiled at Peter's optimism, but inside she doubted he believed in what he was saying. She knew that he knew they were in serious trouble. Thank God Peter seemed to be the kind of man who embraced a challenge, even a life-threatening one.

"I bet Darren reached the fire department by now. So, are you two ready to explore this place, while we're still half-conscious?" Peter asked.

"Yeah, let's go. I'm ready. There's got to be another way out," Amy said hopefully.

"You really think so?" Johnny asked.

"I'd like to think that there are always possibilities."

"I like your enthusiasm," Peter said. "I think the park ranger will hold for now. Johnny, you lead the way."

22

"Grandpa, yes, Dad and Johnny are both down there. And a park ranger too, and he's hurt. Uh-huh. Uh-huh. Yeah, the fire department is coming. Okay, I'll wait by the phones. Please hurry, Grandpa."

"That's cool that your grandpa is coming down," Crayfish said.

"He'll know what to do. He's really smart."

"What time is it? I've got to be home by six o'clock for dinner, or my mom will kill me."

"You can't leave me here alone, Crayfish! So what if your mom gets mad. This is serious, man!"

"You don't know my mom. She'll tan my hide if I don't get home soon. What time is it anyway?"

"I'm not telling you."

"Oh really? We'll see about that!" Crayfish grabbed Darren's wrist.

"Let go, you big goof!" Darren yelled. "Help! I'm being attacked by a giant goofus!"

"It's after six. I'm out of here."

"Wait until I tell Johnny. You're a jerk, Crayfish." Darren was holding his wrist. "Butthead!"

"Well, as long as I'm not a late butthead, then my mom won't get pissed. Later, dude. I'm sorry, man."

Darren gave him a one-finger salute and Crayfish returned the gesture as he walked away, shuffling down the sidewalk toward Forbes Avenue. As Crayfish disappeared into the dusk, a feeling of aloneness swept over Darren. He was snapped out of his reverie by the approaching sirens of the Pittsburgh Fire Department's trucks roaring down Forbes Avenue. He watched as the ladder-truck turned the corner of Forbes and Braddock Avenue, racing toward him. It turned into the parking lot next to the telephones, where the fire truck parked and turned off its siren but kept the red lights flashing. A bunch of yellow-suited, burly fireman jumped off, and one of them made a beeline for Darren.

"Are you Darren Hawn?"

"Yes, sir!"

"We got here as soon as we could. Can you show us where to go?"

"It's way down in the park, but I want to wait for my grandpa. I called him and he's gonna be here any minute."

"Son, we're not waiting for your grandpa. I'm the fire chief, and I"m making the decisions around here. First you're going to take us to that hole you found, after that, you can come back here to wait for your grandpa. Understood?"

"Yes, sir," Darren said emphatically. He desperately wanted to wait for Grandpa, but he couldn't refuse the fire chief.

"I'll take you right now, sir."

"Hey, Jimmy, Pete—follow the boy. Bring the portable lighting and the generator." The men hurried around the back of the truck and unloaded a wheelbarrow-looking device with two handles and knobby wheels.

"Do you think my men can get that generator down to that hole?"

"Yes, sir. We can take the main trail for a ways, then it's up in what my brother said is a 'box canyon.'"

"Good. Darren, is it?"

Darren nodded. "Okay, Darren, let's go. We'll follow you."

23

"It's right over there." Darren pointed. The firemen were exhausted from rolling the generator up and down the trails in the park. They stood bent over, trying to catch their breath.

"Okay, let's get it done, boys!" the chief shouted. The two men snapped to attention and pushed the generator up the hill and past the boulders.

"What's this? Is this where the hole is supposed to be, son?"

Darren stood there, staring. "It's gone. Something happened. It was right here! I swear!" He shouted.

The chief realized there had been a cave-in. All that was left was a huge depression in the ground, nearly ten feet across. He saw a walkie-talkie sitting over by a tree.

"Darren, I want you to listen to me. It looks like the

hole has collapsed. Calm down. Can you tell me if this is your walkie-talkie?"

"Yeah, it is. Johnny! Dad!" Darren screamed.

"This is Pittsburgh Fire and Rescue, over. Does anybody read me, over?"

"Do you read, over?"

"We read, over!" Darren heard Dad's voice on the radio.

"They're okay!" Darren shouted. "They're alive! Dad, I'm here!" Darren tried to grab the walkie-talkie from the chief.

"Sir, my name is Joe Phillips. I'm the acting fire chief on site. What's your situation down there?"

"There are four of us, chief: I'm Dr. Peter Hawn, my son Johnny, Amy Lee, and an injured park ranger Dave Rondinelli. The ranger has a broken leg, but I think he's stable. We are looking for another way out, over."

"I read you loud and clear, sir. Can you tell me how far down you are?"

"Seventy-five feet, repeat, seventy-five, over."

"Thank you, over," the chief replied. "Keep looking for a way out, Dr. Hawn. I'm calling in more backup."

"Roger that. Thank god you're here."

The chief grabbed his two-way radio and called back to the station for more men. He decided to set up the lights at the cave-in site and make that the center of operations. He knew those four people down there were facing some long odds. Seventy-five feet down was a *long ways* down.

The chief had prior experience with a mine cave-in, and it didn't turn out too well. It happened in Somerset County, sixty miles southeast of Pittsburgh. The miners there had accidentally drilled into an abandoned mine filled with water. Soon, the miners were up to their necks in fifty-five-degree water. They died from hypothermia before the rescue crew could reach them. He still got nightmares over that one. The chief hoped, at least, that he wouldn't have to deal with water this time around.

"Excuse me, chief. I've got to get back to the parking lot to see my Grandpa. You should talk to him. He used to own a construction company."

"Is that so? What company, son?"

"Garvey Construction."

"Garvey Construction?" the chief looked surprised. "Well, yes, in that case I certainly will want to talk with him. Please have him come see me when he arrives."

"Yes, sir. I'll bring him right here."

24

The walkie-talkie squawked and the fire chief picked it up.

"Hello, chief? Can you hear me?" Amy's voice cackled over the tiny speaker. "Can you hear me, anyone?"

"Yes, this is the fire chief. Go ahead."

"Chief, my name is Amy Lee. Can you please contact my parents or my grandfather, to tell them I'm okay? Over."

"Yes, no problem. Who should I contact?"

"Better contact my grandfather. I think he can help you. My grandfather is Cecil Stewart. He lives in Fox Chapel, over."

"Did you say Cecil Stewart, ma'am? Over."

"Yes, chief, Cecil Stewart. It's an unlisted number, so please write this down, over."

Amy gave her grandfather's unlisted number to the fire chief. *This just about tops it all*, the chief thought. He really wasn't looking forward to phoning the richest man on the East Coast just to tell him that his granddaughter was buried underground in some kind of abandoned coal mine. He'd read stories in the paper about Cecil Stewart. He was friends with everybody who was somebody. No, this could be a career-killer for sure. *Don't shoot the messenger*, Chief Phillips thought.

"Hey, dispatch, this is Phillips down in Frick Park. Can you guys call this number and connect me, please? Thank you."

It wasn't but five minutes later that his radio beeped and a female dispatchers voice said, "Sir, we have you connected, go ahead."

"This is Cecil Stewart. Is this the person in charge?"

"Yes, sir, Mr. Stewart. I am fire chief Joe Phillips, out of station number six. Your granddaughter and several others are currently trapped in an underground mine of some sort, here in Frick Park. The hole that they used to enter the mine, well, it's collapsed. We are currently deciding what our rescue options are."

"Thank you for calling me, Chief. I want to be personally involved in this operation. I'm sure I don't have to tell you why."

"No, I understand, sir. We are going to do everything possible to save them."

"Yes. WE are going to do everything possible, and that

requires that you follow my explicit orders. Understood, Chief?"

"Yes, sir, understood. What do you have in mind?" He knew that Cecil Stewart, for all intents and purposes, probably bought the fire trucks at station number six. The industrialist made a mid-six-figure donation to the department every year. If the old man was giving orders, Joe was certainly going to follow them.

"I am going to send down one of my experts, Larry Siebert. He is a geologist, among other things, and he will give us an accurate reading of the type of rock that we're dealing with. I would like you to bring him to me when he arrives."

"Yes, sir. I will do that. Thank you, Mr. Stewart. I appreciate you helping us here."

"Larry is my right-hand man, and we are lucky that he is stateside. I will arrive before him, separately, via helicopter. Please have your men mark a suitable landing site with flares. My pilot would appreciate that."

"Yes, sir, Mr. Stewart."

"Amy's well-being is paramount! Do you understand what I am saying, Chief Phillips?"

"Yes Sir!"

"Good. I'm glad we understand each other, Chief. I'll see you shortly."

25

"Grandpa! I'm sorry I wasn't here when you pulled up."

"It's fine, Darren. Were you helping the fire department?"

"Yes. The chief and his men are down there. But something terrible has happened."

"What happened? Here, sit down. Breathe, and then tell me what happened. Slowly."

"Well, Grandpa, the hole we found, it collapsed while I was away calling you and the fire department. Now there's just this big spot in the ground, filled with rocks."

"What about your father, your brother, and you said others?"

"They're alive! I heard Dad on the walkie-talkie with the fire chief, and then I told the chief about you, and he wants to meet you."

"That's good news! That's excellent news. We'll get your dad, Johnny and the others out of there. Listen, it's going to be okay." Darren started crying uncontrollably.

"It's my fault. I helped Johnny plan the whole thing. And if I hadn't put my boot through those boards!" Darren cried.

"Please, stop crying. Accidents happen. You didn't cause the cave-in. It's not your fault, okay?"

Darren settled down a bit, his chest still heaving. "Okay, Grandpa. I just want them to be okay. I'm sorry."

"There, there. I want you to do something for me, okay?"

"Anything, Grandpa."

"I want you to take me down to where the chief is, okay? Can you do that?"

"Yeah, I can do that, but we have to take the trail. Be careful, Grandpa, it's really slippery. Do you have a flashlight?"

"Yes, I brought my own flashlight, dear. Let's get going, but don't go too fast, okay? Your grandpa's legs don't work as well as they used to."

"Okay." Darren held his grandfather's hand and led him from the lights of the fire truck to the stone gravel path that led down into the Frick Park woods. It was nighttime now, and their flashlight beams bobbed and weaved as they walked, passing firemen coming back up the trail. Darren had the route memorized by now, and it helped; the woods were now pitch black.

26

Cecil Stewart immediately called Larry Siebert and told him of the situation. Larry had expertise in a wide variety of fields, an ex-CIA agent, and head of security for Stewart Company. Cecil knew that he would be getting his money's worth from him tonight. As he sat in his brown leather chair in his office, he wondered, *Could they have found* The Pulpit? *What were the chances?* They blew that place to smithereens, hadn't they? The more Cecil thought about it, the more he worried. The location was correct. How many mines were near Regent Square? Of course it wasn't Frick Park then. They'd sold the land to Henry Frick, and then he donated it to the city in 1919. Cecil certainly had never revealed the location of The Pulpit. That left only one person: *Charles!*

"My name is Lou Garvey, nice to meet you, Chief."

"Likewise, Lou. We've got a serious situation here. Can we talk in private?"

"Sure, sure. Darren, would you please wait over there for me?"

"Okay, Grandpa."

The two men moved down the dark trail until they were out of earshot of the other men and Darren.

"Sir, I understand you owned Garvey Construction."

"Yes, I did. Forty-plus years, and I just retired."

"Well, sir, I remember that you did some work on the Fort Pitt tunnels. Is that correct?"

"Yes, it is, Chief. We won a contract to do part of the excavation on that project. Some other companies were involved there, too."

"Well, what if I told you that Cecil Stewart's granddaughter is stuck down there with your son, your grandson and a park ranger? And that Cecil Stewart himself is coming here. What would you think about that?"

"Peter is actually my stepson, though I've raised him since he was ten years old. His real father passed away, unfortunately." He bent his head and then lifted it. "Well, I'd say we're damn lucky, Chief." Grandpa gave the chief an intense look. "Do you know what Stewart has access to? He owns several mining companies around the tri-state area, big coal mining operations. He could probably get us a tunnel-boring machine!"

"Excuse me? A tunnel-boring machine?"

"Yes, they've been used for years to dig tunnels, but now they're getting smaller, more portable. We call them 'TBMs' for short. They can bore a hole right through solid rock, from thirty-six inches up to twelve feet in diameter, to a depth of over two hundred feet. If anybody in the tri-state area would have one, Chief, it would be Stewart, or his friend, Charles Shafer."

"Well, that's useful information, Mr. Garvey. Something like that could make the difference here."

The chief's radio buzzed. "Okay, that's good news, Chief. Out."

"Well, here we go. Cecil Stewart will be here shortly."

"That's good news," Lou Garvey agreed.

"I'd like to be able to count on you for advice, with your experience in construction. What do you think?"

"Certainly, anything I can do to help. Two of the most important people in my life are stuck down there. You can be damn sure I'll do whatever it takes to help them."

27

"Charles. Charles, wake up. It's Cecil Stewart on the phone. Charles!"

Charles Shafer awoke in a fright, only to see his housekeeper, Anna Cleaver, standing over him.

"Jesus, what time is it? You scared me half to death."

"It's ten past seven. I'm sorry to wake you from your nap, sir."

"Cecil? Are you sure?"

"I didn't want to wake you, but…but he kept saying it was urgent."

"Okay, I'll take it in my study. Phew, just give me a minute."

Anna Cleaver watched as Charles Shafer put on his slippers. She'd been his housekeeper for the past nine years and had grown very protective of the man who was so kind and generous with her and her family. There was nothing she wouldn't do for him.

She waited until she heard the line pick up, then she gently hung up the phone.

"Cecil, what's wrong? Are you okay?" Charles fairly shouted into the phone. "What's that blasted noise?"

"Forgive the noise, Charles, I'm in my helicopter. Listen, something's happened. Something terrible. There's been an accident involving The Pulpit."

There was silence on the line. "Charles?"

"Yes, I'm here. What kind of accident?"

"Well, there's been a cave-in. But let me start at the beginning. Some foolish children were playing in Frick Park yesterday, and they discovered a mine tunnel. Ring any bells?"

"Yes, it does, unfortunately."

"I thought it would. Well, these young boys uncovered what we so desperately tried to hide. Now one of these children, his father, a park ranger, and my precious granddaughter, Amy, are trapped underground in that godforsaken place."

"Amy? My God!"

"Yes, Amy. I know the irony is not lost on you. It took our best friend, but I won't allow it to claim Amy. You must help me. I realize we swore that we would never mention that godforsaken place. I know we three swore it. But, Charles, you are the only one who knows more about it than I do. I need your help tonight. Please help me save my granddaughter."

"Of course, of course. But, please, my friend, please calm down. It's imperative that we go about this the right way. Certain institutions must not be allowed to get involved. Agreed?"

"Agreed. Can you be ready in fifteen minutes?"

"Fifteen minutes?"

"Yes, that is when we'll be landing on your front lawn."

"Yes, I'll be ready."

"One more thing?

"Yes, Cecil?"

"Dress warmly, old friend."

The narrow beams of three flashlights crisscrossed the giant, domed ceiling. "Well, let's investigate," Peter said as he closed the first-aid kit. "I don't know how much time we have left, how long we can stay awake. Maybe, if we look hard enough, we might stumble across a way out of here."

He tried to sound as optimistic as he could, but even as the words left his mouth, Peter knew that his last sentence was mostly wishful thinking. He recalled reading a story about a group of Western Pennsylvania coal miners who got trapped underground by a cave-in. A few years before, the *Pittsburgh Press* covered the story in a series of hopeful vignettes that lasted for almost two weeks. But the reports of an impending rescue soon turned out to be painfully unrealistic. By the time the rescue team reached the miners, they found the men dead. He wondered, would this be their fate?

Whatever happened, he thought, he had to stay positive and think through the situation logically. *You've never given up before in your life, Peter Hawn. Use your mind to solve the puzzle.* He looked around with a critical eye at the giant space that stretched before him. *One way in, but only one way out?* he thought. His flashlight beam crossed the ceiling, which was probably near two-stories high. He could see the rubble that was left behind by the tunnel's collapse. Then Johnny yelled out.

"Hey, you guys, over here."

Peter and Amy ran over to where Johnny was standing. There was a hole in the wall that was sealed up with rocks and debris.

"I think it's another tunnel, and this one collapsed too!" Johnny said.

"It looks completely sealed." Amy paused and then threw her flashlight down. "We're not getting any breaks here! I mean, what the hell! What is this place?" Amy started sobbing. "I mean, all the mines I've seen have ventilation shafts, lighting, even telephone lines. There's none of that here! NONE OF IT! I don't understand!"

Peter came up and put his arms around her. "We're going to be okay. We'll find a way out. We can't give up. Please calm down, okay? I need you to be okay."

Amy stopped crying and picked up her flashlight. "These Murphy's Mart flashlights are hard to kill, aren't they?"

Johnny and Peter laughed.

"Yes, they are. They really are." He paused. "Hey guys, come over here and look at this, would you? Look at this wall."

Peter understood the room they were standing in wasn't some naturally occurring cavern; its walls were too smooth, the dimensions too perfect. It felt like being trapped inside a cake dish, only this one was deep underground, and gigantic. Peter walked over and pressed his hand against the slick, gray wall; it wasn't cold to the touch like he expected, instead it was warm. *If it feels slightly warm to my touch, then it's probably close to 100 degrees Fahrenheit*, Peter thought. As he caressed the wall, he guessed that the substance was a matrix of very hard plastic and some kind of metal.

"Amy, have a look at the wall." Peter said as his hand skimmed the surface of it. "I've never felt anything like it."

She walked over and aimed her flashlight where Peter's hand was resting.

"Let's see what my Swiss Army has to say about it." She reached into her jacket pocket and pulled out a shiny red pocketknife that bristled with tools. "It's even got a magnifying glass and a toothpick, though I doubt we'll have much use for them down here." She smiled. "My grandfather tells me to always be prepared, so he buys me things like this." Amy swung out a large blade from the knife and scraped it against the wall. "Whatever this stuff is, it's unbelievably hard. Look! The blade's not even scratching it!"

"It looks like titanium, guys, which is a very hard and lightweight metal that the military is using nowadays. Odd that it won't scratch like titanium will. Let's do a little experiment, shall we? Do you have any flares in that kit of yours?"

"Yes, we've got two flares. Where are you going with this?" Amy kneeled down and started riffling through the first-aid kit.

"I don't think a simple flare would have a chance against this stuff, but if we give it a little boost with pure oxygen…then in effect we'd have ourselves a crude acetylene torch. I think it's worth a try," Peter said.

"Great idea, Dad," Johnny piped in. "But how are you going to add the oxygen from that tank? Won't it blow up?"

"We won't use oxygen directly from the tank. There's a large syringe in the kit, right?"

"Yes, there is. Ahh! I see. That's ingenious!" Amy said. "You're a regular Tesla!"

"I don't know about all that. Tesla? Hmmm. That's some compliment. I'm not in that league."

"What's ingenious, and who's Tesla?" Johnny asked.

"Nikola Tesla was the greatest electrical inventor who ever lived. He worked with George Westinghouse in Pittsburgh. Tesla made Westinghouse what it is today. And ingenious, well, that's just Amy being way too nice to your old man."

"Oh," Johnny said.

"No, your dad IS a genius. See, he figured out how we can use the large syringe from the first-aid kit to add oxygen to the burning flare. The extra oxygen will increase the flame temperature considerably. I'd call that ingenious." Amy shrugged, looked at Peter, and said quietly, "Thanks for calming me down back there. I'm okay now."

"Anytime, no problem." Peter took the syringe from her and showed it to Johnny. "See, a fire's heat is controlled by how much oxygen is available. Basic chemistry. I'm going to add one good burst of pure O2 from the syringe."

"Cool, I hope it burns right through that wall."

"Me too, son. Me too."

Peter and Amy prepared the syringe and flare while Johnny looked on. It didn't take the two of them very long to fill the syringe full of oxygen from the tank. Amy lit the flare and held it right up against the wall.

"Here it goes!" Peter yelled over the sound of the flare.

"Be careful, Dad!"

Johnny watched his dad place the large syringe's needle near the flare's flame. The flare's color instantly changed from a ruby red to a blinding white light. The white-hot flame lasted several seconds, then the flare's color returned to normal. Amy pulled the flare away and all three of them gathered around the spot where it had been.

"Not a smudge, not even a hint of a scorch mark!" Peter said disgustedly.

"I don't believe it," Amy said.

"I believe it," Johnny said. "There's a reason why it won't burn. It's because it's alien metal. Just like Easter Island. Like how scientists can't explain how all those giant statues got moved from one side of the island to the other."

That changes things a bit, Peter thought. *A rescue team is going to have a tough time blasting their way through whatever these walls are made of.*

"That's an interesting hypothesis, Johnny. Alien metal. Hmmm. Let's use logic and see where it takes us, shall we? How long has this place been here, buried deep under Frick Park? If we could radiocarbon date this wall, then we'd have an accurate idea of when it was built. I have a feeling that it is pre-Columbian. Amy, have you seen any mention of this place in your research?"

"No, I haven't. I know this area was a hunting ground for the local Indian tribes, for hundreds of years before the Europeans got here. This room could be six hundred years or six thousand years old for all we know. Carbon dating would help immensely. But what if it's sixty thousand years old? That would certainly lend credence to your son's alien hypothesis."

"It would, wouldn't it? Okay, let's proceed along that line. What if this place wasn't built by humans?"

"That's a wild hypothesis, Doctor. Aliens? We're trapped in an alien-created chamber? I mean there might be another explanation for it. This could be a secret U.S. military project. Like the Minuteman nuclear missile silos that they've got hidden all over the country."

"Oh, yes, the infamous 'they,' or 'them,'" Peter said.

"Is that possible, Dad?"

"Yes, it's possible. There are hundreds of classified military projects that the general public knows nothing about. Some of them are pretty fantastic. I have a good buddy from my Princeton days, Alex Shriver, who works in a government lab in Nevada, outside Las Vegas. It's called S4, and the Department of Naval Intelligence runs it. He told me a few things that put my jaw on the floor, and he said there were things that he was working on that he couldn't…that he was scared to discuss."

"Your friend was scared?" Amy asked.

"When I say that he sounded scared, you'd have to

know more about Alex to understand the gravity of that statement. Alex isn't your usual bookworm scientist. Alex won a heavyweight golden gloves boxing title while we were in college. I went to a few of his fights. He was downright ferocious in the ring." Peter looked at Amy and Johnny. "I've watched Alex beat up muscle-bound, trained boxers, and he looked like he was having fun doing it. So when he told me he was scared, it got my attention."

"Wow," Amy said.

Johnny stood there listening to his dad.

"One of the things that Alex told me was that the Air Force had recovered some unusual objects from Roswell, New Mexico, in 1947. When I started asking specific questions about the objects, he told me that he was breaking the law by even telling me about it. What he did say was that I would be astounded if I saw the metal fragment that he was studying. He told me that this object was constructed from elements not found in our periodic table. He described it as being as thin and light as tinfoil, but completely impervious to damage."

"What does 'impervious' mean?" Johnny asked.

"It means it was resistant to any of the tests that Alex performed on it. And let me tell you, some of the tests were incredible in their own right."

"What kind of tests?" Amy asked.

"They put it at ground zero, and, well..."

"It survived a nuclear blast?" Amy said. "Seriously?"

"It not only survived a five-megaton underground nuclear explosion, but it came out completely unscathed. Alex and his team concluded that the material had quantum shifting properties. Have you ever heard of the multiverse?"

"Wasn't that what Feynman was talking about in his lectures?"

"You've read *Six Easy Pieces*?"

"Yes. I mean, those lectures changed modern physics."

"You're full of surprises, Amy. You really are."

Peter felt the fatigue creep back into his body as the amyl nitrate started to wear off.

"I think it's time for another dose of the wakeup pill." Peter coughed and let out a little smile.

"Very funny. I'm feeling it too. How about you, Johnny?"

"I'm not feeling sleepy. Maybe you feel it more because you're old?"

"Yeah, I'm almost decrepit. Out of the mouths of babes. But he could be right; age might play a factor." Amy said.

"How old are you?" Johnny asked innocently.

"You should never ask a woman her age," Amy said.

"Oh, sorry, I wasn't trying to make you mad."

"I'm only kidding. I'm twenty-four."

"Twenty-four isn't that old. Besides, that puts you in-between my dad and me. So if age matters, my dad will get tired first, you second, and me third. Right?"

"Right. I see your son here not only shares your good looks, Peter, but your brains as well."

Peter felt his cheeks flush, and he looked down at the ground so she wouldn't see the spreading grin on his face.

"First I'm a genius, now I'm good looking?"

He smelled her perfume, and he felt a tingle of excitement. He felt guilty, because Johnny was there. *What is wrong with me?* he thought. He was married, after all. He remembered the first time he saw Laura at Princeton. But this was more intense. Had he ever gotten so excited, so quickly? *Well, okay*, he thought. Maybe those times in eighth grade when he had to use a spiral notebook to cover the front of his jeans whenever a cute girl walked by. But this was getting embarrassing. *Her pheromones are triggering reactions in me*, thought the scientific part of his brain. *It's not such a terrible problem to have*, he thought, *being pursued by a young, wealthy woman who resembles a Penthouse Pet, and is kind, brave and intelligent.* But what happens if they manage to survive? What about Laura? He was still in love with his wife, wasn't he? He remembered the sight of Laura naked with Monica. He felt oddly detached thinking about it. Shouldn't he care more? Shouldn't his pride be hurt? Peter stared at Amy's flowing blonde hair. *What would it be like to kiss her lips? Her skin must be unimaginably soft. She smells so good!* How could she smell so good after all they'd been through? He closed his eyes and imagined Amy running her fingers through his hair. She was holding his head in her hands and looking into his eyes. It felt so good...

"Peter, are you okay?" Amy said as she grabbed his arm. "Johnny, hurry! Hand me the first-aid kit! Your dad's falling asleep!"

28

P eter walked into the room and sat on the edge of the large canopy bed. The white down comforter felt luxuriously soft. He looked around and observed the walls were painted a deep, pleasing tangerine color. He noticed a white lace bra hanging from the doorknob to the master bathroom. A fuzzy, pink sweater lay folded on the bed next to where he sat. He could see the label in the sweater and it read "Saks Fifth Avenue." He reached down and picked up the sweater. The cashmere wool felt incredibly soft to the touch. He brought it up to his nose and smelled a combination of familiar sweet perfume and a woman's light sweat. It wasn't Laura's sweater. He checked the size on the tag: Medium. Correct size, but Laura rarely wore perfume, and when she did, she chose a flowery scent that was more likely to trigger his allergies than turn him on. No, this was a strangely intoxicating fragrance, and he shamelessly took another deep breath as he closed his eyes and buried his nose into the soft fabric.

"Do you have a thing for pink cashmere?" Amy said, walking into the room. She smiled. "If so, I'll make sure I exclusively wear pink cashmere sweaters from now on."

Peter jumped at the sound of her voice, feeling embarrassed, and hurriedly placed the sweater back on the bed.

"I was just, umm, noticing your good taste in clothes, Amy." Peter nervously glanced around the room.

"Oh, well, for a minute there, I thought you were getting off smelling my sweater." Amy grinned. "It's a little kinky, but it's okay if you were. It's really okay, you know." Amy turned around and Peter stared at the tight curves of her Levi jeans.

"Do you mind if I show you something?"

"Of course not." Peter sighed, relieved she was changing the subject.

"I feel like I can share this with you now, after all we've been through together. I want to show you how happy I am that your divorce is final."

Peter was confused. "My divorce is final?"

"You are such a kidder! I never knew you were so funny until we got together. You know, sometimes I can't believe that we're dating. I used to read your articles when I was still in high school. I had this picture of you that I cut out from a *National Geographic*. I kept it in my locker at boarding school. I never dreamed that you'd be in my bedroom someday, smelling my sweater."

"I wasn't smelling your sweater, and one more thing —" Peter was about to tell her that he was pretty sure that he was still married, when she interrupted him.

"Yes, you were," she said, smiling and holding up the sweater. "Confess now, tell me the truth."

"Okay, I was smelling it," he admitted. "It's just that you always smell so good, Amy. I couldn't help myself. Listen—"

She interrupted him again. "You don't have to help yourself, Peter. I want you to smell my sweaters. You can smell anything of mine you want. Okay? I think you're the most fantastic man I've ever met." She stood there for a moment in front of him. "And I want to show you something. Something special. Don't move."

Amy ran into the master bathroom, shutting the door behind her.

"This won't take long. Just sit tight," she shouted from behind the bathroom door. "I think you're really going to like this."

Peter knew that he was dreaming, but it felt somehow more real than any other dream before. It reminded him of a vivid, recurring dream that first started his freshman year in high school. In that dream, an anonymous naked woman came up from behind him and pressed her bare breasts against his back. Then she'd reach around, hook her thumbs under his waistband, and slowly lower his swim trunks. He'd look down and see her beautiful, suntanned fingers take hold of his long, erect penis. He'd stand there and watch as her hands went up and down, up and down. She would masturbate him with a knowing and varied pace, alternating a series of quick strokes and gentle thumb rubs over his swollen glans until he felt himself reaching the point of unbearable tension. He'd awaken with a moan, unable to stop his hot, sticky frustrations as they came pouring out of him, soaking his pajamas. He remembered that particular wet dream, how lifelike it felt. Now, he had that same feeling of realness, where the dream transcends the dream state and takes on a palpable solidity.

"What do you think?"

Peter looked up to see Amy standing there wearing only an unbelievably sexy white lace bra, garter belt and panties.

"Wow."

"So you like it? It took forever to get here from the mail-order place."

He stared at the pretty bra straining to contain her pendulous breasts. He could see her nipples poking through the sheer material. Her breasts were larger than Laura's.

"It's kind of cold in here, isn't it?" She giggled. "I hope you don't mind."

"You're beautiful; that's all I can say."

"Don't speak, I just want to please you. Will you let me do that? Do you like my body? I can tell that you do." She smiled and dropped to her knees. "You're hard!"

Peter looked down as she got between his knees and undid his belt.

"I've been waiting to do this for a long, long time. But I'm a good Christian girl, if you know what I mean? Most people can't believe it when I tell them I'm still a virgin. But I have done other things. Here, let me take off my bra, so you can watch me while I take care of you. I know men like that."

Amy removed her bra and then lowered his jockey shorts to his knees, and his hardness popped out and hit her in the face.

"Hmm, I'm not the only one who was ready, was I? Wow, you're big," she said as she stuck her tongue out and licked the underside of his shaft.

If this is a dream, then I don't want to wake up, Peter thought.

She looked up at him. "I really enjoy giving oral sex, but the guys I've been with haven't lasted very long, once I got them in my mouth."

Peter let out a deep groan as he felt her warm lips cover the head of his cock. He reflexively placed his hands in her thick blonde hair, wanting to push her head down, instinctively wanting to push himself right down her throat. Her tongue swirled in lazy circles as she began to swallow him.

Amy stopped her ministrations. "Whatever you do, don't pull out. I want to taste you."

She lowered her head back down, and kept her big

blue eyes staring up at him as she hungrily took his penis completely down her throat. Peter rode the incredible sensations as her throat kept squeezing him. She was experienced! Amy's relentless blowjob was pulling the orgasm from his body. He stopped fighting the urge to bury himself in her throat, and he let his hips fall forward, sinking his shaft down farther, until her chin bounced against his tightening scrotum. Then he felt his cock get ultra-hard as she pushed him to the edge. She deftly slipped her hand around his testicles and gently squeezed them. He could feel her fingernails as she squeezed his balls harder and held them close to his body. She pulled her mouth off of him and took him in her hand, stroking him furiously.

"Feel it building up? Let it go!" Amy demanded, as she lowered her mouth back down and forced his steely erection down her throat.

"Ahhh! He groaned as he started to ejaculate in her mouth.

"Ummmm. That's it. Ummm. Give it to me," she said as she hungrily sucked, licked and swallowed all she could of Peter's powerful orgasm.

29

L aura was watching television when she heard the shrill ringing of the hotel room telephone. She guessed Peter had just read the note she'd left on the kitchen counter. He was probably going to yell at her for taking off, and Laura didn't want to deal with it right now. She didn't need to hear another "Peter lecture." That's all he seemed to do lately, criticize her.

After their confrontation at the house, she and Monica decided to get away for the night and drive to the lodge at Donegal Springs Resort. *Peter would just have to handle the boys by himself tonight,* she thought. Donegal Springs Resort, located in the Appalachian Mountains, sixty miles outside Pittsburgh, held a special place in Laura's heart because it was here that she and Monica spent their first night together. It happened last winter, when Monica invited Laura to Donegal Springs for a weekend of skiing.

They'd spent a long day on the beautiful slopes, and after dinner, and a few snifters of fine cognac, Monica seduced Laura. It started with a nude back rub, Monica using her training as a professional masseuse to completely relax her. Then she began a tantric massage, manipulating the energy in Laura's Chakra points. She told Laura that she needed a Chakra cleansing. As Monica worked her magic fingers over her lower back, Laura succumbed to the sensations; soon she was dripping wet with excitement. It surprised them both, when Laura sat up and pulled Monica into her arms. But that was months ago, and they'd been sneaking their sexual liaisons behind their husbands' backs ever since. Now Peter was calling to lay a guilt trip on her, and Laura wasn't in the mood. The phone finally stopped ringing. *Good*, she thought. *Why can't he understand that I've changed? I'm sick and tired of him trying to control me!* The phone started ringing again. *Ring! I hate that phone*, she thought. Monica was still in the shower, and Laura was glad she wouldn't hear her argue with Peter.

"Peter, can't you just take care of the kids for once? It's just one night for chrissakes!"

"Ah ma'am, my name is Sergeant Charles Heiderman with the Pennsylvania State Police. I'm trying to reach Mrs. Laura Hawn."

"This is Laura Hawn."

"Mrs. Hawn, there's been an accident involving your husband and your son, John."

"Oh, my God! What happened? A car accident?" Laura started crying. She had been so ready to start fighting. Suddenly, she felt a tidal wave of guilt sweep over her.

"No, ma'am, it's hard to explain the situation over the phone. What I can tell you right now is that your husband and your son had an accident in an underground tunnel in Frick Park. That's in Regent Square."

"I know where Frick Park is, Sergeant. I live in Squirrel Hill."

"Ah, yes, ma'am. I can understand you're upset. There is a rescue effort underway."

Laura let the sergeant's words sink in. *Underground tunnel? Rescue effort?*

"Ma'am, are you still there?"

"Yes, I'm here. I don't understand. This is unbelievable!"

"M'am, we've sent a Somerset County Sheriff police car to escort you to the park. It'll be there in five minutes, right in front of the main lodge. Just bring your car around, okay?"

"Yes. Yes. I'll be there right away. Thank you. What was your name?"

"Sergeant Heiderman, ma'am. A patrol car will be there shortly. Goodbye."

Laura stood there shaking, tightly holding the phone in her hand. She heard the shower turn off.

"Laura, who was that?" Monica called from the bathroom. "Was it Peter?"

"No, that was the state police. There's been some kind of accident with Peter and Johnny." Each word came out in a dry, monotone voice. "I have to get to Pittsburgh." Laura headed for the door. "I'm taking the car. I have to go now!"

30

C harles Shafer looked out the window of the Huey Bell and watched the bright lights of Three Rivers Stadium along the Ohio River. He didn't like to fly and felt a bit queasy as Cecil's pilot swooped the Bell jet helicopter across the Pittsburgh skyline from Sewickly, past the Incline on Mt. Washington on their way to Regent Square and Frick Park. He looked over at Cecil, who sat there with his head in his hands. Cecil was his best friend, but tonight he might be forced to abruptly end their friendship. He wondered what kind of Judas he'd become, and how far he was prepared to go? His life had become a complex series of sacrifices and secrets, each in turn bringing him more wealth and power, but forcing him to alienate those he loved. He felt disgusted with himself, though he couldn't confide that in anyone. He also couldn't tell a soul about the things he knew. The U.S.

government had long ago given him the highest classified intelligence rating. He hoped to God that tonight his usually infallible gut instinct was wrong. As the helicopter flew onward, he hoped he wouldn't have to betray the one true friend he had left.

"We could use Bill's help right now," Cecil yelled. "Right, Charles?"

"Yes, I wish he was here," Charles agreed. "Bill would have been useful in this situation. No doubt about that." The two men stared at each other. "Are these headsets secured?" Charles asked.

"Yes, the pilot cannot hear what we're saying, unless we push the orange button. Speak freely, my friend."

"Good. It's hard to believe they found it. Isn't it, Cecil?"

"Damn that place, damn it to hell," Cecil said.

"I thought Bill's nitroglycerin buried it forever, but The Pulpit seems to have a life of its own, an invincibility."

"Yes, it surely does. But also some kind of dreadful curse above our very heads."

"It hasn't taken Amy yet, Cecil, and we're not going to let it. I will spare no expense or resource in her rescue." Charles was lying. Of course, he had no intention saving any of the unfortunate people trapped with The Pulpit. Cecil's granddaughter and the others would unfortunately have to be sacrificed, a small price to pay in order to keep one of the country's biggest secrets safe. Even Charles didn't have the authority to change what was almost certainly going to happen. The intelligence community couldn't afford another high-profile bungling like Roswell. He knew the government protocols concerning alien technology, a non-negotiable policy of denial and misinformation, using force, intimidation and assassination if necessary to keep the information secure. Careers were intentionally ruined, and honest people discredited, all in the name of national security. He knew from experience, as he was there at Wright-Patterson when they brought in the craft and bodies from that ranch in New Mexico, back in 1947. He was already firmly entrenched in the intelligence world by then, con gratis, after Shafer Industries participated in the Lend Lease Act. The company provided millions of dollars of aid to England in the form of ships and munitions. Also, Shafer Industries' applied technologies division helped the U.S. government develop their first radar systems. This brought Charles patriotic bragging rights in the press but, more importantly, ensured his company's backdoor lock on several lucrative government contracts post-war. Those military contracts quadrupled the fortunes of men like Charles Shafer and Howard Hughes. But Charles held an advantage that the eccentric Mr. Hughes lacked: he had prior knowledge of the outcome of World War II. In one of his "deep dreams" using The Pulpit, he had seen the second war in Europe and how the allies' armor and aircraft turned the war to their advantage. He had witnessed the secret government work at Los Alamos and the forth-coming strides in practical nuclear physics. Yes, this supernormal foresight gave Shafer Industries a crushing advantage over their competitors.

"I knew I could count on you, Charles." Cecil smiled. "I feel better knowing you are right by my side, once again."

"Think nothing of it. We'll get your granddaughter out of this mess, and we'll put an end to this affair, once and for all."

31

"Peter, Peter! Wake up, dammit! Wake up!" Amy held Peter by the shoulders, shaking him. "We need another one of those capsules, Johnny. Hand me one."

Peter opened his eyes while shaking his head. "Okay, okay. That's enough!"

"Thank heaven. We couldn't wake you."

"Yeah, Dad, it was super hard to wake you up this time."

"Whoa. Was I out long?"

"You've been asleep for almost twenty minutes, and I was worried because your breathing became erratic."

Images from the erotic dream with Amy flashed across his mind. Usually Peter only remembered bits and pieces of his dreams, but this time it was different. He could recall every single detail. And it was so *good!* He never realized sex could be that intense. Had he just had the wrong partner all these years? How could he ever go back to Laura's arms after experiencing *that*? Peter couldn't help staring at Amy as he remembered the dream.

"Well, actually you were moaning. Yes, um, it must have been a very intense dream."

"Umm, can we talk, in private? Johnny, can you excuse us for a minute? This is adult conversation."

"Oh, sure. No problem." He walked away slowly, his head lowered. "I'll be right over here, checking on the ranger."

"Don't worry, he'll get over it," Peter whispered to Amy. "He just wants to be included in everything."

"Yeah, I was like that at his age. Well, what's going on? What's up?"

"Well, I don't know how to say this, umm, properly. You might have to help me here."

"Okay, I'll do the best I can."

"I just had one of those intense dreams that this place seems to foster, only mine had more of an adult nature. Get my drift?"

"You had a sex dream? Is that what you're trying to say? Well, that would explain the heavy breathing and moaning," she said with a laugh.

"Yes, but there's more. You see, you were in my dream. I mean really with me. Get it? You and I?"

"Okay, Umm." Amy started turning red. "Now I'm embarrassed. That's some confession." Then she turned a bit bolder. "Can I ask you if it was a good dream? Was it good? I mean, I may be out of line here. I realize you're married."

"It was more than good. To be honest, it was amazing." Peter bunched up his face. "And it was quite graphic. Of course with my luck, it had to happen in a dream. But here I am, trying to describe how vivid it was, how lifelike!" Peter started gesturing with his hands now. "It felt as real as you and I being here, talking together in this moment. I'm probably going to throw you some strange looks and, well, I don't want there to be any secrets between us. I just had to tell you."

"Really? It was good?"

"You're a very attractive girl. I mean, that's not the question."

"But do YOU find me attractive?"

"Amy, that's not the point. I'm thinking it's because of what we're going through. You know, like when hostages emotionally bond with their kidnappers. Remember Patty Hearst? She robbed a bank with her abductors. I'm feeling this way because you..."

"Shush," she said as she pressed her lips to Peter's. He felt the heat of her mouth and the softness of her full lips. Her long blonde hair fell over his face as she kissed him. Her sweet scent was intoxicating. Then she pulled away and left him standing there, his heart beating wildly and his mind racing.

She smiled at him. "I've had a crush on you for a long time, Dr. Hawn—I mean, Peter." She shoved her hands in the back pockets of her jeans. She looked at the ground as she spoke to him.

"Really?" was all he could muster.

"I don't really know you, but I can't help feeling what I feel around you," she said, taking a deep breath. "You're an amazing man. You remind me of my grandpa; you're a good man. I've fantasized about what it'd be like to sleep with you, and… well, I've honestly thought about it for a while. I don't know exactly what I'm trying to say. Am I making any sense?"

"Yes." Peter's face was beet red now. "I feel it too. It's just that I feel guilty about being attracted to you. I think my marriage is ending, but I'm not sure it is. Just listen to me. It's different when you have children. It complicates things. I guess what I want to say is, I think you're an incredible young woman, but if anything were to happen between us, I'd want it to happen the right way, at the right time. Does that make sense?"

"Sort of." Amy turned her eyes away from Peter's, trying to hide the hurt.

"That kiss was incredible, don't get me wrong. I'm never going to forget it." He reached out and brushed a few silky strands of hair from her face. "But please understand, I am still married. You know, it's hard to think clearly, especially when you're standing this close to me, and you smell this good, okay?"

"Okay, Peter."

"Good. Phew! I'm glad we talked about it. Cleared the air."

"Me too. I just want you to know that I'm here for you." Amy smiled at him.

"Who knows what will happen. But right now, we need every ounce of our concentration to get out of this mess. So let's take another look around, shall we?"

"Just one more thing?"

"Yes?"

"That was some kiss, mister."

32

The bright landing light pierced the light fog and gently falling rain, blinding the firemen standing below as they looked up and watched the jet helicopter's descent. The pilot performed a somewhat difficult but perfect landing as he carefully avoided the Forbes Avenue Bridge, placing the craft squarely in the middle of the soccer field in upper Frick Park. One tall man emerged holding a cane, his head lowered as he slowly made his way past the spinning rotor. Then the rear door of the helicopter opened and an elderly man in a slightly odd-looking wheelchair was lowered to the ground by some kind of mechanical arm. The two men cleared the rotor's wash and headed straight for the work lights surrounding the red Pittsburgh City fire truck parked at the edge of the field. The fire chief saw the duo approaching him, and it suddenly dawned on him that he was about to meet two of the most powerful men in America. He recognized their faces as they drew nearer. Uncharacteristically, the fire chief straightened his hat.

"Welcome, Mr. Stewart, Mr. Shafer. I'm Pittsburgh Fire Chief, Joe Phillips. Please follow me, gentlemen, to the command center tent. Let's get out of this drizzle and grab a cup of hot coffee, if you'd like." He turned and looked at Cecil. "Do you need additional assistance?"

Cecil smiled. "That's very kind of you, Chief, but my wheelchair is designed to maneuver over the roughest terrain. Should come in handy tonight I suppose." The fire chief looked nervous. Had he managed to insult the man?

As if reading his mind, Cecil said, "Relax, Chief. We're here to do one thing: safely retrieve my granddaughter and her friends from this predicament. Charles and I are eager to hear your plans, so let's get going. Oh, one more thing."

"Yes, Mr. Stewart?" The chief's voice wavered.

"Like I said before, more of our people will arrive shortly. Will you send a man up to the parking lot to greet them, and bring them here?"

"Of course, Mr. Stewart. I'll send someone immediately. Oh, and before I forget, there are two fellas from the FBI here. Over there, wearing the black coats."

"Yes, thank you, Chief." Cecil hid his surprise under a smile.

Charles stood, leaning lightly on his rosewood cane, a grin stretching his thin lips. Cecil's eyes narrowed, "I wish

I found that bit of news as amusing as you do. Personally, I've never cared much for government, too many damn secrets and red tape."

"You have a point, but suppose they can help us rescue Amy?"

"Well, in that case, they can send in the U.S. Cavalry for all I care."

"That's the spirit, Cecil! Perhaps the cavalry is on its way."

Lou Garvey sat by a heater in one of the large tents that the fire department had set up. He was curiously watching the two men in black coats. They had arrived without much fanfare, but they'd nonetheless attracted his attention. They looked military, with the requisite high-and-tight haircuts. Lou noticed they kept to themselves, standing in the far corner of the tent, sipping coffee. *They are conspicuous for their inconspicuousness*, he thought, and it got him thinking. Like, why would the government send its stoolies out to the collapse of an old coal mine? Had Cecil Stewart brought these men here? After all, the Stewarts were an incredibly powerful and connected family. Lou had once seen a picture in the Pittsburgh Press of Cecil Stewart and President Ford having breakfast at the White House. That could be the connection, an explanation for the government men. Lou wondered as he sat there in the folding chair, sipping his somewhat bitter, lukewarm coffee. He was determined to help get the rescue operation off and running in high gear, but he feared the government's involvement would slow it down. *While these idiots are busy checking their manuals, they still don't have a solid rescue plan!*

One of the government men walked over to the coffee machine, next to where Lou was sitting. He thought, *time to introduce myself, and maybe get a few questions answered.*

"Hello, I'm Lou Garvey, the boys' grandfather." Lou extended his hand, and it was met in a firm handshake.

"Agent Robert Ray, FBI. Nice to meet you. Terrible situation we have here, Mr. Garvey, just terrible. I want you to know the U.S. government is doing all we can to help."

"That's certainly good news, Mr. Ray, because we need all the help we can get. Uh, hey, maybe you can answer a question that I've been tossing around in the old food processor." Lou pointed to his head.

"Sure, I'll do the best I can."

"Good, well, can I ask you what you're doing here? See, I've been sitting here wondering why exactly the U.S. government is interested in a mine collapse on the east side of Pittsburgh—interested enough to send two federal agents down here. Care to enlighten me?"

"That's a good question, Mr. Garvey, and I understand your concern. Honestly right now, all I've been told is that your son and the others might have stumbled upon an illegal interstate waste disposal site. Nuclear waste."

"You're telling me this place is some kind of radioactive trash dump?"

"Well, we've seen this kind of thing before, and of course the FBI works hand in hand with the EPA. We're here to ascertain the situation, and report back to headquarters. Right now, you probably know as much, or maybe more, than we do."

Lou listened carefully as the FBI agent spoke. Not much of what he said made sense, but he let the man ramble on about EPA certificates and groundwater contamination.

Lou nodded his head. "That sounds pretty serious, EPA violations, contamination and all, but what I care about is getting my son and grandson back. You know, I used to own a construction company, Agent Ray. If there's anything I can do to help, please don't hesitate to ask."

"We're doing everything we can to help them, sir. I promise you that. And I'll inform my superiors of your generous offer. Thank you." Then the agent looked into Lou's eyes, firmly shook his hand again, and turned and walked away.

Lou looked down at his cup of coffee while his mind raced ahead. From employees that stole, to suppliers intentionally shorting him, he had firsthand experience with liars. He'd just been lied to, he was sure of it. As he mentally sifted through their conversation, he tried to sort the facts from the lies. His thoughts drifted to the time he hired a foreman named David Dyson. The guy used to cheat on his wife and then brag about it in the office. Lou ignored Dyson's infidelity because he was a good job-site manager. That changed when Lou caught him embezzling money from his cement orders. In retrospect, Dyson's marriage infidelity taught Lou a lesson; *a liar will lie in all parts of their life.*

It nagged Lou's mind—what was so important here that the agent would lie about it? Whatever was going on, he decided to play dumb for a while and keep close to the action.

Lou sat down in the chair, feeling tired, and feeling incredibly old. What mess had his boys gotten into? He breathed a heavy sigh and took another sip of the terrible tasting coffee. As the temperature dropped, he wished he'd worn his good wool sweater. He shivered, pulled up the collar of his coat, and braced himself for whatever was to come.

33

P eter closed his notebook and took a break from working. He'd spent the last hour studying the obelisk's symbols and markings, and honestly, he needed a little rest. He was beginning to understand, but inside, he was fighting self-doubt. He'd always had a weakness for solving puzzles, and now he was faced with the greatest puzzle of all.

He stood there for a few minutes, appraising the situation, and then he remembered something.

"It's a giant puzzle, isn't it? Twelve symbols, and they look Sumerian. If Zecharia Sitchin could only see this!"

"But you like puzzles Dad." Johnny stood up. "Sitchin? Who's that?"

"Sorry son, I was thinking out loud. Well, Sitchin is a scientist obsessed with Sumer and Mesopotamia. You know, I even met him once, in the New York City library.

He was doing research and we literally bumped into each other. What an interesting guy."

"Dad, I still don't know what you're talking about."

"Remember that book I showed you last month? The one with the stars and the planets on the cover?"

"Yeah, I remember. That's what you're talking about?"

"That's his latest book. It's called *The 12ᵗʰ Planet*. Have you read it, Amy?"

"I've never heard of him before. What's *The 12ᵗʰ Planet* about?"

"Zecharia thinks aliens gifted ancient man with technology and made genetic alterations on our ancestors. He says mankind's existence is an ongoing alien experiment. Kind of out there, huh? But, he's also an expert in ancient Sumerian and Hebrew texts."

"That's pretty far out," Amy said.

"Yeah, he's anything but mainstream. But the guy is intelligent, and to me, his theories are intriguing. We talked for two hours straight, as I remember."

"Do you think that these symbols really are Sumerian?" Amy said.

"I think they're related. Take this symbol for example."

"What does it mean?" Johnny asked.

"I think it represents one of the months in the calendar. See? Twelve symbols."

"So you think this is a giant calendar?" Amy asked.

"I suppose it could be a calendar, but I suspect it's more than that. Hold on a second. What's this?"

"What, Dad?"

"Hmm. Hold on. I'm counting. Fifty-five, fifty-six, fifty-seven... Hmm. Sixty."

"Sixty what?" Amy asked

"Sixty hash marks on each side of this pictogram. See? They're right on the border. Subtle, but important."

"I see them, Dad."

"Me too," Amy said. "What's the significance of sixty?"

"Six times sixty is three hundred and sixty. I'd wager it means either degrees or days. See, the Sumerian's mathematical structure was based on the number sixty, and there are still vestiges of their mathematics present in our society today. Like the three hundred and sixty-five days in our calendar, or three hundred and sixty degrees in a circle. Also twelve inches in a foot is two times six, or how about a dozen eggs? You can blame the Sumerians for all of it, and I think we're seeing that system, right here."

"It could be a record of crops or commerce, like the Egyptian hieroglyphs. The ones I've seen were placed in royal burial chambers. They celebrated a certain god or gods, or they were records of crop yields and such," Amy said.

"I'm thinking about the Rosetta Stone, how it helped decipher the Egyptian hieroglyphs. Let's see if we can't decipher what's been written here. Johnny, you'll be the light holder, okay?"

"Okay. Do you really think you guys can figure out what this means?"

"I got it! It's an almanac!" Amy said triumphantly.

"You're close, but take a look at this." Peter pointed to one of the symbols. "This must be one of the Sumerian gods. Sitchin called them *Nephilim*. He argued in his book that the carvings of the Nephilim depicted them wearing some kind of space suit. This one looks like something right out of Sitchin's book. And look at this." Peter pointed to another of the symbols set in the unknown metal. He touched the symbol with his index finger, and for a split-second he felt something odd. "Did you guys feel that?"

"What?" Amy said.

"I don't know, like a vibration or something. There it is again!"

"I felt it. Wow!" Johnny shouted.

"Was that a tremor?" Amy asked.

"I don't think so. It's a pulse. Feel it now?"

"Yes, I feel it! It's got a rhythm. Wait a minute, what's happening?" Amy screamed. "I can't see my hand!" As she watched in horror, her left hand began to slowly dissolve. *No, not dissolving*, she thought. She reached out with her right hand and she could feel the fingers of her left hand, perfectly intact.

"Here!" She grabbed Peter's hand and shoved it past

her vanishing wrist. "Feel! Oh, my God, I'm turning invisible!"

"I feel your hand, it's still there," Peter said as he blinked his eyes. He could feel her hand, could feel her nails, but he couldn't see any of what he was touching. Oddly enough, he thought about the mimes that performed at the Three Rivers Arts Festival. Then he looked at her stricken face. She was crying, and she grabbed Peter with her other arm.

"Hold on. Don't cry, okay? There's got to be an explanation for this." He pulled Amy closer to him, wanting desperately to protect her. "I think I started some kind of reaction. It must have activated when I touched the symbols."

"Ahhhh!" Johnny screamed. "Dad, it's happening to you!"

Peter brought his hand up, and though he could feel his arm and hand moving upward, his right arm had disappeared up to his elbow. He held his invisible arm up, more curious than terrified. "This is amazing. Just like in the movie, *The Invisible Man*." Then he started to laugh. "Ha, Ha, Ha!" And then Amy started to laugh.

"Stop laughing!" Amy said. "This isn't funny. Is it?" She laughed again.

"Dad, it's happening to me!" Johnny shouted. His hands were invisible, his arms ended in dissolving stumps.

"If this keeps up," Amy looked at him. "We're all going to disappear."

Peter thought for a moment. "I think this thing is rearranging the atoms in our body."

"Peter! I'm scared," Amy cried.

"I'm scared too, but let's not panic yet. I think we're dealing with a quantum-rearranging device." He nodded his head to one side. "Let's move this way, away from it."

They stumbled backward, awkwardly retreating from the obelisk. Each of them was partially invisible now, and as the three of them held onto each other, they looked like one strange, moving, multi-limbed human. Gradually, their arms and legs began to reappear.

"Look at that! We're coming back!" Amy screamed.

"That's what I was hoping for," Peter said.

"Wow! Look at my hand, guys!" Johnny was holding his hand up, and at first they could see only the blank stump of his wrist. Then his hand began to appear in what looked like time-elapsed photography. "Awesome!" he screamed.

"This proves its effects are proximity based, and they're reversible. That's a relief. It would have made life very interesting if it wasn't." Peter held up his own hand, and watched the same process repeat itself. Then he looked at Amy. "You okay?"

Amy's limbs were almost fully visible now. "It's working. Thank God."

"Keep moving back, okay?" Peter said. The three of them moved farther away, until they were standing about fifty feet from the machine. They each held up their hands and arms, and smiled at each other.

"How did you know?" Amy asked.

"It was a simple hypothesis, and luckily I was right. I think we'll be okay now. Are you guys ready to hear my other hypothesis about this machine? Hold onto your hats, this is going to sound crazy."

Just then a bright blue light came up from the floor of the room and started moving over the three of them.

"Don't be scared, everybody." Peter said. Johnny ran over and grabbed his dad, burying his face in his jacket.

"We're being scanned right now. I don't think the blue light will hurt us. This must be part of the process."

"What process?" Amy asked.

Peter absorbed the scene for a moment. "I'm guessing the light is some kind of advanced X-ray. That thing is gathering information about us. What I was going to say, and I know this will sound far-fetched, is that I think we've discovered some kind of time and/or teleportation machine! I don't know how it got here, or who built it, but only one thing can explain what just happened...a quantum breakdown! That explains the invisibility. Our photons were being rearranged."

The blue light stopped.

"No more blue light." Peter shrugged. "I guess it has all the information it needs."

"But it doesn't look like a machine. There are no gears or wires or anything. There are no buttons." Johnny said.

"It's a machine alright, but maybe a machine that no man has ever seen before. This technology is far beyond what modern-day science is capable of."

"Peter, are you thinking what I'm thinking? Is that why you've got a smile on your face?"

"Yes, that's exactly why I'm smiling. You read my mind." His face was animated. "If we could figure out how to operate it, we could use it to get out of here. I read somewhere that quantum physicists are convinced that all the material in the universe is made up of photons. They believe everything is basically the same thing atomically, from a rock to a human being. This thing rearranges photons, so it must operate using the principles of quantum entanglement."

"Okay, you're losing me." Amy said, tapping her head.

"Like on *Star Trek*, Dad? Is this thing like a transporter or something?"

"Yes, that's a good analogy. But let's back up a minute, okay? I'll try to explain it the easiest way I know how. See, some physicists have theorized that there are an infinite number of universes that exist, worlds like ours, but each subtly different. Even the past and the future might be just different universes, and not immovable places on a one-way timeline. If that's true, then it'd be possible to build a machine that manipulates matter on an atomic scale, thereby allowing time travel or teleportation. It all comes down to the fact that an electron can be two places at once; scientists have proven that. This hypothetical electron I was talking about, well, it's in two *universes* at once. Others say it's in an infinite number of universes at once. Okay, stay with me here; what if this is a quantum device? That would explain the rearranging of our photons, and the invisibility! I think we just witnessed atomic disassembly, a prerequisite for quantum travel."

"Isn't it dangerous? Could it kill us? I mean, even on *Star Trek* they sometimes have accidents with the transporter." Johnny's voice sounded tentative.

"Yes, it's dangerous because we're dealing with a powerful unknown. But, I think it's our best chance at the moment. What do you say?"

"I don't see that we have much choice, Doc. We're trapped down here, no way out. The batteries in the radios are pretty much toast. I'm not even sure how much breathable air is left. I say yes, let's continue."

"Do it, Dad." Johnny said.

"Okay then, it's unanimous. I'll get to work on translating the symbols."

34

L ou Garvey watched curiously as the fire chief introduced Cecil Stewart and Charles Shafer to the rescue team. He guessed there were two-dozen firefighters, a dozen or so policemen, himself, the FBI guys, and a few more fellas he didn't recognize, all sitting there under the tent, listening to the chief. Lou ignored the chief and the rescue team and instead focused his gaze on Stewart and Shafer. He recognized the two of them, even though he'd never met them before. He'd seen their faces on the covers of *Time*, *Newsweek*, and the Pittsburgh newspapers, so they were quite familiar. *What fortune*, he thought, *could bring two of the most powerful industrialists of the twentieth century to Frick Park on this cold and rainy October night?* These two men were J. Paul Getty wealthy. They were politically connected, too, and he'd seen them on television attending the Republican presidential convention. As he discretely studied Cecil Stewart, sitting there in an unusual-looking wheelchair, he noticed the man was genuinely upset. *A natural reaction*, Lou thought, *upon hearing the news that your granddaughter was trapped in a mineshaft.* Then he looked at Charles Shafer. He was an imposing figure, much taller than Lou had imagined. Shafer stood there leaning on a cane, but even so, Lou guessed he stood well over six feet four and had the shoulders of a linebacker. He exuded a strange physical prowess, somewhat shocking considering the man's age.

As he watched, he caught Shafer making eye contact with one of the FBI agents; it was Agent Ray, the one that Lou had met earlier. The gesture was subtle, but he caught it. The FBI agent casually nodded his head and then quickly exited the tent. The other agent followed soon after, and Lou noticed him carrying a black duffel bag. *This isn't good*, he thought. What was going on between that FBI agent and Charles Shafer? Why keep it a secret from the rest of the rescue team? The more he thought about it, the more he realized he needed an ally. As the meeting adjourned, Lou made his way through the crowd to the well-dressed man seated in the wheelchair.

"Hello, Mr. Stewart? Excuse me."

"Yes?"

"My name's Lou Garvey, Mr. Stewart. My son and grandson are down there with your granddaughter."

"Ah, Mr. Garvey. Well now, it looks like we have something in common, don't we? This is a terrible thing we share, just terrible. I can promise you—Lou, is it?— Lou, I will do everything in my power to rescue them. We WILL get them out of there safe and sound." There was a tension in Cecil's voice.

"I appreciate that, sir, and I'm relieved that you're here to help. But I was wondering if I could talk with you in private? I have a few questions, though I don't want to keep you from your friend here."

"Excuse my rudeness, Mr. Garvey, meet my assistant, Tom Daley."

Daley shrugged. "Would you like me to leave you two alone, Mr. Stewart?"

"I won't take much of your time." Lou added. "Just a few questions, that's all."

"Yes, Tom. Give us a few minutes, please, and thank you for bringing the car down. I'll page you when we're done."

"Yes, sir."

The two men watched Daley walk away.

"Okay. You have your privacy. Now what is on your mind?"

Lou pulled up a folding chair and brought his hands

up to his chin. It was risky to trust this powerful man, but he had to take the chance. He spoke hesitantly. "I think there might be something else going on, Mr. Stewart, something besides the rescue."

"Is that so? Please elaborate."

"I know this is going to sound crazy, but I think that your friend Shafer is in cahoots with those two FBI agents."

"Well, Mr. Garvey, my friend Charles has many connections in the government. I'm not surprised to see that these men are consulting him. I would expect nothing less, in fact." He paused. "Like it or not, Charles is an influential man, so I don't count that as unusual."

"Well, Mr. Stewart, I was talking with one of the FBI agents earlier, and he told me a story that frankly doesn't make any sense. In fact, I think he was lying. As a former business owner, I learned to spot a liar a mile away."

"What did he tell you?" Cecil touched a shaky hand to his chin. "Please continue."

"To put it bluntly, he told me a fairy tale about how the EPA is concerned this could be a dumping ground for radioactive waste. It just sounds preposterous. I was wondering if you knew about this?"

"No, I didn't." He watched as Cecil Stewart's expression changed. His rheumy blue eyes looked on the verge of tears. "Thank you for coming to me with this information."

"I was hoping you'd help me find out what's really going on, Mr. Stewart."

"Call me Cecil, all my friends do."

"Okay, Cecil. My friends call me Lou."

"Well, Lou, I don't believe you can hang a man on rumor or supposition, do you? You see, Charles and I have been friends for the better part of this century. I believe in that man's integrity like I believe the sun will rise tomorrow. I'm sure this is all a misunderstanding, and we'll find that the EPA does in fact have reason to be here. But I will make the appropriate inquiries, and we will know soon enough if that FBI agent was telling you the truth. For now, let's keep this between us, shall we? Does that sound agreeable?"

Lou was stunned by his response. He feared the wealthy industrialist might laugh him right out of the tent. "Yes, that sounds very agreeable. I just hope I'm being paranoid. Thanks for hearing me out. It's been a pleasure, a real pleasure."

"Thank you, Lou. Likewise. Now, will you accompany me to the other tent? I'd like to introduce you to a friend of mine." Cecil pushed a button on a small control pad under his right hand. There was a whirring sound and then his wheelchair started gliding toward the tent's exit. "This rescue means as much to you as it does to me, Lou." He kept talking as his he scooted along. "Follow me, as I think you will like Larry Siebert. He's a well-regarded expert in the fields of geology and mining, among other things."

"I'm honored, thank you. I just want my son and my grandson to be okay. I'll do whatever it takes to make that happen. Anything at all."

"I'm sure you're wrong about Charles; nonetheless, I can assure you, the people we love will be rescued!"

35

Peter Hawn was busy scribbling in the small notebook that he usually kept in his pocket. His head bent down, he was obviously concentrating intensely. Johnny didn't want to disturb his dad in the middle of his work, but he knew this couldn't wait.

"I found something, dad, something weird."

"Sure, one second. Okay, I'm just finishing up. What did you find?" Peter walked over.

"I asked your friend to lend me her Swiss Army knife, and I was messing around with it when I saw this." He pointed to the floor. "I opened the knife's magnifying glass, and, well, look." Johnny lowered the knife's tiny magnifying glass, and when it got to within an inch of the ground, a bright blue light appeared in a criss-cross pattern, illuminating the floor around them.

"See, what's that?" As Johnny lifted the knife back up, the blue light vanished.

"I don't know. Let's get her over here. Amy!" Peter hollered. "I think you should see this!"

"What's up?"

"Johnny found something. Show her."

Johnny again brought the knife's magnifying glass down near the ground, and the grid pattern of neon-blue light reappeared.

"Well, look at that. Is it some kind of laser?" Amy asked.

"That's what I was thinking…a laser with a wavelength that can't be seen by the naked eye, unless it's refracted. I've never seen anything quite like it, although I've been around lasers before. The boys over in the physics department are always thinking up new ways to use them. The ones in the lab operate on precise wavelengths, and different wavelength lasers are used for different applications." Peter had a far-off look in his eyes.

"What are you thinking?"

"I don't know." He rubbed his chin with his hand and shook his head. "You're going to think I'm crazy if I tell you." He laughed. "The whole thing sounds crazy! You know this is science fiction stuff, right?"

"Nothing would surprise me now. I can handle it." She shook her head and studied Peter's face.

"What do you think, Dad?"

"I'm thinking that this light, because that's what a

laser basically is, this very powerful and concentrated light, functions as a measuring tool. Kind of like what happened to us a few hours ago. I was wrong about the X-rays, though. I have a feeling that whoever built this would regard X-rays as primitive and dangerous. Lasers are light sources more focused than X-rays, and they emit very little radiation. I think this machine is using lasers for its quantum functions."

"That's ironic!" Amy laughed.

"It sure is." Peter laughed too.

"What's so funny about that?" Johnny asked.

"Remember when you were talking about *Star Trek*?"

"Yeah."

"Well, I think you proved your own analogy, and that's why I was laughing. You're a bright kid."

"Thanks, Dad."

"What I mean is, I think you were right about the whole *Star Trek* thing. This machine could act like a transporter. But let me ask something."

"Sure."

"The transporter they have on *Star Trek*…does it move the characters through time?"

"Nope. It won't do that. The crew on the *Enterprise* uses the transporter to beam people and supplies from ship to ship, or up and down from whatever planet they're orbiting."

"I think this machine can help us," he said, gesturing to the towering obelisk.

Amy squinted her eyes. "I have a bad feeling about what you're gonna say next."

He smiled and nodded. "Uh-huh. Yes, I'm thinking that we can use the machine to teleport us out of here!"

"That's a great name for it, Dad. *The Machine*!"

"Okay, then it's official!" Peter said.

"I like the name, but how do we start?" Amy said.

He ruffled his fingers through his thick brown hair and smiled confidently. "It's time to start our experiments!"

36

Cecil swallowed his heart medication, wincing as one of the pills stuck in his throat. He took another gulp of water from the paper cup, and finally, the last pill went down. The stuck pill left a bitter aftertaste that reminded him of Charles. Charles was not the easiest person to get along with... that was for certain. He was headstrong, unusually intelligent, and sometimes brisk in his manners. *Somewhat of a bitter pill*, he thought. Charles always fought to lead, no matter what the situation. That was his way. Cecil stroked his chin and thought about Lou's observations.

Cecil looked around to make sure his was alone, then he reached down and opened a black box that hung from the side of the wheelchair. He removed what appeared to be a handset to a portable army radio (a disguise), and spoke softly into the mobile satellite phone with voice-recognition software, "Number one." The futuristic telephone instantly speed-dialed Larry Siebert, and Cecil thought about what to say to his Chief of Security. Of course that was an incomplete title, as Larry Siebert's primary job was liaison from Stewart Enterprises to the federal government. Larry performed various duties: lobbyist, lawyer, and sometimes salesman to the CIA, the Pentagon and other government agencies. His Washington connections were invaluable, and tonight, they would help verify the FBI's story. Cecil knew in his heart that Charles was capable of lying. He'd seen him do it to others, often very casually. Cecil contemplated the sheer power of The Pulpit. The ability to see into the future was addicting and yet destructive at the same time. He worried about Amy. The more time she spent around that…that *thing,* the more chance she might fall asleep, and *dream.* And the dreams could be so destructive! They affected the lives of three intelligent young men over sixty years ago, killing one of them.

"Larry, good evening. I realize you are on your way, but I need you to check something for me. Yes, it's urgent; I need to know if the EPA has or had any operations on the east side of Pittsburgh. I also need you to search for any classified files that reference this area with Shafer Industries. Yes, thank you. I'll take your report when you arrive. Thank you, Larry."

He still gripped the strange-looking phone in his hand when he spoke into it once again. "Joseph, please." His grandson was much more than just a harmless playboy. Cecil had carefully cultivated his shallow public image as a disguise. In reality, Joe had trained with the SOF, Special Operations Forces in San Diego, using a CIA cover story that Larry had come up with. Joe had completed basic training, A.I.T. and Airborne School as the requirement to work with the precursor to our modern Navy Seals. Eight weeks of survival training, land navigation, repelling, hand-to-hand combat and constant running will test any man. But Joseph passed with flying colors and turned out to be one of the best performing SF babies, as they called him, that they ever saw. Being six-foot-three and 225 pounds of muscle helped him as he went through the physically demanding Phase 1 of the SOF training: swimming, weight-lifting and anaerobic and toughness training. He spent another eight weeks in Phase 2 of what the military calls MOS, which stands for Military Occupation and Skill training. Joe received the world's best instruction in handling various weapons and then cross-trained in demolition. Cecil remembered how Larry was able to convince the CIA to allow his grandson into the U.S. military's most elite training regime.

"Joseph, good evening. I have some bad news. Your cousin Amy is in trouble. No, I'm taking care of it. But please listen carefully; I need you to pay a covert visit to

Charles' house. Remember the safe he showed us? Ah, yes. Please bring me its contents. Yes, all of it. I'm at the Regent Square side of Frick Park. You'll see the lights. And, Joseph, please bring your black duffel bags. Yes, Larry will be here. Thank you, and Godspeed."

37

P eter was studying the symbols on the strange obelisk. He had Amy hold the flashlight as he copied the twelve symbols into the small notebook.

"Just ignore it," he instructed as their limbs disappeared and reappeared in a strange rhythm. They had grown accustomed to the intermittent invisibility that made their limbs flicker like a 1920's silent film. As Amy watched over Peter's shoulder, he jotted down a series of equations that she didn't understand. The numbers 60 and 360 appeared over and over again.

"If this is what I think it is, then we're standing next to a multiverse access machine. I'm determining how these units of measurement correlate with our own measurements of space and time. To be sure, we're going to need to do a little experiment," Peter said. "Come here, Johnny."

"You're going to send an object somewhere, aren't you?" Amy crooked an eyebrow.

"Great!" Johnny yelled.

"Yes, WE are going to perform a test of The Machine, by sending a small object from one location to another. Just across this room, if my calculations are correct. Johnny, your house key please."

"Sure. I really hope this works."

"Me, too," Amy said.

"Me, three," Peter said.

"I'm starting to feel the sleepies. Amy, would you do the honors?" Peter said, his eyes squinting.

"Yes, happily." She opened the first-aid kit. "This should do the trick. Okay, everybody gather around." They stood in a tight circle as she cracked an amyl nitrate capsule open and passed it under their noses.

"Whew, that stuff is wicked!" Johnny's eyes got big.

"Quite powerful," Peter said as he wrinkled his nose.

"Be thankful we have them, or we'd be just like Rip Van Winkle over there," Amy pointed to the snoring ranger.

"Yes, I am thankful. Now, let's get on with the experiment, shall we? Where to start… Well, guys, we're probably going to be the first humans to witness quantum teleportation."

"What's that?" Johnny said.

"Yes, please explain 'quantum teleportation.'" Amy said.

"We're going to attempt to send my son's house key from one side of the room to the other. Do you see this symbol?" He asked as he pointed to the machine. "This symbol represents the x, y, and z axis. This other symbol with the marks on the side—that represents time, our seconds, days, months and years. Location, time, basically all four dimensions. It's only logical that whatever advanced civilization built this machine, they'd be able to control it using not just touch, but with telepathy. An advanced civilization would have discarded the need for manual inputs, like how we operate just about everything. Imagine driving a car, or setting an alarm clock, not by using your hands and fingers, but by using your thoughts! Considering our strange dreams about the future, my hypothesis is that The Machine interacts with any intelligent mind. Even our primitive noggins!" Peter smiled and shrugged his shoulders.

"If I'm correct, The Machine can transport not only the mind, but also matter, through space and time," he continued. "In other words, we would be disassembled and then reassembled in another location, another time, or both. The real trick will be controlling it so we don't end up in the middle of the Atlantic Ocean, or teleported into the cone of an active volcano. It's all depends on the accuracy of the coordinates we input, and if I was smart enough to have correctly interpreted the symbols in the first place. So we're going to test it first, with inorganic matter."

"How, Dad?"

"Let's start with your house key."

Johnny handed over his key, and Peter placed the bronze-colored key in his jean's pocket, stepping closer to the machine.

"I'm going to touch the machine with both hands, and try to initiate a telepathic link. Then, I'll command it using my mind to move the key from my pocket to a precise location across the room. Harry Houdini would be proud, as this should be the world's best magic trick."

He stepped up to the black obelisk and placed one hand on each side of the tower. Almost instantly the symbols on the side started to flash intermittently, and then they heard a low humming noise. Peter's right pant pocket was suddenly illuminated by a blue beam coming from the obelisk. A few seconds later, The Machine went dark again. Peter stepped away and patted his pocket.

"It's gone!" he said.

"Wow. That's amazing!" Johnny yelled.

"It really worked?" Amy asked.

"Well, hopefully it did. Follow me, guys."

As they crossed the giant room, their flashlights pierced the inky blackness. "It should be right over here," Peter said, pointing. He knew their survival depended on a successful test.

"I don't see it," Amy said.

"Keep looking," Peter said. "It's got to be over here,"

he added, trying to sound confident, but feeling a bit weak inside.

"I found it!" Johnny held the shiny key in the beam of his flashlight.

"Good work! Oh, my God, Peter, you did it!" Amy shouted.

"The Machine did it!" Peter huffed. "And it is exactly where I 'thought' it to be. I imagined Johnny's key traveling to this particular corner of the room, then it felt like the key was melting in my pocket. I think we've found the 'key' to our escape."

"Oh, bad pun!" She laughed.

"Granted, but I couldn't resist." Peter laughed too.

"I get it, Dad, very funny!"

"I'm just relieved, guys, really. This was the first step. The next experiment we'll use organic matter. Something much larger."

"I know what you're going to say, Peter."

"That's right. The next test involves teleporting one of us."

38

C ecil was adjusting the blanket across his lap when he felt the vibration from his satellite phone at his side.

"Yes, Joseph? Ah, that's very interesting. Yes, bring it here. I will see you soon." He put away the device.

Cecil whispered to himself, "Damn him! He thinks I have no inkling as to what he is up to." Then he thought, *Not quite, Charles; this deadly game has only just begun!*

"Mr. Shafer, the president is on the phone, sir," one of the government agents whispered. "Follow me, please, to a secure line."

Charles followed the unnamed agent in black to the farthest tent, which now had two more agents standing guard at the entrance. Charles walked in and picked up the handset.

"Yes, Mr. President? I can arrange that, sir. Nobody will know. We have the devices here. Yes, sir. That will be the official explanation. Yes, Mr. President, goodnight, sir." Charles got off the military encrypted phone. He thought to himself that it was a shame that Cecil's beautiful granddaughter had to die, but sacrifices had to be made when it came to The Pulpit. And it was too bad for the archeologist, his son, and that park ranger. Just four unlucky souls caught up in machinations much bigger than they could ever imagine.

Laura followed the police car from Somerset County, down the Pennsylvania Turnpike to the Parkway East, then rest of the way to the Swissvale/Regent Square exit. The patrol car maintained the fifty-five mph speed limit the entire way, and she cursed their lackadaisical pace in between worrying about her sons and Peter. The police hadn't given her much information. They only told her that they were caught in some kind of mine collapse, and that rescuers were trying to reach them. It all seemed like a nightmare, made worse by the fact she'd gone to Donegal Springs with Monica. Laura castigated herself on the drive, waves of guilt washing over her. How could she be so selfish?

Frick Park looked like Times Square when Laura

arrived. Bright lights running on generators lit up a scene of fire trucks, ambulances, police cars and TV station trucks. Her police escort directed her to a parking space that was marked "police only." She parked and stepped out of her car, adjusted her coat, and the policeman from Somerset took her to an unmarked green military-style tent. The officer was gone before she had a chance to thank him. In the tent, she saw a few folding chairs, a table with a stack of heavy-duty looking flashlights, a large chrome coffee machine, a pair of large, gray-colored radio transceivers connected to telephones, and a terrain map of Frick Park hung on one side of the tent. The map was about five by five feet, and there was a yellow tack surrounded by red tacks near the center of the map. As she got up to take a closer look, a tall fireman walked into the tent.

"Mrs. Hawn?"

"Yes?"

"Your father-in-law is here."

Lou walked into the tent, and Laura burst into tears.

"Oh, Lou! Tell me they're okay!" She said with tears streaming down her face. Lou walked up to her and put his arms around her.

"Laura, it's a serious situation. Johnny, Darren and that neighbor boy, Mike, they went digging here in the park, looking for fossils. Anyway, they found an abandoned mineshaft or well. Honestly, we're not sure exactly what they found. Johnny went down there, by himself, and found an injured park ranger. Soon after that, Darren and Mike lost radio contact with Johnny. That's when they called Peter at the school. Of course, you know how Peter is; he couldn't wait for the fire department. Peter made it safely down there, but he, too, stopped responding on the radio. The fire department thinks they've been overcome by carbon monoxide gas."

"Carbon monoxide? Oh, my God! That can kill them!"

"I know, but we're praying the CO levels aren't that high. And there's more. One of your husband's grad students rappelled down there, and then the hole...it collapsed. I'm sorry to be the one to have to tell you all this."

"Oh, my God!" she screamed. "Oh, my God!" Her pulse escalated.

"Please, calm down. We've got the best men and equipment in the world helping us, thanks to Cecil Stewart. You see, the grad student I mentioned is Mr. Stewart's granddaughter," he added. "Mr. Stewart and his friend, Charles Shafer, are bringing in a tunnel-boring machine. Laura, we're going to drill our way in and save them."

"What are the odds...will it work?"

"I think we've got a good chance. It all depends on how fast we can drill through the strata. If everything goes right, it should work. We can't give up hope right now, because we don't know the situation down there. It's even possible there's another way out, and if there is, you and I both know Peter will find it."

She sat and held her head in her hands and took a series of deep breaths.

"Mom!" Darren screamed as he burst through the tent door.

"Darren! Oh, my darling!" Laura cried as she ran over and grabbed her youngest son. The relief of holding him in her arms swept over her. "Oh, honey, I love you so much."

"I love you too, Mom. Listen, we went to Frick Park looking for fossils. That's when we found it. We thought it would be fun to explore down there. We brought walkie-talkies and everything. We got rope at the hardware store, and food at Crayfish's house." Darren's words came rapid-fire now.

"But something went wrong, and Johnny just…I lost him on the walkie-talkie. I know we should have told you and Dad. It's my fault. If I just hadn't…"

"Honey, please, it's okay. You didn't know this would happen. Yes, you should have told us, but we have to be strong right now. For Dad and Johnny's sake, okay?"

"I'll try, but I'm really scared. Even the firemen look worried, and that's making it worse! What do you think, Grandpa?"

"I think we've got a lot of good people trying to help us right now. There are men here who have seen this type of thing before. We're just waiting on a special drilling machine that can help us reach your dad and brother."

"Grandpa is right, honey. We have to be patient. Now,

I want you take me to where this place is. Mommy needs to see it for herself. Can you do that?"

"Yeah, Mom. We gotta get you a flashlight." Darren moved to one of the tables in the tent and placed his hand on the handle of one of the large green military flashlights.

"Do you think they'll mind if we borrow one of these? I think it'll be better than the one I got."

"I don't think these military types will miss one flashlight. There are twenty more like it on the table. Besides, hopefully soon they'll have enough lights on the trails that we won't need these anymore," Lou said, pointing to his own chrome flashlight.

"Okay, Mom, Grandpa, let's go."

"Okay, honey," Laura said.

They left the tent and walked past the brightly lit tennis courts to the unlit entrance of the trail system of east Frick Park. The newly laid asphalt of the upper part of the trail soon gave way to a narrower, crushed-gravel path. They passed firemen who were busy installing a series of generators and field lights along the way. They slowly made their way down, descending past dark towering oak and black cherry trees, down into the park's Stygian valley.

Laura held onto Lou's arm the entire time. She realized that Lou was helping her family once again. He had helped them financially on several occasions, not the least of which was a $30,000 wedding present that they used as the down payment on their house. *Thank God for Lou*, she thought. He was more than Peter's stepfather, and her boy's favorite grandfather, he was their guardian angel.

As they walked by two large boulders, four men in military fatigues passed them going the other way, looking like they were in a hurry. Laura was surprised to see soldiers, but then she thought maybe the National Guard was helping with the rescue. The area up ahead was lit up by klieg lights, with several Pittsburgh firefighters walking around. *It looks so surreal*, she thought, *like a scene out of a Hollywood action movie*. She felt a chill slowly rise along the length of her back as she saw orange hazard cones surrounding a small crater in the earth. She walked closer and saw the drilling equipment. She remembered seeing a similar scene when she was a little girl. Her father had hired a drilling company to drill their farm's well. She was lost in memory, when suddenly the earth began to rise and lift her off her feet. The ground became a roiling sea, and she screamed as the three of them were pitched headfirst into the bushes surrounding the canyon.

"What was that?" Darren yelled.

"Darren, something's wrong," Lou said. "Get your mother back up to that tent and wait for me, okay? Do it now!" he commanded more firmly.

"Okay. Mom, c'mon!"

"I'm staying, Lou, I don't know what just happened, but I'm staying," she said.

"No, you're not, that's an order. That was an explosion. Probably methane. It's not safe here. This whole place could go. Now, take him and get out of here, please. Run!"

"Okay, okay! Darren, let's go!"

Lou watched them turn and disappear down the dusky trail.

Now what in blazes was that? Lou thought. Methane? *It didn't feel right*, he thought. Explosives? Lou was part of a demo team in WWII as the 1st Battalion pushed its way into Germany. His instinctual alarm bell was ringing loud and clear. He decided it was time to revisit Cecil.

Joseph pulled his Porsche into the Frick Park parking lot. He showed one of the police officers his driver's license, and he was promptly waved through. It hadn't been easy to crack the lock on old Charles's wall safe. Safely hidden behind his prized Van Gogh, Charles had proudly showed off the hidden safe one night, after downing several glasses of Lagavulin. Thank God Charles had a weakness for fine single malt scotch, Joe thought, or he wouldn't be here holding the papers that would forever change his grandfather's opinion of his life-long friend.

39

In the darkness, Amy held Peter's arm. She wondered, *Does Peter really have it figured out?* Would they teleport to safety in time, before they fell asleep?

Peter said, "This way," and he started moving across the room.

"Don't let go of my arms, guys." They crossed the room slowly, the only remaining light being the faint glowing halo that surrounded The Machine. Peter was the first to reach the sleeping body of Dave Rondinelli.

"We need to search him. Maybe he's got a flashlight, a lighter, or at least some matches," Peter said.

They all knelt down, and began rifling through the pockets of the fallen ranger. "Check the ground around him, too," Peter commanded.

"I got it!" Johnny yelled. "It's one of them Zippos."

He shook the lighter. "It's almost full too!" He flipped up the hood of the Zippo and flicked the lighter's wheel with his thumb. A two-inch flame suddenly lit up the dark, their shadows dancing on the chamber's walls.

"That's better," Amy and Peter said at exactly the same time. They both laughed. "Great minds think alike!" Peter exclaimed.

"So, you think I have a great mind?"

He tried not to think about the dream with Amy on her knees, but his mind started wandering through progressively more erotic scenes.

"Well, you are one of CMU's brightest graduate students," he said, his pat response all he could muster as he valiantly tried to suppress the thought of her taking off her bra and panties.

"Well, thank you, Professor!" she said, cocking her head to one side. "And you're not so bad yourself!"

Peter finally snapped out of his reverie. "Well, let's get the teleportation show on the road, shall we? One more experiment, and then we'll know for sure if my calculations are correct."

"What's the next experiment?" Johnny asked.

"Moving a key is one thing. Moving a person is… more challenging. We must know if the disassembly and reassembly process is harmful to organic matter. Well, namely me, because I'm volunteering to try and teleport across the room."

"Dad, I'm worried, if this thing is like the transporter on *Star Trek*. Most of the time it works okay, but there's this one show where it killed one of the crew."

"Yes, Johnny's right, and I don't want him losing his father. Why don't I go?"

"Listen, despite the danger, I'm reasonably sure that my measurements are correct. I'm the oldest one here by a long shot, so I hereby nominate myself."

Just as Peter said "myself," there was a bright orange flash and a thunderous sound. Peter, Amy and Johnny were thrown from their feet. Rocks, dirt and dust peppered them as they lay sprawled across each other, like a soot-covered barrel of monkeys.

"What the heck was that?" Amy said, coughing.

"That was an explosion, and it came from the hole. If it wasn't clogged from the collapse earlier, now it's completely destroyed. What the hell?" Peter said.

"Dad, I thought you said that since there was no methane that we didn't have to worry about explosions?"

"There isn't any methane. Remember the Zippo?"

"Then what was THAT?" Amy's eyes caught Peter's.

"Maybe they used dynamite to try and rescue us," Johnny said.

"They didn't do a very good job, 'cause it looks like the hole is now completely destroyed," Peter said, choking on the dust. "It doesn't make any sense. Anyway, let's check to see if The Machine is okay. If it's damaged, there goes our ticket out of here."

40

C ecil and Charles were talking when they felt a violent jolt shake the earth.

"What was that?" Cecil said.

"It came from the bottom of the park. I was afraid of that. There must have been methane gas in that tunnel. It probably ignited when the fire department started drilling."

"Jesus, Charles, you know very well that we never encountered any methane gas near The Pulpit. You even said yourself that The Pulpit controlled the environment surrounding it, that it protected itself from the elements."

"I realize I said that once—yes, but how many years has it been? Perhaps The Pulpit is malfunctioning. Surely that's a possibility."

"No, I do not believe it's possible. And I have to question why all of a sudden you've changed your mind. You were the one who hypothesized The Pulpit was indestructible. You yourself sponsored each of the tests. Methane gas? The Pulpit malfunctioning? It doesn't make any sense!"

Joseph cut across the compound of green army tents and saw his grandfather and Charles standing outside the farthest tent. They looked like they were arguing. He quickly tucked the manila envelope under the back of his polo shirt, down below the waistband of his blue jeans. Joseph could hear their voices rising and falling. As he got closer, he could tell his grandfather was upset.

"Grandpa, I got here as fast as I could."

"Thank you for coming, Joseph. Ah, Charles and I were just discussing a few things."

"Joseph, my boy," Charles said.

"It's good to see you, Mr. Shafer. What's going on?"

"There's been a recent setback, some kind of explosion, but we don't know the details. Gentlemen, excuse me. I must go and make a few phone calls. We're going to need more equipment here. I'll return shortly. Goodbye."

"Thank you, Charles." Cecil said.

Bright lights lit up the area surrounding the tents as Cecil and Joseph watched two black-coat-wearing FBI agents join Charles, their distant voices unintelligible as they walked away.

"Now, what did you find, my boy?"

"First, tell me what's going on? There was an explosion? Is Amy okay?"

"Yes, just before you arrived, there was an explosion of some kind. Charles believes it was caused by methane gas, but I'm not buying that cockamamie story. Regardless, I have my reasons for believing that Amy and her friends are safe. Now, what did you find?"

"I took whatever I thought looked important. Classified documents, foreign bank accounts, I grabbed it all, and well, here it is." Joe lifted up his shirt and pulled the inch-thick envelope from behind his back.

"Good work. Now, go down to the rescue site, and find out exactly what just happened. Talk to the fire crew, and here, take this with you." Cecil handed Joseph a black, Walther PPK .380ACP pistol. "It's loaded, with one in the chamber. I don't trust any of the players here tonight, so please watch your back."

"I will. Are you staying here?"

"Yes, right now I need to study these documents. Whatever happened down there will serve as a distraction and allow me some time. I trust you, Joseph, and now more than ever, I need you to be my extra set of eyes and ears. Understand?"

"Of course. Is your wheelchair functioning properly?"

He tucked the small pistol under his waistband, in the small of his back.

"Yes, all systems are online. Ah, the element of surprise. One of the benefits of appearing as a frail old man in a wheelchair, I suppose."

"Okay then, I won't worry."

"No, don't worry, just find out what happened, and report back to me. Go!"

41

"Wait, what's this?" Peter said as he lifted up a small piece of silvery metal. "It can't be."

Peter realized what he held in his hand was part of a detonator, the kind he used in his army days. He had trained in the use of C-4 explosives, which was cutting-edge stuff in 1963 Vietnam. The tiny fragment of metal was definitely military-spec.

"What's that?" Amy said.

"What is that?" Johnny said. "It looks like a gum wrapper."

"This explains the explosion. It was deliberate. This is part of a detonator, the kind we used in Vietnam."

"Are you saying someone up there doesn't want us to be rescued?" Amy said.

"That's exactly what I'm saying. That leads me to another thought; somebody up there knows about The

Machine. Call me paranoid, but I'd bet this 'guardian angel' is part of our so-called rescue team."

"What are we going to do?" Amy said.

Peter brushed some dirt from his hair. "Let's keep digging. We've almost got all the debris cleared away."

"I'm scared," Johnny said.

Peter went over and hugged his boy. "Now, now. We're going to get out of this, honey. We've got air, we've got plenty of water, and more importantly, we've got each other. Let's stay calm and get through the next experiment. At least The Machine doesn't look any worse for wear. I don't see a single scratch on it. Whoa, look at that! Bring the lighter over, Johnny."

As the flickering flame of the Zippo lit up the side of The Machine, they watched in fascination as dirt and dust slowly slid off the obelisk, as if swept by a giant, invisible feather duster.

"I guess I'm not surprised. Our Machine is self-cleaning! Will you look at that?" Peter shook his head.

"Look! It's moving the stones!" Johnny pointed to the ground.

Sure enough, small rocks slowly slid away from The Machine, each one leaving a trail as it moved through the dirt.

"Looks like it's going to finish cleaning up this mess, all on its own. Okay, that means we can move on to our next experiment. I'm going to *think* the same coordinates as I did with the key. Only this time, I'm going to *see* myself being moved. My guess is that there are few limits to what The Machine can do, and we're probably only tapping into a small portion of its potential. Today our most advanced computers are bathroom-sized. But, if we imagine how far technology will progress in, let's say, a thousand years, it's easy to see mankind making machines like this. What I'm most worried about are the side effects." Peter slowly walked around The Machine. "This is alien technology, or at least tech from the future; we're sure of that. But what's it doing to our primitive minds and bodies as we interact with it?

"I feel okay," Johnny said.

"My blonde hair is brown from the dust, but besides that, I guess I'm okay as well. You know, I think your theories about The Machine make sense. I mean, how much air was left in the chamber after the collapse, after the explosion? We're not having any trouble breathing. Is The Machine manufacturing an atmosphere?"

"Why not? I mean, let's suppose we had the technology to build a teleportation machine. We'd probably give it healing powers and some kind of protective force field, like how a space capsule protects the astronauts, only The Machine's protection is invisible."

"I don't mean to interrupt, Dad and Amy, but I'm super hungry. Before you got down here, I ate all the food I brought with me. I should've brought more. I should've listened to Darren when he tried to give me more food to carry."

"You couldn't have predicted what happened tonight. Please don't worry about that now, son. It's actually my fault. I've been so preoccupied with staying awake, and then decoding the machine, that I forgot about making a plan to conserve the food. I'm sorry."

"Wait!" Johnny said with surprising energy. "I put a PowerHouse candy bar in my pocket after school. Hold on." Johnny pushed his hand into the right front pocket of his Levis. "Yup! It's flat as a pancake, but I got it!"

"Yeah! You are my hero! PowerHouse! Mana from the gods. Thank you, thank you, thank you!" Amy clapped him on the shoulder.

They divided the candy bar into thirds, and eagerly gobbled up their portions. They scooped water with their hands from the small stream running through the middle of the room and washed it down.

"Well, thanks to Johnny's sweet tooth, that should hold us for a little while. And that water tastes great. Anyone got any more candy bars hiding in their pockets?" Peter said.

"Not me, but that sure helped. Thank you Johnny!" Amy said.

42

Cecil held in his hand a contract from Shafer Industries, partnered with a company called Gemini Contractors. The date on the top of the page read "1942." "Top Secret" was stamped on the borders of the page, and a disclaimer read, "For security clearance 11 or above only."

Hmm, he thought, a security clearance equal to the president and the joint chiefs? As he read further, the details of his best friend's betrayal became evident.

Cecil sipped his black coffee and thought about the significance of the year 1942. It was true, Shafer Industries had partnered with the U.S. government to build the secret lab at Los Alamos. Charles had been very proud of his patriotic contributions towards the war effort. But this contract revealed Charles's company received $250 million dollars, an astronomical figure by 1942 standards.

Had Charles used The Pulpit to speed up development of the first nuclear weapons?

Cecil laughed out loud as he looked at the next document. Another set of lucrative contracts! $500 million dollars of PaineWebber stock in exchange for consultation work! He read the contracts and payment receipts that spanned decades: 1955, 1961, 1969 and finally, 1974. Cecil shook his head as he quickly calculated the funds. As a graduate of the Wharton School of Finance and Commerce in Philadelphia, it was easy for him to apply some rough "forensic accounting" of Charles's secret accounts.

He marveled at the thought of his friend secretly creating and maintaining that access hole to The Pulpit in Frick Park. The bastard! And the contracts proved Charles had the financial motive to keep The Pulpit a secret. And what about the explosion a few minutes ago? Was Charles involved? Was his old friend such a cold-blooded fiend that he would sacrifice the lives of his granddaughter and her friends, just to preserve his secret "cash cow"? He knew in his heart the answer to that question was "yes."

Cecil remembered that Charles was the one who most vociferously championed The Pulpit. And it was Charles who had so passionately objected to Bill and Cecil's determination to destroy it. The facts indeed pointed to Charles as a devious mastermind, plotting to kill at all costs to protect his prize. Cecil realized he must stop his old friend, a fight to the death, if need be.

He gathered up the contracts, put them safely in his lap, and moved his wheelchair to the entrance of the tent. He heard footsteps, and Joseph appeared.

"The hole is completely destroyed. The firemen are convinced it was a methane gas explosion, but they didn't see this." Joseph held up a tiny piece of silvery metal between his thumb and index finger.

"What is that?"

"It's a piece of a detonator. They're used in conjunction with plastic explosives…C-4. You mold the charge the way you want and then push the detonator into the plastic explosive. It wouldn't have taken much to blow that hole. This is proof it was deliberate." Joe stared at Cecil with his green eyes.

"Come here," Cecil said, a subtle smile coming on his wrinkled cheek.

"Yes, Grandpa?"

"You have done well tonight. You've proven yourself in two difficult missions. You've revealed a conspiracy!" Cecil pounded his fist on the wheelchair's arm. "That tiny piece of metal and all of these contracts and receipts prove Charles is responsible for this mischief. I will deal with Charles later. Right now, we have to focus our energies on rescuing Amy and her friends. We will use Charles to get his tunnel-boring machine. Let's assume he will sabotage it and make it look like an accident. It's our job to make sure that doesn't happen. Once the boring machine arrives, that is when I want you to intervene. Do you understand?"

"Yes, I understand, but we're a little outnumbered at the moment. A Special Forces team usually has at least six soldiers. We've only got Larry and myself. I'd feel better if we had at least half a team tonight." Joe kicked at the tent's dirt floor. "Wait a minute! I can call my SEAL friend, Josh Parks. He lives on the South Side. He can help us, Grandpa, and I can get him here ASAP."

"Excellent, Joseph. Go get your friend. I'll inform Larry of the change of plans. We must stop Charles!"

43

In the golden glow of the strange machine, Peter was taking notes. As he ran his fingers along the symbols on the sides, the machine's luminosity bathed his hands in a multitude of vivid colors—shades of greens, blues, reds, oranges and yellows, seemingly every hue possible in a rainbow. He noticed that the surface was covered in millions of perfectly symmetrical squares, one millimeter across. They stretched from one at the very tip of the machine, to many thousands covering the base; tiny, glowing squares that constantly kept changing colors. Peter deduced that each square was a year, and he hoped that The Machine's creators enabled it to automatically calibrate to the end-user's calendar. He hypothesized The Machine would "grow" taller with each year; perhaps starting out as a one tiny single cube and evolving into the towering obelisk before him. He pondered the technology:

wireless and direct machine-to-brain interface. How amazing, but how accurate? *It'd better be damn accurate*, he thought, *or this experiment will be my funeral.* He felt Amy approach from behind.

"I know what you're thinking," she said.

"You do?"

"Yes, you're worried you're going to teleport yourself right into solid bedrock. Am I right?"

"Well, miss psychic, you are exactly right. How did you know?"

She reached out and touched his hand. "It doesn't take a psychic to realize how serious this next experiment is. You're either brave, crazy, or a little of both."

Peter thought for a moment. "We don't have any choice. Somebody on the surface is trying their darndest to keep us down here permanently, and, we're running out of time. We're also out of food, and once those amyl capsules are gone...The Machine looks like our only ticket out."

Amy hesitated. "I know you're right. I'm just worried, that's all."

Peter moved close to the machine, placing his hands on the sides of the obelisk. At that moment he looked like a galactic preacher holding on to an otherworldly pulpit. If he only knew it was nicknamed "The Pulpit" by three enterprising young men sixty years before.

He carefully used his palms to feel the symbols on the sides. Then, using his fingertips, he felt for the many finer, tiny raised squares. He closed his eyes and immediately felt a strange power pulse, spreading from his fingers upward into his arms and body, a feeling of omnipotence that was both delicious and unnerving at the same time. Was this how Superman felt? Like he could go anywhere and do anything, with the power of the universe itself coursing through his body?

He imagined teleporting across the room, reappearing twenty feet away. There was a flash of blue light, and he saw Amy and Johnny's shocked expressions as his body began rapidly disassembling right in front of their eyes. He felt bodiless for a moment, and knowledge was transmitted to his brain telling him he could wish himself anywhere in the universe. The Machine was capable of so much! He was physically and psychically joined with The Machine now; he and The Machine were one!

In an instant, he was pulled away from the room, traveling up through the rock walls and into the night sky. He thought the word *soul*, as he rocketed out of Earth's atmosphere and zoomed across the galaxy. Peter visited Earth-like worlds scattered across the Milky Way, felt the life forms on each of them. He saw planets with two and three suns, and watched others with a dozen moons glowing in their night skies. Yes, he felt he could travel even farther now, reach across the universe if he wanted to. He was pure energy; he was pure light!

Then he remembered. It seemed like a thousand years ago. He felt the love for his son. He remembered being human, a father with more life to live. He saw a kaleidoscope of images of the people he loved. He saw Darren and Johnny laughing. He saw his real father, Charlie, lying peacefully in the casket. He saw Lou, standing with his mother in their back yard, both eagerly exchanging vows in front of the preacher. He saw Laura in grade school, and then he saw Amy as a little girl playing in a field. Oh, she had such an angelic face! Peter began to fight, to will himself back to Earth, back to Frick Park, back to the underground chamber. He tapped into a will he never knew he had, to reassemble his body using The Machine. Peter felt a great and unexpected sadness sweep over him as he slowly came back into corporality. Johnny and Amy came running over with their arms outstretched, their mouths moved silently until their words filtered in as his hearing returned.

"Dad, you did it! When I saw you...dissolve, I was so scared. I thought you'd left us here. Then Amy said *look*, and we saw your body reappearing!"

"You pulled it off, Peter! You disappeared for a few seconds, and then reappeared over here. Are you okay?"

"I saw the universe. I saw other planets just like ours. I could feel every life form living on each of them. There is so much life out there! I traveled across the galaxy as pure energy, seeing everything, but I almost didn't make it back. I almost forgot."

Johnny watched his Dad closely. "Forgot?"

"I almost forgot who I was. I felt no pain, no fear or limitations. It's terribly seductive. I was pure light, just zooming across the universe. But something brought me back. Now I understand this profound, powerful force. It's a force as real as gravity."

"What force?" Amy asked.

"Love! Love is what brought me back. I saw my sons laughing; I saw your face, Amy. I saw my stepdad and my mom getting married. I felt the love I have for each one of you. I had to fight to come back, but love was on my side, and I made it." Peter staggered, his face pale and sweating. "I need to sit down now. I'm exhausted."

"Here, sit over here." Amy sat down beside him and moved her face close to his. She said in a low voice, "I have to ask you, what if you hadn't returned? What then? And what about us, when we try? I don't want to disappear into the cosmos. I've got my whole life ahead of me, and so does your son, right here on Earth. What if we're not as strong as you?" She stopped; her voice changed from hard to soft. "Wait a minute. You love me? I helped to bring you back? How can you love me when you barely know me?" A feeling of strangeness fell over her.

"I'm telling you the truth. Yes, I love you. I don't understand why or how, but I saw everything. And I do mean everything. I saw you as a little girl, playing in that green grassy field, near the creek below Shadyside Academy, beside Fox Chapel road. You wore a yellow dress, and you were chasing butterflies. Do you remember?"

Amy looked stunned. "Oh, my God, how could you know that? That was so, so long ago." She paused. "I must have been six years old, and I used to beg Grandpa to take me to that creek to catch snakes and turtles. How could you know?" Her eyes were wide now.

"I saw EVERYTHING!" Peter shouted. "I saw you playing in your house with your dolls. You sat in your closet with a flashlight, and lined the dolls up according to size. I saw your mom and dad leaving for a vacation, and you had tears in your eyes. I saw your first kiss with that shy, dark-haired boy at some camp in Canada, and you had cake in your mouth. I saw it all! And I felt love for you the whole time, pure love. I realized, at that moment, I do love you, Amy."

She looked away. "I have to think about this."

"I have something else to confess. Part of me didn't want to come back. It's like a drug, the ultimate drug. I almost got lost in it, lost in the power and freedom. The omnipotence I felt was almost irresistible. I'm ashamed to admit I almost stopped caring about anything on this tiny blue world. But love pulled me back, Amy! Love! I know it sounds crazy, but you'll understand once you've teleported. We're going to use The Machine to escape, but we have to trust that we won't forget the people we love. All the conventions that we use to avoid expressing love are ridiculous! We should revel in it every day, and never forget the power of love. I traveled across the universe, and love brought me back. I'm not afraid anymore. We get to spend such a tiny sliver of time here on Earth, and love is the best part of it."

Amy looked directly at Peter. "I'm trying to take in what you're saying. I'm trying to imagine what it's like to shed the physical form, become pure energy and travel the universe like you did. It's almost too much to think about right now. I'm just relieved you made it back, like you said, that you were strong enough to fight to return."

"I think I understand, Dad. There was a *Star Trek* episode like what you're talking about. I'm serious! And I'm not afraid to teleport now, because you did it! You moved yourself across the room using The Machine, so I know you can get us out of here."

"Oh, Johnny, you're the best son a dad could ever ask for. I love you so much!" Peter grabbed him in a bear hug, lifting him off his feet.

"Your love brought me back to Earth, son. I learned that love is a force that spans the universe, that's how powerful it is! Well, now…I need to rest. I'm so tired."

"Peter!" Amy yelled.

"I'm so sleepy. I just want to shut my eyes for a minute…"

Peter fell into a sleep bordering on unconsciousness. A sleep that even amyl nitrate couldn't wake him from. The strain of the teleporting had pushed him past the point of exhaustion, back to dreaming.

44

Laura sat silently in her car, a thousand thoughts running through her mind. She watched as the firemen moved from their trucks to the tents. She watched the frenetic commotion in the lower Frick Park parking lot. She held her small black purse tightly in her hands, as if she were guarding the Holy Grail itself. In her purse lay an amber-colored plastic bottle. She had gotten the prescription for Valium from her psychiatrist, Dr. Colbert. She had taken very few of them during the past few months, just the occasional one to knock back her insomnia. In the meantime, she'd refilled the prescription three times over, so now she had eighty of the blue ten-milligram tablets, filling the plastic bottle to the very top.

She sat there, berating herself over Johnny and Peter. Would she ever see them again? Why was she so damn selfish? She'd run off with Monica to Donegal Springs while Peter and Johnny's lives were in peril. *Selfish, selfish, selfish!* Laura chewed her lip. *But Darren is okay. Darren is fine. I still have Darren! That's enough, isn't it?*

Laura reached into her glove compartment, fumbling with the lock until it suddenly opened. There, under her car registration and the Volvo owner's manual, was a fine silver hip flask. It was filled with her favorite Cognac, Chateau de Beaulon XO. She unscrewed the cap to the flask and took a deep swallow. She felt the burn travel down her throat and into her stomach. It felt good. She took another, larger swallow. Her mind slowed down a fraction from the intense worry that was consuming her. She opened the bottle and removed two blue pills. She swallowed those with another slug of Cognac.

She thought about her marriage, and after the hormonal hell of menopause, her desire for Peter died with it. She'd be publicly humiliated in Squirrel Hill if word got out she was a closet lesbian. There would be the incriminating stares at the tennis club. "There's that lesbian who was out screwing around while her son and husband were dying in a hole in Frick Park." She could imagine people saying it!

Laura felt the warmth of the Valium and the Cognac concoction, traveling through her bloodstream, the rush of the high easing her worried mind. She looked at the bottle of pills sitting in her lap. It would be so easy to pop four or five more in her mouth and wash them down with another swig. She thought about her regular doctor,

Richard Pauley. He was sympathetic to her struggles through menopause; he was the one who had referred her to Dr. Colbert after her near nervous breakdown.

She could hear Dr. Pauley's kind, Harvard-educated voice giving her advice: "Now Laura, you must NOT consume any alcohol while taking Valium! The combination of the two can be lethal. Do you understand, Laura?" Oh, he had a sweet voice, and he was so handsome!

Wow, the drugs were really affecting her now. Now her mind was taking off on the high. She opened the bottle again and took out two more pills. *Let's see*, she thought. That's just twenty milligrams. She popped them in her mouth and swallowed another bolt of the Cognac. God, it burned on the way down! She felt herself starting to care less and less.

Looking around, she thought the bright white lights in the parking lot looked pretty. She saw the people running around like so many ants, and then she remembered why they were there. How many little blue-pill friends would it take to make this ugly reality vanish? Who cared about her anyway? Monica just dug the sex with her. It wasn't any different from the attention men had given her since her teens. Laura always knew she was prettier than the average girl, that she'd been blessed/cursed with the curves of Sophia Loren. "My tall, slim, busty dark-haired beauty," Peter used to say. Strangely, even though she possessed the visage that most women craved, it never meant much to Laura herself. She had a brilliant mind that longed for recognition, but it was constantly overshadowed by her stunning shell. *Stupid people*, she thought.

She felt the Valium high ratchet up another notch. She took out four more blue pills and washed them down with the last of the Cognac. She closed her eyes and thought back to the family vacation they had taken to Beach Haven, New Jersey, a few years ago. She saw Johnny and Darren running in the sand, and Peter looked so handsome in his swim trunks and aviator sunglasses! Oh, life was perfect then. Why did it all have to change?

Life could be so cruel. A tear ran down her cheek as she closed her eyes and went back to thinking about Beach Haven. Laura passed out in the front seat of her Volvo, thinking about herself and Peter making love to the sound of the waves crashing on the shore.

45

Cecil waited outside of the last tent, breathing in the cool night air. He glanced down at the control panel under his left hand.

A large knob rested under his right palm, and he pushed down on it to check the status of the weapons on board. A small screen appeared in the cornea of his right eye, of course invisible to anyone but him. Neurotoxin darts were ready to go, both lethal and non-lethal doses. He wondered which one he would be forced to use when he confronted Charles. A bank of small green LED lights glowed under his left hand. That meant that all the batteries on board the wheelchair were fully charged.

To the untrained eye, Cecil's custom wheelchair looked fairly innocuous. He had designed the chair himself, with the help of his best engineers at Stewart Aerospace. The frame was made of T-7075 aluminum.

The wheels were forged magnesium with run-flat all-terrain tires. The on-board batteries were a top-secret lithium design that was first introduced on the Minuteman nuclear missiles. Propulsion was provided by an extremely powerful electric motor, with a top speed of thirty miles per hour. Cecil laughed at the thought of going that fast in a wheelchair, when his usual pace was that of a brisk walk. But tonight...*tonight* he thought, anything could happen. Cecil heard footsteps and saw Larry Siebert approaching.

"I'm sorry I'm late, Cecil. The helicopter was grounded with an engine problem, so I actually had to catch a cab here. I have the information you requested. Can we go somewhere a bit more private? Is the limo here?"

"Yes, it is, Larry, and I can't wait to hear what you found. It turns out Joseph also had a productive night. Let's compare notes to see exactly what Charles has been up to."

Larry opened the rear door of the black Mercedes 600 limousine by pushing a hidden button on the inside of the doorframe, starting the sound of small whirring motors. A jointed aluminum arm slowly extended from the bottom of the car and hooked into a recess in the back of Cecil's wheelchair.

"It makes things easier," Cecil said.

"It certainly is ingenious, sir. I think the engineers at Mercedes were quite impressed when you showed them your blueprints. To say they were skeptical at first, well, that would be putting it mildly."

"There are far more exciting inventions in store for disabled people than this automatic lift. Things like implanted computer chips that will cure paraplegia, bypassing the spinal cord altogether. Inter-species cross-genetics. That's not just comic book fantasy, you know. Ah, but they're a wee bit farther off in the future. Anyway, it's a convenience just be able to stay in my wheelchair and with a push of a button be automatically placed inside the car, and its speed helps me avoid those damn paparazzi."

"Yes, sir. I'm not a fan of the photographers either, but you are quite famous, Cecil." Larry leaned back in the Mercedes' plush, black leather rear seat. "Is this coffee?"

"Yes, I had Tom prepare some for both of us. Sugar and cream as you like it, of course. I have a feeling we're in for a long night."

"Thank you, sir; that's very thoughtful." Larry opened the tall, silver thermos and poured a cup. He smiled at the old man's preparedness. "Well, are you ready?"

"Yes, go ahead, Larry."

"Okay, here goes. I found Charles has been exchanging exotic technological expertise with our government and the private sector for the past sixty years. My sources inside the Pentagon confirmed that your old friend has the highest security clearance of any civilian. Basically, he has access to any government resource, short of launching a ballistic nuclear missile. Even then, he could probably get one launched using his influence over The Joint Chiefs. He currently has contracts with all of the major computer corporations and several nuclear engineering companies. As for The Pulpit, I can only assume he's been in constant contact with it, taking advantage of its unique properties, i.e., traveling into the future and bringing back advanced technology." Larry leaned back in his seat and looked directly into Cecil's eyes. "I'm assuming it's here?"

"Yes, Larry. I took an oath to keep its location secret. I'm sorry I couldn't tell you. The fact that I am confirming your deduction is simply because I trust you with my life."

"I am honored, sir. I understand your need for secrecy." He nodded and was quiet for a moment. "It's too bad Charles didn't share your point of view."

Cecil's lips grew tight. "I trusted Charles. We made a gentlemen's agreement. You realize it killed one of my dear friends?"

"Bill Nollem." Larry took a sip of coffee.

"That's correct, he was my closest friend. He was more sensitive than Charles and I. He couldn't handle the information the The Pulpit showed him. He confided in me that he cared little for the present, once he witnessed the deaths of his children. And who could blame him?"

Cecil took a deep breath. "He believed that he saw Heaven—actually visited Heaven. He said he wanted to go live there, that he tired of life here on Earth. And, that's exactly what he did." A tear slid down Cecil's wrinkled cheek.

"Terrible, sir." Larry waited a minute before continuing. "So, tell me what Joseph found."

Cecil wiped his face with the back of his hand. "Joseph did well tonight. He infiltrated Charles's safe and returned with a folder full of contracts and receipts, a mixture of government and private sector. Before you arrived, I was sorting through it. It corroborates what you said, Larry. But the situation has become even more dire, I'm afraid."

"How's that?"

"There was an explosion about an hour ago," Cecil said with a disgusted look. "It completely demolished whatever was left of the access hole leading to The Pulpit. I'm afraid Charles is protecting his cash cow, at the expense of my Amy and her friends' lives."

Cecil went on, beginning to get even more upset. "He's guilty of attempted murder, or murder if they are dead already!" He shouted. "The so-called 'FBI agents' we've seen most definitely work for a different three-letter agency, and they're most definitely under Charles's command." Cecil took a deep breath. "In all likelihood they are assassins."

Larry intertwined his fingers, flexing them. "I see, sir.

The situation is more critical. So what do you have in mind?"

"Joseph is fetching one of his well trained friends. I am putting you in charge of them, Larry. What do you call it? 'Team leader'?"

"Yes, sir, the military term is team leader."

"Well, the position is yours. My plan is that once we have eliminated these nefarious forces and isolated Charles, then we will confront him. Don't underestimate him. He is an extremely sly and resourceful man." Cecil paused and motioned for Larry to hand him the silver-colored thermos. "But, of course, so am I." As he unscrewed the lid, he spoke. "I feel we're headed for an old-fashioned showdown with Charles. I suppose it has to be this way, and Frick Park is going to be our O.K. Corral." He laughed. "Tell me, what is the status of the boring machine?"

"It's almost here. Shafer has a Sikorsky helicopter bringing it in. The excavation could start by morning. From my understanding, it takes a while to anchor it properly. Then, the site will be radar mapped before they start drilling." Larry watched as Cecil poured himself a cup of coffee, his hands amazingly steady for his age.

"And how long will it take to drill to that depth?"

"Seventy-five feet could take up to eight hours."

"I'm worried about the time, Larry. That means four-teen more hours until we reach them?"

"I know."

"Consider this, Larry. The Pulpit has a hypnotic effect. It induces narcolepsy in humans, and the closer one is, the stronger the effect. That was one of the first things we experienced when we discovered it. Unless they have a way to counteract it, then they are all asleep by now. And, of course, there are other side effects." Cecil sipped his coffee. "This is good."

"What other side effects?"

"Well, The Pulpit is in some ways a fountain of youth. For instance, the three of us had the beginnings of androgenic alopecia, male pattern baldness. There's nothing more distressing to a young man than watching his hair slowly disappear, day by day. But soon after we began working around The Pulpit, we noticed our hair growing back! And look at me today! I still have a full head of hair!" Cecil said with a half-laugh.

"All these years, and The Pulpit's effects are still with me," Cecil continued. "It heals the human body, strengthens it." He lifted his left hand and made a firm fist. "I've never been sick a day in my life, and Charles the same. I'm well into my eighties, and I am in better shape than most sixty-year-olds. At my yearly physicals, my doctor just shakes his head, says I'm perfectly fine. This gives me hope, hope that they're still alive down there. The Pulpit ought to be protecting them. I'm telling you, its powers are vast, so we must adjust our expectations accordingly."

"I hope you're right, and thank you trusting me with

details of the device. If what you say is true, then they're probably still alive. It should buy us valuable time."

"Yes, but proceed with haste, Larry. The Pulpit affects not only the anatomy, but also neurological and psychological systems. That is why I am so worried. Though, truth be told, perhaps she inherited some of my resistance to its effects. For instance, I was the last to fall asleep out of the three while we worked near it."

"I understand, sir. We'll work as fast as we can. I'll let you know when the boring machine arrives, but you'll hear the helicopter's thump." Larry rose from his chair, shook Cecil's hand, and tried to force a thin smile. "I'm not going anywhere, Cecil. I'm here to see this through."

Larry exited the limousine, thinking to himself that the rescue was a long shot. He began walking, his mind calculating the effort to eliminate Charles Shafer and his associates. Through the chilly October night air, he watched his steady breath blow puffs of fog as he made his way to the rescue site. Things were getting interesting.

46

D arren walked along Braddock Avenue, looking for his mom's blue Volvo. He didn't see it, and he made it almost halfway up to the Regent Square Movie Theater before doubling back to the park's parking lot. As each moment passed, his worry grew. Then he saw her car. It was parked in the unlit southwest corner of the parking lot, and that's why he must've missed seeing it the first time around. A wave of relief swept over him as he started walking faster. He was twenty yards away when he saw that his mom's head was slumped to the side. *She must be sleeping*, he thought. He sprinted to the car window and knocked hard on the glass; once, twice… nothing. "Mom!" he shouted. "Mom, wake up!" His mother didn't move. "Mom, wake up! Please!" But she remained still. He tried the driver's door. Locked. He circled the car, trying each door. All locked. This wasn't right. His mom's face was pale and turned toward the driver's side window, a lock of her dark brown hair swept across one eye. Then Darren saw the pharmacy bottle in her lap. It was open, the cap to one side. Several blue pills lay scattered on the seat. "Oh, no," he said as his legs buckled. He turned and willed his legs to run, but they felt slowed in molasses. He screamed, "Grandpa! Grandpa!" The strength in his body seeped away as he realized what she'd done. His legs buckled as his world turned to black, and he slowly twirled into an enveloping darkness.

Joe slipped the dark red Porsche 911 into fifth gear as he sped through the Squirrel Hill tunnels. Cruising at eighty miles an hour was a breeze in the 2.7-litre, six-cylinder, rear-engine German sport coupe, and he was making good time toward Carson Street on the South Side of Pittsburgh. He reached into the small glove box and removed a compact black satellite phone. His grandfather had given him the silver Porsche as a gift for completing the Special Forces Q-Course, and the phone came installed.

"Hello, is Josh there?"

"Is this Joseph?"

"Yes, Mrs. Parks."

Josh's mom was a kindly, blonde and gray-haired woman, whose voice was soft when she spoke. "Okay, hold on a second, dear. I'll get him."

Joe heard her say, "Josh, it's Joseph."

"Hey, Joe, what's up?"

"Sorry to bug you so late, Josh, but I need your help."

"You mean tonight?"

"Yup, tonight, old buddy. And it's a full-on TS-SCI. I'm glad you're still 11th Special Forces. We're going to need jungles and all of our gear. Believe it or not, it's going down in Frick Park."

"Holy smokes! Frick Park?"

"Yeah, I know, and one of our rescue targets is my cousin, Amy."

Josh raised the pitch of his voice. "Oh man. Yeah, I can be ready in about fifteen. Where are you now?"

"I'm on my way, buddy, just exiting the Parkway onto the Brady Street Bridge. Make it ten minutes, and I'll be there. We're going to need a Terrain Analysis of the lower side of the park, near Forbes Avenue and Braddock. We'll also need to recon and set up an ambush of at least six targets. Two of them are highly trained, but that wasn't too hard to figure. They're carrying FBI badges, but also toting around .45 automatics. From that, I'm assuming they're SF or ex-SF. Then there's four other regular army guys, but they could be disguised SF. We're going to need suppressed weapons. Do you still have that pair of High Standards?"

"Aw, come on. You know I'd never sell those! They're my pride and joy, Joe." Josh laughed. "Yeah, I got 'em. I also got a few other surprises you haven't seen before. Should help tonight."

"Good, good. My grandfather is onsite, and of course, Larry's there."

Josh chuckled grimly. "Ah, Siebert. That dude is seriously spooky. He's about as CIA as you get."

"Yeah, but if we need an F-4 strike, you know we'll get it."

"For sure. You almost here?"

"Turning onto your street now. Hey, tell your mom something, okay?"

"She doesn't ask questions anymore, Joe. I don't think she liked the answers I gave her. Went too heavy on the gory details. But hey, she asked, you know?"

"Civilians can't understand. But that's okay. Just tell her I've got you set up on another hot date. How could she forget that brunette she found in your kitchen that morning? That must have been a sight!"

"Yeah, thanks for that one. I got in so much trouble over that. My mom's devout Catholic, dude. She almost had a heart attack when she found a half-naked girl making coffee in her kitchen!"

"You're welcome. Well, I'm here. Oh yeah, almost forgot, we're going to need the rappelling gear, all of it."

"Already got it packed, Joe. We're not taking the Porsche, are we?"

"Nope, fire up the Jeep. Not sure if we're going to need four-wheel drive, but better safe than sorry."

"Okay, meet you out back."

47

C harles knew what had to be done. The Pulpit had to be protected. When the boring machine arrived, it would be scuttled...carefully. That would end the charade of mounting a rescue for the poor fools who discovered the access tunnel. After a week or so, the rescue would be called off. Eventually Cecil's niece and her friends would be declared dead. Of course, there'd be a public outcry that the bodies should be recovered. He could see it now; every bleeding-heart liberal within thirty miles of Pittsburgh would flock to Frick Park with their "bring them back" signs and candlelight vigils. That scenario would not do, as it could inspire the authorities to try and recover the bodies.

Charles sat in his limousine and pondered the riddle. How to protect the secret of The Pulpit and make it so that a recovery effort could never take place? The EPA cover story bristled with possibility. What if it were true? What if nuclear waste was actually discovered at the site? Then the area would be placed under federal control. That scenario had merit. Charles was very familiar with nuclear weapon production, as Shafer Industries was one of the leading contributors to the country's nuclear defense research. Public opinion was already turning against nuclear waste. Would it be that hard to convince the media that a rogue agent had somehow buried nuclear materials in the heart of Frick Park?

Charles reached over to the crystal decanter half-full with Lagavulin, and grabbed a sparkling glass, engraved with his initials. Yes, then there it was. A plan just as neat as a pin! That area of the park would be doused with contaminated nuclear wastewater from the old Hartford weapons plant. How much would it take to get the rem counts skyrocketing, the old Geiger counter needles climbing? Those were details he could leave to the NSA. Charles could even provide a patsy to take the fall. Yes, he would choose an employee of his with a troubled past. Oh, the shame of ruining Frick Park for, let's say, the next century? He could imagine the press conference already. Charles would name the employee and then vow to commit Shafer Industries to the cleanup of Frick Park. Charles might even come out of this whole thing looking like a hero. And most importantly, the existence of The

Pulpit would remain a secret! That would be a fitting end to the life story of Charles Shafer.

Charles smiled and picked up the encrypted satellite phone and made the call. Things were going to work out fine, just fine.

48

"So what are we talking about here? You want to repel into the park from the Forbes Avenue Bridge?"

"I think that's the fastest way in, Josh. We can park the Jeep in the little neighborhood next to the bridge. I used to date this girl that lived over there. She eventually moved away, but I know just the place to go."

"Sounds good. It'll be fun. Just like old times, huh?"

"Yeah, just like old times. Here, make the left here on Beechwood Boulevard. Yeah, just like San Diego. Only this time, we're playing for keeps."

"We'll do the recon first, find out where they have their checkpoints. It won't be that hard to take out the regular army guys. You want to detain them, or send them back upstairs?"

"I've been thinking about that. I'm sure Larry has it covered. He always has it covered. The recon is something that's already been decided, so once we get it done, we'll get out and meet up with Larry and my grandfather."

"Once we get down there, buddy, let's set up the LP/OP. I brought the sensors and the whole shebang."

"Okay, I know where to put the listening post/observation post. Uh, make the right here at Forbes."

"Got it, we're close now. That graveyard on the left, isn't that Homewood Cemetery?"

"Yeah, Josh. You know the East Side pretty well for someone born and raised on the South Side. Ya know, old Mr. Frick himself is buried there. My friends from Allderdice and I walked through there a couple of times. It's got a pond, and a big stone house where the cemetery keeper lives. The place kind of gives me the creeps, but at the same time it has this strange beauty. Ah, here's the bridge. Okay, see that street up there, just past the bridge? Hang a left there."

"Got it, boss. Oh yeah, I can see the lights down there on the right. Hear that? That's the thump of a big chopper."

"They're bringing in a high-tech boring machine, called a TBM. That's probably the Sikorsky. They're going to try and use the TBM to drill a six-foot wide hole down to Amy and the others. We're here to make sure nothing happens to that machine. After reading some of the papers in Shafer's safe, I'm pretty sure he's never going to allow the rescue to happen. But guess what? We're the surprise element!"

"Uh-huh. Everyone thinks you're just this spoiled playboy. Well you are, but you're a well-trained spoiled playboy."

"That's right. Thanks to my grandfather and Larry. Oh, and we can't forget Sergeant Kolb."

"Nope, we won't ever forget Sergeant Kolb. He's aces, man. That dude knows his weapons!"

"Sure does. He's probably the world's authority on Soviet bloc weapons; even the Russkies don't know their own weapons systems as well as Sergeant Kolb. In fact, thanks to him, I brought a few silenced Makarovs for tonight's mission. Nine-millimeter Makarovs I picked up on one of my Saudi trips. Clean serial numbers, untraceable. One for you, and one for me."

"Thanks, Joe, you shouldn't have!"

"Anytime, brother. Okay, park over here. These people are never home. The guy runs some kind of import/export business, and he's always out of the country. See that house? That was her house."

"Alright, let's get the duffel bags down to the bridge, and then we'll come back for the ropes and the rest."

49

"What happened? Where am I?"

"You're okay, Darren, you just fainted in the parking lot. You're in an ambulance here in the park."

"Mom! Mom! Is she okay?"

"She's fine, honey, thanks to you. She's on her way to Mercy Hospital. We'll go visit her in just a little bit. You know what happened, huh?"

"I know, Grandpa. I saw the pills and the bottle. I tried to run and find you, but that's…that's when it all went black."

"You passed out, honey, and you hit your head. The medics say you have a mild concussion, but amazingly you didn't even suffer one cut. You have a hard head!"

"That's what Johnny always says. He says I'm hardheaded."

"He's right. The important thing is your mom is going

to be okay, and you're okay. Here, hold this icepack right there. That will reduce the swelling."

"It's cold!"

"I know, but trust me. Okay?"

"Okay."

"That's a good boy. Just lay back and relax. I have to go and help with the rescue."

"Grandpa, I want to see mom."

"Pretty soon we'll go visit her, but I need you to rest, okay?"

"Okay. I love you."

"I love you too, Darren. I'll be back very soon."

The Sikorsky S-64 Skycrane helicopter's main six-blade rotor's deep whooping sound penetrated the cold and cloudy October night sky as it approached Frick Park. Dangling on high-strength stainless steel cables far below was the prototype boring machine—or TBM—from Shafer Industries. The pilot scanned the area with his night-vision monocle and checked the infrared display on the Sikorsky's gauge panel. No other Sikorsky but this one was equipped with the advanced infrared system, making it the first computerized twenty-four-hour, all-weather helicopter in the world. The pilot had made the trip from Shafer's nuclear power plant construction site in North Carolina in three hours, record time for carrying such a heavy load. Modified engines on the helicopter helped increase the cruising speed to one hundred miles an hour. The pilot checked the coordinates on the small green DOS computer screen, confirming he was on target.

"Mr. Shafer, sir, this is Charlie 7144. Do you read me, over?"

"Yes, Mr. Stout. We read you loud and clear. Please set the machine down on the coordinates given. My men will guide you in on the descent, over."

"Roger that, sir. Beginning our approach, over."

"My God, it's a lot bigger than I'd imagined," Lou said as he watched the boring machine being slowly carried over the park by the helicopter.

"There isn't anything else like it in the world, Mr. Garvey," Charles said. "You're looking at the world's lightest and fastest hard rock TBM, and I invented it. Imagine a machine that can bore a man-sized, perfectly symmetrical hole twice as fast and twice as deep as any machine before it. Well, she can do it! It took ten years to go from prototype to the field unit you see here. You could say it was a pet project of mine. Just look at her! Now, let's hope it all goes to plan."

"Thank you for getting it here. I can't thank you enough."

"Don't thank me yet, Lou. Thank me when we pull four healthy people out of the ground. Excuse me now, as

I must attend to the delivery. The Sikorsky can be quite a handful, especially with such a heavy payload."

"If I can help in any way, please don't hesitate to ask."

"Yes, yes, I'll keep that in mind. Excuse me."

Two white vans proceeded in formation, driving slowly down the dark, curvy, lonely road that descends into the lower Frick Park parking lot. The beams from their headlights created a glaring wall standing in the eerie fog hovering over the access road. The vans duly drove to the north end of the lot and parked. After a time, eight men in white lab coats exited the vehicles.

The crew of men unloaded a hoard of large black waterproof utility cases and black duffel bags. Unbeknownst to the others, two of the men were carrying Browning High Power 9mm pistols under their jackets, tucked neatly into brown leather shoulder holsters, each equipped with an advanced, compact disposable suppressor. The armed duo was in charge of one particular case that differed from all the others. Their lead-lined case contained two, 4-ounce unmarked vials of what looked like harmless water, but what was instead transuranic radioactive wastewater, full of plutonium-based radionuclides from the Hartford Connecticut weapons plant. With a half-life of one hundred years, this was some of the most toxic nuclear waste ever created by man, short of actual plutonium pellets. Without fanfare, but with noticeable care, the two men carried the case away from the others. Then they began walking up a dark, unmarked trail into the west part of the park.

The Sikorsky Skycrane slowly lowered the cylindrical, white-colored TBM directly below to the rescue site. Charles Shafer and several Shafer Industry technicians held two-way radios in their hands and watched as the TBM got closer to the ground.

"That's it, that's it," Charles said. "Keep it going. About one meter now, you've almost got it! Adjust half a meter left. That's perfect. Now straight down a half-meter. Slowly, slowly, perfect! She's down and safe. Great job, men. Give us a few minutes to unhook the cables."

White-coated technicians climbed on top of the gleaming white TBM. It stood just over six feet tall, perfectly cylindrical and as long as a school bus.

"That is an impressive piece of hardware," Lou said as he walked up.

"You like following me around Mr. Garvey?"

"Sorry if I'm bugging you, but I'm curious. That's all."

"As long as you don't interfere, I guess it's okay.

"Thanks," Lou said.

"It weighs nearly five tons, you know. It's a lucky thing I have that Sikorsky and some fantastic pilots. They made the trip from North Carolina in only three hours.

Anyway, with this we could reach them by tomorrow evening, depending on how dense the stratum is."

"I'm not sure a layman would appreciate how fast that is, Mr. Schafer. You're going to have to punch through thick layers of shale, then straight through anthracite coal. Not the softest rock in the world. And correct me if I'm wrong, but your machine can't drill straight down. You have to work at an angle, right?"

"That's correct. So you're familiar with TBMs?"

"Somewhat. I worked a few contracts on tunnel projects in my time. I've seen TBMs before, but not one like this. Will you look at the teeth on that baby? You said diamond carbide? They're arranged in a cross-pattern. Interesting. Anyway, in the old days, it could take weeks to dig fifty or sixty feet."

"This is an order of magnitude faster. Did you know the cutting teeth can be changed from inside the machine? It helps speed up the drilling process considerably. And you are correct; we will dig at a forty-five-degree angle."

"Again, I appreciate you showing me around. Do you mind if I watch your men set up the drill? I'll stay out of the way, and I won't ask any more questions, I promise."

"Well, the military informed me they are setting up perimeters: one here at the site, a few on the main trails and access road, and one up at the trailhead by the parking lot. The soldiers will be in charge of security then."

"To be honest, I understand why you'd want to keep the media from clogging up the trails. The first checkpoint makes sense to me, Mr. Shafer, but why another checkpoint way down here by the digging? You don't believe the rumor that this is a nuclear waste site? I mean, where are the guys in contamination suits holding Geiger counters?"

"Listen, Mr. Garvey, I'm no expert on nuclear waste and waste sites. Sure, my company has built nuclear reactors, but we don't get involved in their day-to-day operations nor the disposal of nuclear waste. I'm not one to question the EPA, or the NRC for that matter. I am sure they have their reasons for being here. And concerning men in contamination suits, don't you think we should leave that up to the federal authorities?"

"I'm just saying it's odd, Mr. Shafer."

"You're not one of those conspiracy theorists, are you? Let's not get ahead of ourselves."

"I suppose you're right. You're right. I don't work for the EPA or the NRC, and all I know about radiation I learned from a Reader's Digest. But I've lived in Pittsburgh my whole life, and I've never heard a whisper about nuclear waste being buried in Regent Square. For the record, until I see a Geiger counter needle swinging high, I'm not buying the EPA's fairy tale."

"Yes, Yes. We're all on the same page here, Mr. Garvey. No need to worry. The government has a job to do, and we have our own job to do. I'm sure we can all get along. Over the years, I've had to deal with different administrations, Congress, and regulatory agencies sprouting up all over Capitol Hill. I know my way around D.C. Trust me, we're going to get your loved ones back, safe and sound. That's what the TBM is for, and that's our first priority." Charles motioned to one of his men. "Jim, come over here. Please show this young man around our prized possession. He's apparently well-versed in the construction trade. Perhaps we can use an extra set of hands. This man's son and grandson are trapped down there."

"Why thank you, Mr. Shafer, but I'm not qualified..."

"Nonsense. Jim here will show you around. He's one of my best men."

"This way, Mr?" Jim said.

"Lou Garvey, nice to meet you."

"Okay, Mr. Garvey, how are you at reading hydraulic pressure indicators?"

"I think I can do that," Lou said.

"Take good care of our friend, Jim." Charles smiled.

Charles looked back as he walked away from the boring machine. Everything was going to plan, but he was quickly tiring of the old man's questions. *We can't afford any liabilities during the operation*, he thought. Of course, there were ways to take care of such problems, and Charles considered his options. He decided to keep Garvey close, and if he needed to dispose of him, then so be it. *A shame*, he thought. The old man seemed genuinely concerned for his son and grandson. But he was a busy-body—a nosey busybody. There was far too much at stake to let a bumbling old fool get in the way.

A very tall Pittsburgh firefighter approached Lou Garvey and put a hand on his shoulder. He leaned down and whispered in his ear.

"Excuse me, Mr. Garvey?"

"Yes."

"Sir, could you come with me?"

"I'm busy helping with the rescue. What's this about?"

"Sir, we have information that your life is in danger. I'm not at liberty to say much more than that. Cecil Stewart sent me to get you. Please, follow me."

"I knew it!" Lou whispered. "It's Charles Shafer, isn't it?"

"Mr. Garvey, my job is to get you to safety. We have a car waiting in the parking lot. It's marked 'fire department,' but I assure you, it belongs to Mr. Stewart, and we must leave now!"

"Okay, okay. I'm coming. My grandson, Darren, he's being treated at the ambulance."

"I know, sir, we'll go to him now. Thank you for cooperating."

50

"How long was I out?"

"An hour this time. I had to use two capsules to wake you, and even then it wasn't easy." Amy gave him a look. "Any more dreams?"

"No dreams. Listen, we're going to have to try soon," Peter said. He put down his notebook, turned and looked at Amy, really looked at her full in the face. God, she was pretty, with high cheekbones, blazing blue eyes, and that lustrous blonde mane of hers. Even though she was filthy from all they'd been through, somehow the sweat and dirt combined with her perfectly tanned skin made her look like an exotic Amazon goddess.

"I know, Peter. We're down to two capsules of the amyl nitrate. I should have brought more."

"I'm just glad you brought them at all. They should be part of any decent first-aid kit, but unfortunately, most don't include them. You're quite the smarty, Ms. Lee, and quite beautiful."

"Why thank you, Dr. Hawn. You're not so bad yourself. You look like Humphrey Bogart right now, very *Maltese Falcon*. I mean, you don't actually look like Bogart, you're much more handsome. I mean, you have that hero quality."

"Well, I'm just doing the best job I can. Maybe after all this is over, you and I can have a long talk together. What do you say?"

"I'd like that, Peter. I'd like that very much. You fascinate me. You're much different than I expected."

"Oh really? How so?"

"You're so real. You say exactly what's on your mind. You're a man of action, yet you're also tender and loving. I've watched you around your son. You're so protective, and it's easy to see how much you love him. I find all of that attractive. Am I making any sense?"

"Yes, you're just getting to know the real me, I suppose."

As they sat close together, Johnny looked over and smiled.

"Dad, when are we leaving? I'm hungry. I'm starting to feel sleepy again."

"We're leaving soon. I'm just finishing up calculating the coordinates. In the meantime, we're going to have to either drag that guy over to The Machine, or use part of a capsule to try and wake him. What's his name? Rondinelli?"

"Yeah, Dad. His name is Dave Rondinelli. Isn't that Italian?"

"Correct, Italian. What do you think, Amy? Time to open one of the last capsules?"

"Yes, good idea. I'm getting sleepy too. Let's include him in our sniffing circle." She motioned with a wave of her hand to follow her over to the sleeping ranger.

"Okay, we can hunch over him. When I break the capsule, we'll each take a quick, deep sniff like before, but I'm going to give him a bigger dose than the rest of us. I hope it works."

They all looked at each other as Amy brought the green box containing the yellow-white amyl nitrate capsules out of her pocket.

"It's hard to believe that this stuff wouldn't wake him. I see stars every single time."

"It's quite strong. I guess that's the point."

"Yeah, I see stars too," Johnny added.

"Okay, here goes," Amy said as she quickly snapped the capsule between the forefingers of her hands. She inhaled briefly, and then passed the jagged capsule around. Each one took a short sniff, then she passed it under the ranger's nose.

"C'mon. C'mon. Wake up!" she said. A few tense seconds passed.

"What's going on here?" The ranger opened his eyes. "Where am I?"

"Mr. Rondinelli," Peter said. "Sir, just relax. You've been injured in a fall, and you've been unconscious. Are you in any pain?"

"Call me Dave, and yes damn it, my leg hurts. Is it broken?"

"Let me have a look," Peter said. He bent down close to the torn pant leg.

"I need more light. Son, bring the lighter."

"Hey, kid, that's my lighter!"

"I know, I know," Peter said. "We had to borrow it. Now keep still while I examine your leg."

"Dad, look! I can't believe it!"

Incredibly, the ranger's leg was no longer broken. The once exposed, cracked femur and the gaping wound surrounding the compound fracture had healed over. All that remained was a small purply-green, watermelon-sized bruise.

"Unbelieveable," Peter said, rubbing his eyes.

"What?" Amy asked.

"His leg is perfectly healed. Not even a scar, just a bruise."

"Maybe he can stand on it. Let's help him up guys."

"Dave, this might hurt a little," Peter said.

Dave grunted an "okay," and Amy, Peter and Johnny grabbed his arms.

"Here we go. On three. One, two…three! Lift!" Peter yelled.

With grunts and groans, they pulled the big man up.

"Oww. Man!" Dave cringed as he took a few steps.

"Go easy on it. Say, do you remember how you ended up down here?" Peter asked.

"Well, I was making my rounds when I saw that someone had moved this wood I bought for a project we're working on, building a new bridge over the creek. Anyway, I went to get our board back, and that's the last thing I remember."

"Well, would you believe the femur in your left leg was snapped clean in two when I last checked on you? Peter said.

"That's impossible," Dave said.

"Not when it comes to The Machine," Johnny said. "It's from outer space! Alien technology," he added.

"What's he talking about? Is the kid serious?"

"We don't know where it's from, but we think the alien part is most likely true. That thing over there has been down here a long time, maybe since the last Ice Age, maybe longer. The Machine—as we've named it."

"It has powers?" Dave asked, now curious and looking over at the obelisk.

"It healed you, for one," Peter said. "It causes narcolepsy and strange futuristic dreams. It can teleport objects. It generates an invisible, protective shield with a breathable atmosphere. This is what we know so far, and there's probably much more that we don't know."

"Where the hell are we?" Dave asked, looking more alert.

"We're standing about seventy-five feet under Frick Park. This room we're in, I believe was created by or for The Machine. You fell down here, Dave."

"Yeah, sure," Dave said, looking uncertain.

"No, Dave, you fell. You broke your leg, badly. You went unconscious, and that's how we found you when we got down here. Amy and I repelled down after my son Johnny, but the hole collapsed and you'd better believe it, we are trapped."

"Does anyone know we're here? Tell me the National Guard is up there right now, with the Mayor and everyone."

"My other son and his friend alerted the authorities. I'm sure there's plenty of people, working as hard as they can to get us the heck out of here."

"But it's more complicated than that," Amy chimed in.

"How so?" Dave said. "What else?"

Peter winced, "We're convinced somebody on the surface doesn't want us to be rescued. They used plastic explosives, C-4, to seal the hole. I found pieces of an electrical detonator. Here." Peter reached into his pocket and retrieved a small piece of jagged silvery metal.

"I know what that is. My uncle works in the coal mine

in Republic, PA. That's a detonator alright. Bastards!" Dave's shoulders dropped. "Why would someone want to trap us here?"

"That's the sixty-four thousand dollar question, isn't it? But I think the answer is right over there." Peter pointed to The Machine.

"Alien technology," Dave said. "That would explain it. Somebody doesn't want it to be found?"

"Bingo, Dave," Peter said. "And we're just beginning to understand what The Machine can do. Somebody up there knows."

"Hmm. I can see why they'd want to keep it to themselves. You said it can teleport. Isn't that moving something from one place to another, just like that?" Dave snapped his fingers. "You guys figured out how it works?"

"It was Dr. Hawn here—Peter—who translated the symbols on the machine and got it to work."

"Is this your wife? She looks kind of young." Dave smiled and pointed at Amy.

"No, she's my student and umm, colleague."

"She's sure a looker."

"I'm standing right here, in case you haven't noticed. I don't appreciate the blatant sexism. Can we keep this conversation on topic?"

"Relax, lady. It was a compliment, a blatant compliment." Dave shrugged. "Well, we're screwed, huh? Hey, wait a minute. You're gonna try and teleport us out of here, aren't you? You guys are serious. You weren't kidding with the *Star Trek* stuff?"

"Yeah, that's my dad. He's a genius."

"Apparently so, kid. So what's the plan?" Dave asked.

"The plan is exactly what you surmised. We're going to use The Machine to get us out of here. I'm fairly sure my calculations are correct."

"'Fairly sure'? Doc, don't you have to be more than fairly sure? If you make a mistake, ain't we dead?"

"Not necessarily. I'm concerned with the accuracy of my coordinates. What I mean is, I'd rather err on the side of caution when it comes down to it. I'd rather have us rematerialize four feet above the surface than six feet under."

"Yeah, you and me both, Doc," Dave said.

"There's more. Worst-case scenario, we could end up in another time, or another country, or end up treading water in middle of the Atlantic. This is quantum physics, and frankly, in our time, we've just begun our understanding of it. The Machine is a quantum spaceship for all intents and purposes."

"We could end up in the ocean, Dad?"

"I just used that for an example, honey. Don't worry, that's not going to happen."

51

The technician's nametag simply read "Dobbs," one of the six male Shafer Industry employees working to set up the command center on the far south side of Frick Park. Located two miles from the rescue site, through a forest of heavy oak and poplar trees, this was a choice site to launch the operation. Dobbs and the five other technicians all carried top-secret or TS-SCI clearance with the Pentagon. Tonight would be the first real-world test of the Hornet drones.

Dobbs undid the five butterfly latches on the aluminum waterproof flight case and swung the lid open. Nestled inside the black, heavy foam liner, were eight silvery mechanical insect-like devices. He pulled one out, carried it outside the green tent and placed it on the parking lot's dark macadam. Dobbs noticed the soldiers nearby watching him, but he didn't care. He removed a small device that looked like a pocket calculator from his lab coat pocket. He thought if he told his wife what he was working on, she'd sure be impressed. Then again, if he told his wife what he was working on, they'd both soon be dead. Shafer Industries made every higher-level employee sign a confidentiality agreement that guaranteed jail time for any employee with loose lips, but over the years, Dobbs had heard a few unsettling rumors.

No, he could never tell anyone about the tiny robot he was about to activate. The size of a small hummingbird, this insect-looking device was nicknamed "The Hornet." Equipped with regular and infrared cameras, and several types of weapons, it was a tiny all-weather tactical flying robot. Wirelessly controlled, no less. Not even the Russians had technology like this, and it was all courtesy of Charles Shafer. Rumor in the company was that he was one of the original Groom Lake scientists, that the old man himself was in charge of a secret government lab called S4, located near Las Vegas in the Nevada desert. It wasn't Dobbs's concern tonight. Tonight he was excited to deploy The Hornet, to see what it could do. He thought it was odd that its first outing was going to be domestic. He always envisioned being sent to the Middle East, or to the East German border for the first real-world test. No matter, because the old man himself had given the order.

He flipped the small toggle on the upper right part of

the slim black box in his hand. The Hornet's "eye," a single LED on the nose of the robot, began glowing a bright yellow. The yellow color had been Dobbs's idea, as he had remembered catching fireflies at night when he was a boy growing up in Lancaster, Pennsylvania. The Hornet's LED accurately mimicked the hue and brightness of a firefly. His left thumb clicked another small metal toggle switch, and two small black propellers began rotating—one on top and one on the tail of the Hornet. The Hornet utilized a top-secret, incredibly tiny microchip for all of its control functions. The device had a range of five miles before it would automatically start circling to reacquire a signal.

Dobbs pushed the left joystick up, and the tiny metal robot lifted ten feet into the air. He moved the right joystick and The Hornet took off across the parking lot. Dobbs decided 'why not,' and he buzzed the Hornet just past the top of one of the soldier's heads who was guarding the parking lot checkpoint. He quickly ducked, raised his head and said, "What the hell?" Dobbs laughed. "Sorry about that." But he wasn't sorry, just amazed at the ease with which he could control it. Dobbs flicked another toggle, and a five-inch screen lit up on the black box. The photovoltaic sensor had automatically turned on the infrared, and he quickly got a nice aerial picture of the park, with every heat source glowing a bright white.

He flew the Hornet higher to see more of the park.

That's when he noticed two human heat signatures at the north end of the valley. He flew the Hornet closer and saw two stocky men repelling down from a bridge. *Not good*, Dobbs thought. He pushed the return-to-home button on the box and simultaneously reached into his coat pocket.

52

"Damn, this is cool!"

"Not every day we get to repel off a city bridge, huh Josh?"

"Nope, not every day. And not every day we go to full-on attack mode in the middle of Pittsburgh. This should be real interesting."

"Hey, do you hear that?"

"Yeah, I do. Sounds like a big dragonfly, like a two-pound dragonfly. What the hell?"

"Hey, there it is! See the yellow?" Joe pointed to the dark treetops.

"I see it! What is it? It's tiny!"

"I don't know, but damn it's fast! Look at thing motor!"

"Maybe it's a toy helicopter or something. Remote control? We don't have anything like that, do we, Joe?"

"It's not ours, as far as I know. And….It's gone! Look at that! It took off to the south side of the park. I have a bad feeling about our little yellow friend."

"Yeah, me too. If it was some kind of recon device, then I'm pretty sure it saw us. Well, we'd better hurry if they know we're here. I was hoping for the element of surprise, and I'd hate to think we just lost it."

"Don't worry. We have new toys of our own to play with."

"I like anything that gives us the advantage, Joe."

"Okay, we're almost down. Get ready."

They lowered themselves the final few feet to the dirt trail below. Joe realized Josh was right. They'd lost their advantage.

"Let's hide the ropes. I don't think we'll need them again."

They stashed the ropes behind one of the bridge's supports.

"Come here, I want to show you what Larry gave me."

Joe reached in his backpack and brought out two pairs of goggles.

"Ever see one of these?"

"What's that?" Josh examined the goggle set in the darkness. "Wait a minute." Josh brought a small flashlight out with a red filter on it, and then clicked it on.

"What the heck are these?"

"They're advanced night-vision goggles," Joe said.

"Ah, yeah. They're tiny. Dude, they look like swimming goggles. Here goes." Josh slipped the black goggles over his head.

"The switch is on the left side, so is the brightness knob."

"Holy crap! These are sweet!" Josh said in an excited whisper. "I can see everything, just like it's daytime! Oh, man, these are definitely radical, my friend, seriously radical!"

"Glad you like 'em. Now, my turn." Joe slipped the goggles on and clicked the switch. "Wow! Just wow! The forest looks as clear as day! I love Larry Siebert!"

"Me too! Thank the lord for Larry! We've got what they used to call in school a 'tactical advantage.'"

"I'm thinking it's more like we evened up the playing field. Whatever was flying around up there a few minutes ago, it damn well saw us. You can bet things are going to heat up here in a few minutes, so let's get the weapons unpacked. What did you bring?"

"Follow me. We're gonna celebrate Christmas early."

Joe and Josh walked over to where two black duffel bags were sitting beside the trail.

"Oh, you're gonna like this, buddy. Here, this one's for you. It's a Heckler and Koch, or just HK MP9, fully suppressed, of course. It's a select-fire nine-millimeter sub-machine gun, and I loaded up the twenty-five-round magazines with some very unique hollow points. We each have four loaded magazines, including the fully loaded one in the gun. Make 'em count, okay?"

"I will! Thank you! What's with this sight? Is it electronic?"

"Oh, yeah, almost forgot. Just turn this knob. There you go, now look."

"Oh yeah! Just put the red dot on the target?"

"Yep, that's it. It's accurate out to about a hundred yards. Limited range, but it should be just about right for this mission."

"What are you carrying, Josh?"

"Another fine HK item. It's called a HK33, but there aren't many around like this one. It's fully suppressed, has a night-vision scope, and fires a 5.56 NATO or .223 round. Accurate out to about three hundred yards, but it's louder than the MP5."

"You always have the latest trick gear, and I'm especially glad you brought it tonight. Thanks. Now, let's deploy those sensors and set up our listening post. I'm expecting company soon."

53

D r. Hawn checked his calculations one last time. This was the critical test. He was confident he could get them out of the cave, but he had his doubts about *where* they would end up. He shuddered at the thought of their bodies reassembling into the middle of a frigid ocean; the irony of surviving all they'd been through, only to drown pointlessly. Heck, he might be slightly off target, and they'd end up in the cold Allegheny or Monongahela Rivers, drowning just the same.

Stop worrying, Peter! he thought. He sighed and touched The Machine, thinking there had to be safeguards built in, some kind of alien computer program that prevented such mishaps. He marveled at the intricate details and the seemingly indestructible nature of it. How long had it sat in the chamber undiscovered? Why was it left here? So many questions, but the time for questioning was over. It was time for action, and he looked at Johnny and Amy. Then he looked at Dave, and the man was staring right back at him.

"I know what you're thinking, Doc," Dave said.

"You're a mind-reader? Do tell."

"Yeah, you're afraid. I can see it on your face."

"That obvious, huh?"

"Yeah, it is, and you'd better quit it," Dave whispered. "Someone here has got to play the hero, and guess what, Doc? It's you! Pull your shit together, because I sure ain't got what it takes. You were the geek in high school, huh? While I was chasing chicks and playing rock 'n roll, you were cracking books. Listen, no matter what happens, Doc, at least the man upstairs knows you tried. That's all you can do...try your best. If we don't make it, then it's just our fate."

"Okay, point taken, Dave. Philosophy major?"

"I actually did take Philosophy 101 at Pitt, but I'm just another frustrated musician and Renaissance man who has a talent for reading people. One thing I learned as a musician, though, is that once you get up on stage, you give it your all. Science is your stage. Get it?"

"Yes, got it. Thanks. You're okay, Rondinelli. Would you go get Johnny and Amy? I think we're ready."

"Sure, Doc."

"This is going to be interesting," Peter murmured to himself.

He flipped his notebook shut, memorizing the coordinates. *Is it really that simple?* he thought.

"We're ready!" Johnny said brightly.

"Let's go, Peter. I'm really getting sick of the decor around here," Amy said.

"Okay, everyone, here's the plan. We're all going to put our hands on The Machine, overlapping each other's. I want each of you to clear your mind. You've heard of meditation? Well, we're going to focus our minds using a Tibetan chant that I picked up on one of my adventures. We're going to say 'Om' together, and concentrate on that sound. I think you're all going to be surprised at how freeing it is to lose your physical form, even for just a brief journey through space-time. Since I've already been through it once, I must warn that it's incredibly difficult to resist the temptation to leave this plane of existence, to go astral-surfing."

"What's astral-surfing, Dad?"

"Johnny, the best way to describe it is that it's like going to Heaven. It's incredibly beautiful, peaceful and exciting all at the same time. When The Machine teleported me, I felt I could go anywhere in the universe, just by thinking about it. I was aware of all the life forms on all the planets throughout the galaxy. Son, imagine having all this at your command, then having to force yourself to give up that power to come back to Earth. Heaven is a difficult place to leave, believe me! Love brought me back, and that might sound far-fetched, but it's true. But I was alone during the last test; it might be different teleporting as a group. I'd say we should be ready for anything. Okay?"

"Okay, Peter," Amy said.

"Okay, Dad."

"Okay, Doc. This sounds better than some of the candy we had back at Woodstock," Dave said with a wink.

"Thanks for the memory, Dave. Now let's join hands on The Machine."

54

The Starlight scope lit up the forest in Frick Park, turning night into day. Josh pulled the bolt back on his rifle and checked to see if a round was in and the magazine full. He could see the back of a 5.56mm case snuggled into the rifle's chamber. He closed the bolt then leveled the scope's crosshairs on one of the two soldiers at the far north side of the park. He could clearly see them standing next to the wooden "Kensington Trail" sign, holding their black M16s loosely, their fingers off the trigger.

Josh whispered into his radio, "Joe, I've got two bogeys in my sights. I can take them out no problem. I'm two hundred and fifty yards uphill and awaiting your orders."

"Hold your fire. Contacting Larry now."

Joe picked up his encrypted satellite phone. He

wondered if being so deep in the valley in Frick Park would affect reception. *Ring, Ring.*

"Yes, are you in position?"

"We are in position. What's the order?"

"It seems we're a bit outnumbered here at the moment. Let's even-up the playing field, shall we? Take out the guards close to your position. We can't have you two being discovered, now can we?"

"Roger that. Just the two soldiers closest to us?"

"Yes, just those two for now. Make it quick and silent."

"Roger that."

Joe picked up the other radio that linked him to Josh. "It's a go, repeat, go on those two targets."

"Roger. Will do."

Private James Jones looked down at the rifle slung across the front of his body, a black, automatic M16. The eight-pound gun was fully loaded with a 30-round magazine of NATO spec FMJ 55-grain bullets. Jones wasn't a big fan of the M16, even though he had become intimate with his weapon during boot camp at Fort Hood. He could tear it down and reassemble it in his sleep. Jones loved how easy the M16 was to fieldstrip, just pull two pins and the whole thing came apart. This was the latest version with forward-assist, but even his instructors at basic training had disdain for the M16 because they had seen them jam during firefights in Vietnam. Rumor had it that the plastic grip and forearm of the M16 was made by a toy company. No matter, the rifle felt comforting in his hands.

Jones looked out into the black night and suddenly had the odd sensation that he was being observed. *Top secret my ass,* he thought. Just then he heard a pop, like a soda can opening. He turned to look at Miller. And Miller was gone.

"Private Miller!" Jones shouted out. "Don't mess around, Andrew!" Jones took a breath and searched the area where Miller had been standing. That's when he saw Miller slumped over. It looked like he was in position to heave up the beers they drank the night before. "Aw nah, Miller. Are you all right? Tough night last night, huh? You'll feel better after you get it all out, puke-boy." Miller didn't move. *That's strange*, Jones thought. He reached his hand out to pat Miller on the back, and felt Miller's shirt. It was warm and sticky. That's when Jones heard another soda can opening, and before he could turn around, a 5.56 mm bullet entered Jones's skull and he was dead.

The giant room was eerily quiet, except for the faint humming sound produced by The Machine. Peter, Amy, Johnny and Dave all surrounded the glowing obelisk, hugging it with their hands overlapping. Dr. Hawn was standing beside Johnny when The Machine began to glow a bright blue light.

"Just keep holding my hand, honey. It'll be okay." The Machine started to hum and Johnny felt his skin start to crawl with a low-voltage electric shock.

"Dad, I'm scared. I'm scared!" Johnny yelled over the humming sound.

"It's okay. You're doing fine. We're going through this together. Just stay with me!"

"Peter!" Amy screamed. "Oh, my God!" Peter looked at Amy and she was glowing yellow-white, like a small sun. A kaleidoscope of light poured out of The Machine, blinding Peter, forcing his eyes to shut.

"Hold on, guys, this is it!" Peter yelled. A series of four incredibly bright flashes lit up the cavern around The Machine. Four people being turned into so much quantum data, essentially vaporized to travel through the multiverse. Four loud bangs rang out in the room and then suddenly, they were gone.

55

The Decade was crowded that Friday night. Billy Price and the Keystone Rhythm Band were about to start their first set at the new nightclub at the corner of Atwood and Sennott Streets in Oakland. Billy had worked with the legendary blues guitarist Roy Buchanan, and his raspy, soulful vocals were like a cross between Sam Cooke and Otis Redding.

The Decade had just recently switched from fifties-type music to a more modern hard rock, soul and blues-oriented lineup of acts. Upstairs in the tiny Green Room, Billy was nervously pacing in his gold shirt and black pinstripe pants.

"It's gonna be a good show tonight, fellas! Yeah, it's crowded down there. It's gonna be a packed house! You ready, Glenn?" Glenn Pavone was the hot new lead guitarist for the band, and he was busy finishing restringing his 1963 Fender Stratocaster.

"Yeah, Billy, I'm ready. New strings," Glenn said, holding up his guitar.

"Alright, guys, we're going on. Let's tear it up!"

The five members of the band walked downstairs and made a quick left turn at the busy bar. "You guys ready?" the bartender shouted. Just a nod from Billy, and the bartender nodded back.

Glenn walked onstage and plugged into his brand new Marshall JMP 50-watt combo amp. No effects, not even reverb—Glenn Pavone was a guitarist who preferred going guitar to cable to amp. Glenn checked the master volume and preamp volumes on the Marshall and checked the EQ settings. Even though they had done sound-check hours before, he wanted to be sure nothing had changed. Billy was right, the room was packed, full of University of Pittsburgh and Charles Masters students smoking and getting pleasantly buzzed on Iron City and Rolling Rock beer. Glenn heard a roar and turned around. Billy had walked up to the mike and just stood there smiling, zoot suit, sunglasses and all.

"Hello, Decade!" Billy shouted. Another roar.

"I'm Billy Price, and this is the amazing Keystone Rhythm Band!"

"Are you ready for some blues and soul music?"

The crowd screamed, "Yeah!"

"Alright then. We're going to preach the blues and

rock your socks off! This is called, 'Good Time Charlie'!" Billy pulled the microphone stand towards him and counted off the tune.

One...two...three, and the band started in with their saxophone and lead guitar sound, with Billy smiling to the dancing crowd.

"Good Time Charlie!" Billy sang. Glenn looked out at the crowd as he played his sunburst Fender Stratocaster. *This is going to be a great show*, he thought.

All of a sudden, Glenn saw a giant flash and heard a series of four popping sounds just behind his guitar amp. "What the...?" he said as he kept playing. *Did my amp just go? Did I just blow a tube?* he thought. *Hey, what are those people doing back there?* The flash and noise had sounded like firecrackers going off, and even Billy was looking toward the rear of the stage. Four people were standing there, kind of hunched over and disheveled. The blue-green stage lights made them look like ghouls. Glenn noticed that their faces and clothes were streaked with dirt: two men, a woman and a young boy.

"Hey, you four, off the stage!" Billy yelled, moving away from the microphone.

"That kid's too young to be in here!" Billy yelled back again.

How'd they even get up on stage? Glenn thought. The four people didn't move; they seemed frozen. *That's weird*, Glenn thought again. Then one of them began to move. One of the dirt-covered men walked around the amps and over to Glenn.

"Where are we?" the man yelled into Glenn's ear.

"Man, you're in The Decade, in Oakland!" Glenn yelled back over the pulsing music.

"In Pittsburgh, right?" the man shouted into Glenn's ear.

"Yeah, man, Pittsburgh. But you gotta get off the stage. Billy is going to go nuts. Please."

"Thank you!" the man yelled back.

Billy Price watched Glenn talk to the grimy intruders on his stage. *This is a new one*, he thought. Then he watched one of the men usher the other three off the bandstand. Billy strutted over to Glenn.

"What the hell was that? How'd that kid make it past the bouncer?"

"I dunno, Billy. But it's cool. They're leaving, alright?"

"Good job, Glenn. Man, the freaks are out tonight!" Billy said as he swung the microphone around and went back into another chorus of "Good Time Charlie."

Peter grabbed Johnny's hand and then Amy's and nodded to Dave.

"We're in The Decade!" he yelled. "C'mon, follow me!"

"I knew this place looked familiar! Hey, that's Billy Price!" Dave said, pointing his finger as they walked down the stage stairs to the dance floor.

"You did it, Peter!" Amy yelled excitedly.

"Dad, you saved us!"

"C'mon, let's get out of here. We'll talk outside," Peter yelled over the music.

The four of them made their way through a heavy blue haze of cigarette smoke, pushed past the drunk and swaying college kids. Finally they reached a startled bouncer standing at the entrance, and the four of them spilled out on the sidewalk.

"We've got to get to a phone. Amy, does your grandfather have a mobile phone?" Peter said.

"Yes, he has a satellite phone mounted on his wheelchair."

"Okay, we've got to call him."

"Hey, Doc, lemme call my friend Jimmy," Dave said. "He'll come get us. He lives up near Craig Street. I've known him since we was eleven."

"Hold on, let's see what Amy finds out first, okay?"

"There're some payphones over by the Pitt Law building," Amy said.

"I want to call Mom," Johnny said.

"We will honey. We will," Peter said.

56

J oe observed the two men in white lab coats coming up the trail toward the rescue site. He watched as they stopped and put two small cases they were carrying gently on the ground. Then they each reached up and turned on small flashlights mounted to their white hardhats. The bright glare momentarily blinded Joe through the night-vision goggles.

What are they up to? he wondered.

Joe moved down the hill to get a better view. He watched the men holding in their hands what looked like white modeling clay.

"Aw, man, plastique," Joe said to himself. He knew what was about to happen. Sure enough, the men removed dull silver-colored, lipstick tube looking thingies from their coat pockets.

Complete with detonators, Joe thought. He watched as

the two men inserted the silver tubes into the white clay-like substance, now armed and ready to go. *Oh, shit.* Joe shook his head and decided to retreat up the hill to alert Josh and Larry. Things were starting to get red hot in Frick Park.

Cecil sat in his wheelchair in his limousine, talking with Larry. As he heard the news of the soldiers that Joe and Josh had taken out, Cecil smiled grimly. *The costs are piling up tonight*, he thought. He heard the telltale beep on his phone, alerting him of an incoming call.

"Hold on, Larry. It's Joseph. Meet me back here, later, for a conference. I will let you know. Thank you." Larry nodded and exited the car. Cecil pushed a button on the small phone.

"Joseph, what is going on down there?"

"Bad news, Grandpa. I just saw something peculiar."

"Go ahead, son."

"I observed two men sneaking into the park from the south side trail, carrying two unmarked cases. They removed two bombs from the cases and armed the devices. They're dressed in white lab coats, just like the rest of Shafer's men."

"Please maintain surveillance on them, at least for the time being. Do not engage, yet," Cecil said.

Cecil heard a knock on the limousine window. "Understand, Joseph?"

"Yes. I got it. We'll keep them under observation."

"Okay, son, I have to go now." Cecil pushed another button on the phone to end the call.

Cecil motioned for Tom Daley, his driver, to lower the window. A small envelope was passed into Cecil's hands. *It must be from Charles*, Cecil thought.

"Sir, a message from Mr. Shafer."

"Yes, Tom, let me see it."

Cecil slowly shook his head as he read the handwritten note. "Perhaps we should have a private meeting, old friend. Meet me in the upper Frick Park parking lot in 15 minutes. Just you and I, and we can discuss The Pulpit. I know you are aware of my recent *explorations* of the device. I am truly sorry that for all these years you actually believed I would just walk away from such a treasure. But the past is past, my friend. Let's meet and discuss how we can best pool our resources in order to rescue your dear granddaughter. Sincerely, Charles."

Pool our resources! "Damn you to hell, Charles!" Cecil raged out loud.

"Tom, take me to the upper Frick Park parking lot. Yes, take Forbes to Beechwood Blvd, that's the most direct route. It's time for Charles Shafer to pay the devil his due!"

Charles Shafer checked his watch. It would all be over soon, as the TBM was about to be destroyed. You never knew when another methane pocket could erupt when boring into such unstable strata. A few carefully placed charges on the TBM with wireless detonators, and Charles himself would initiate the next explosion. Charles reached in his pocket and pulled out an oblong black device. *The Taser*, he thought. Good old twenty-first century technology right here in the twentieth century. Cecil would never know what hit him. *Once he's unconscious and immobilized in his fancy wheelchair, he will be placed next to the TMB and at ground zero for the explosion.* Then, Charles thought, *Cecil's driver will have to suffer a fatal overdose of heroin. Poor chap's gone back to the White Tiger.* He'll be found dead at the wheel in the upper Frick Park parking lot. Nice and tidy, and the press will make a martyr out of Cecil. *A fitting end to a long and sometimes strained friendship*, he thought. Charles sat smiling at the cleverness of his plan when his mobile phone rang in his pocket.

"Yes."

"Sir, this is Bergen. We've got a problem. Two of our regular soldiers are gone. They're not responding to radio calls at their checkpoint on the north side of the park. Our team has also detected two unknown intruders within the park. I recommend we employ the entire squad of Hornets to eliminate the threat."

"I agree. Deploy the Hornets! That shall be a nice surprise for our two new friends. Keep me updated on the situation."

"I will, sir. Thank you. Bergen out."

Charles sat in his limousine and thought logically about these new developments. The first question in Charles's mind was: who were these intruders? Surely working for Cecil, but how capable were they? The answer was they were highly trained, because they had successfully taken out two regular army soldiers, and they had done so swiftly and silently. The second question was: could these two unknowns defeat a dozen well-armed men and an army of deadly flying robots and then successfully diffuse two sophisticated bombs, all within a period of an hour or so? Answer: very unlikely. The time constraints alone and the difficult terrain would limit their movements, and then there were the Hornets.

They'll never see them coming, thought Charles. He took a deep breath and removed the Taser from his pocket. He slid open the small plastic cover to check the battery level. As he did so, he activated the built-in red laser and white LED flashlight. He danced the red laser beam around the black interior of the limousine and waited for Cecil's car to arrive.

Two Shafer Industries technicians removed the remaining six Hornets from their foam-lined cases. One of the men thought that the robots really did resemble an actual hornet. There were two antennae protruding from the front of the little beasts, actual microwave receivers and emitters, and infrared detectors. Then of course the wings, made to resemble real insect wings at rest that morphed into tiny helicopter blades when activated. *And the coup de grace*, thought the technician, *is the stinger*. Located at the rear of the robot's tiny golden-brown forged magnesium body was a two-inch long titanium needle. Any type of anesthetic, hallucinogenic, or poison could be administered via the needle, and it would be nearly untraceable during an autopsy. *The ultimate stealthy killing machine*, thought the technician. *Man mimicking nature and upping the ante with advanced technology.*

"Are we ready to release the remaining Hornets?" asked the other technician.

"Yes, they're loaded with the GABA receptor-blocking serum. They've got enough to take down an elephant."

"Good, good. Release them and set their detectors to infrared. We've got to find these targets quickly and take them out. That's the order, right from the very top. Set their computers to a five-square-mile search grid directly over the park."

"Yes, okay done. Ready for launch!"

The two men watched as the six Hornets lit up, their yellow eyes glowed and their "wings" began to spin. Then all six lifted off from the asphalt and flew off in six different directions to search for their targets, hiding in the forest.

57

"Joe, come in."

"Read you. Go ahead."

"I've got the men with the explosives in sight, and they're nearing the rescue area. What do you recommend?"

"Use your knife."

"No, they're too close already. I'm three hundred yards away now, observing. Man, these goggles are incredible! Hey, wait a minute. I see something flying, it's one of those things we saw earlier!"

"Okay, take it out. Wait. Oh man, I got one coming in too. It looks like a giant fly. Hold it…it has a stinger! Holy crap! The flying bugs are weapons! Kill it! Kill it, Josh! Do it now!"

Josh's gun fired. There was a low flash and a hushed

clack-clack-clack sound of the bolt in the HK rifle slamming home thrice.

Josh pulled the trigger two more times, tracking the flying robot with three-round bursts. Bull's eye.

"Got mine! Holy smokes! It's like shooting skeet with a rifle!"

"Hold on, Josh. I got one coming in. It's making straight for me!"

Joe fired. He missed.

The flying robot with the glowing yellow eye was so close now, almost on top of him. He instinctively ducked, rolled and kicked with his boot. He connected! The attacker flew off wobbling and crashed into a nearby tree.

"I got it!" Joe whispered into his mike. "Oh, man, that was too close. Hold on. I'm going to recon that thing. It looks intact, but I'd say its flying days are over, buddy. Okay, meet me at the north end of the park, under the bridge. You've got to see this thing! Over."

"Roger that, Joe. Be there in a few minutes, over."

Amy, Peter, Johnny and Dave walked down the concrete sidewalk on Forbes Avenue in Oakland. Along the way, college students passed them, some of them turning to stare at the ragtag group. Almost trancelike, the four ambled along, their collective thought to reach a pay phone.

"The phones are down here, guys," Amy said. "My grandfather must be worried sick by now."

"We gotta call Mom, Dad. She's probably worried sick too! And what about Darren?"

"We're going to call Mom and Darren. Don't worry, Johnny."

"Okay, I'm trying not to."

"After you guys, I'm calling my buddy Jimmy to come pick us up."

"Well, we might take you up on a ride if you're offering," Peter said.

"I'm offering, Doc. I owe you more than just a ride in Jimmy's Cadillac, that's for sure."

"Okay, we're here. Is it okay if I call first?"

"Yes, of course, Amy. Do you have change?"

"Umm, I don't. Can I borrow a dime?"

"Sure. Sure thing," Peter said as he reached in his pocket and handed her one.

Amy pushed the buttons on the payphone and dialed the familiar phone number.

Cecil's phone rang, just as his limousine turned onto Forbes Avenue.

"This is Cecil."

"Grandpa, it's me! Amy!"

"Amy! My God, where are you? Are you okay?"

"Yes, I'm fine, Grandpa. We made it out!"

"You made it out! Oh, dear child, miracles do happen! We've been working non-stop to get you out of there. How? How did you do it?"

"It was Dr. Hawn, Grandpa. There's an incredible… machine down there! I know it sounds crazy, but we think it's some kind of alien technology. Dr. Hawn figured out how to use it, and we escaped!"

"Dear child, I am so glad you are safe. Listen carefully, you must stay away from Frick Park; it's not safe here."

"But, Grandpa, I want to come see you. I'm with three amazing people who helped save my life. I want you to meet them. We can be there soon."

"Amy, listen to me. There are dark forces working against us tonight. That machine you found…they want it to stay hidden, and they will stop at nothing to keep it a secret. Please wait for my word, as I am taking care of the situation. It's complicated, but believe me when I tell you it's not safe here. Wait where you are, and I will send a car for you when the danger clears."

"Grandpa, are you okay? No, I won't wait here. We're in Oakland, by the University of Pittsburgh. Listen, you can't make me stay here. I'm coming to find you."

"No, I'm fine, Amy; please, listen to what I say. I have to go now. I'm so relieved you are safe, but do not come to the park! I love you more than life itself! Goodbye, Amy."

"Not goodbye, Grandpa! Grandpa!" Amy screamed into the telephone.

Amy looked at Peter, Johnny and Dave. "He's in danger. My Grandpa's stubborn, and he's in danger. I could hear it in his voice. And we're in danger. He said "dark forces" want The Machine to stay hidden, and we should stay away from Frick Park. But we have to go! I think he's in trouble."

"Okay, then we're going. First, I have to call home and let my wife know that Johnny and I are safe. I also need to check on Darren. This will only take a minute." Peter dropped a dime in the payphone and dialed. After thirty seconds, he hung up the phone and said, "There's no answer. She's not there. She's probably already at the park."

"Where's Mom and Darren?" Johnny said.

"I'm not sure, but they must be at the park. I'm sure they're safe, Johnny. I need you to be calm right now, okay?"

"Okay, I'm just worried. That's all," Johnny said.

"I know, son. I am too. We'll see them soon, I promise, but first we need a ride. Well, Dave, looks like it's your turn. Better call your friend."

58

L arry Siebert finished changing into his "jungles"—
U.S. Army Special Forces mottled-green camou-
flaged shirt, pants and boots, and a green cap. He was
looking forward to playing his part in this mission, to be
Cecil Stewart's Trojan Horse. Dressed as he was, he could
pass for the lieutenant colonel that the bars on his
shoulder proclaimed. He reached in his pocket, pulled out
his encrypted mobile phone and called Joe.

"Joe, what's the situation? Yes, I can be there in five.
Okay, see you then."

Joe had just finished talking to Larry, when he heard the
snap of a twig. He scanned the dense forest from his
vantage point, perched high up on one of the Forbes
Bridge's massive concrete supports. He saw an

approaching figure with the aid of his night-vision goggles and was ninety-nine percent sure it was Josh, but he called out anyway. "Identify yourself. Make it snappy or meet your maker," he commanded.

"I came all the way from the South Side to see the world's first flying artificial bug. How's that?" Josh said loudly.

"Up here." Joe whispered.

"Ah-ha, thinking in three dimensions. I like that! Well, get your butt down here and show me your new toy. I can't wait to see what just tried to waste us."

"Alright." Joe moved down the slope and jumped the last few feet down to the muddy trail. He took off his black backpack and brought out the metal insect.

"Look at that!" Josh said.

"Yeah, c'mon, follow me to take a closer look."

"Okay." Joe and Josh walked up the densely forested hill until they crossed behind one of the giant gray concrete supports for the bridge.

"Here it is." Joe said, as they shined their low-intensity tactical flashlights on their prize.

"I think this is what they mean by exotic hardware. Wow, what's it made out of? And holy Moses, look at that stinger! Hey, what's this marking mean?"

"It says 'H8,' Josh. A wild guess is the 'H' might stand for hornet."

"Hornet makes sense, and it sure has a temper like one."

"Umm, I think the body is made out of magnesium. It's light, see?" Joe picked up the Hornet with one finger. "Anyway, Old Larry will be here soon. Boy, he's going to love this!

"Yeah, this is right up his alley."

"Well if 'H' stands for hornet, which makes sense, then the '8' could be its serial number. As in maybe this guy has seven more ugly friends flying around?"

"If that's the case, then we've got some major exterminating to do. Hey, listen. I think I hear Larry."

Approaching from the opposite ridge above the trail, Larry Siebert saw Joe and Josh behind the bridge supports. He removed his army regulation flashlight, set it to red, and flashed it in on/off series pointed across the valley.

"He's sending Morse code. Larry's a real card. He's asking if it's safe to cross over." Josh exhaled sharply. "Dude's really old-school, huh? Okay, if he wants Morse, he'll get Morse."Josh brought up his red-light flashlight, and using the on/off switch, sent a return message, saying that yes, it was safe.

"He's coming," Josh said.

"What's that?" Joe pointed down the trail.

"Oh, crap. Another one!" Josh hissed.

"You got the rifle, brother. Take it out! It's headed for Larry!"

Larry Siebert's head was down, using all of his concentration to keep his footing as he made his way down the muddy slope toward the trail below. He boots were sliding here and there, despite their heavy Vibram combat soles. That's when he first heard the faint but high-pitched whirring noise. He jumped and landed just on the edge of the trail and quickly looked around. He soon spotted a bobbing pinpoint of glowing yellow light, moving quickly through the trees and closing fast on his position from fifty yards away. Then he heard a set of three rapid muffled gunshots coming from above his head.

"Get down, Larry! Get down now!" a distant voice yelled.

Larry jack-pulled his Hi-Power pistol from his cross-draw holster and dropped face down, flat on the gravelly trail.

Three more quick shots rang out.

"Dammit, Joe, I can't get it!" Josh yelled.

Siebert quickly flipped over, and in one smooth motion leveled his pistol at the approaching yellow dot. He tracked the flying yellow-eyed thing with the fluorescent green tritium front sight of his pistol. *Bang...bang... bang...bang*. He timed his pistol shots, but still it kept coming. Then the rest happened so fast. He felt something land on his chest, and then he felt a sharp pressure on his sternum. As he looked down at his chest, he saw a bright flash, and the pressure was suddenly gone.

"Good shooting! That was close!" Joe clapped his hand on his friend's back.

"It wasn't good enough. It stung Larry before I nailed it. Let's go."

As the two of them came down the hill, Larry rose to a sitting position. He felt his chest, opened a Velcro compartment, and removed a black steel magazine.

"Are you okay?" Joe said, approaching and kneeling down.

"That was close, Joseph. Take a look at this." Larry pointed to a tiny hole in the magazine.

"I was right, it must be titanium. Look at that, right through a steel magazine! Did it puncture any of the rounds?"

"Let's see," Larry said. He used his right thumb to eject the first six 9mm NATO cartridges from the top of the magazine.

"Well, will you look at that?" Josh said. "Went right through that shell there, and that one too!" He pointed to the mangled cartridges in Larry's open hand.

"I'm thankful Josh is one heck of a shot, and to Cecil for this prototype vest."

"Looks like it's got pockets for everything, and luckily

for you it's got the magazine pockets right front and center."

"It's called a Tactical Vest, fellas, the latest in battle-field clothing. It's designed to give the soldier plenty of carrying capacity, and a little more protection for his vitals."

"I want one of those vests!" Josh said.

"That can be arranged, Josh. Listen, Charles Shafer didn't send those things to give us a flu shot, that I can assure you. What do you say we take a closer look at the one you captured? There's not much left of the one Josh KO'd."

Joe removed his backpack and pulled out the damaged Hornet.

"Here it is. Cute, huh? Notice the 'H' in the serial number, right here." He pointed. "We're thinking it stands for 'hornet.'"

"Guys, 'cute,' is not the word I'd use. This is abso-lutely amazing, futuristic engineering. Oh, and FYI, what-ever we discuss, and whatever happens tonight is classified, okay?"

Both Josh and Joe nodded in agreement. "We're in."

"Good. We're looking at a miniaturized drone. Flight systems, guidance systems, radar, and infrared too, I'm sure. Look at that tail; it's fully articulated, along with a titanium hypodermic needle. Not only can this thing sting you, but it's able to move its tail around like a real hornet to sting you over and over. Damn lethal, and certainly not from our time."

"What do you mean 'not from our time?'" Joe asked.

"It's from the future. Shafer must have brought it here, using what your grandfather calls 'The Pulpit.' Stay with me, guys. There's an alien machine called The Pulpit, sitting in an alien built room, seven stories under our feet. Amy and her friends unfortunately stumbled upon it, and that's what this whole shebang is all about. Shafer is trying to protect this Pulpit, to keep it for himself. We're here to save your cousin and her friends, and put an end to Shafer's plans to rule the world with this thing."

"Okay, this is getting really heavy. Are you saying we're fighting over an alien time-machine?" Josh said.

"It's much more than a time machine, and that's why Shafer is willing to kill for it. This flying attack robot he sent, tells me we better be ready for more surprises tonight," Larry said.

"We think there's more of them. Read the lettering. 'H8' could mean Hornet number eight. We've killed three so far, but who knows how many more are out there," Joe said.

"We better grow some eyes in the backs of our heads, fellas. What do you say I set up some radar tracking to help locate these things before they find us?"

"Excellent idea, boss," Joe said. "What's our part?"

"You two head over to the rescue site. We must prevent Shafer's men from blowing up the TBM. I want you to take out the rest of the soldiers at each of the checkpoints, but do it quietly. That will level the playing field considerably. You both are authorized to use lethal force, as I've cleared it with the president."

"THE PRESIDENT?" Josh said, blinking and wide-eyed.

"Yes, our commander-in-chief. He's an old friend and trusted ally. Now, get going, and keep me updated. Also, don't forget about our two friends carrying those mysterious bombs. Joe, that's right up your alley. I've got other business to attend to, but I'll keep a radio nearby."

"Got it, Larry. We're on it."

59

They heard the car approaching before they saw it. Jimmy Page's heavy guitar riff intro to Led Zeppelin's "Good Times, Bad Times" came drifting over the Oakland night, then Robert Plant's soaring opening vocal. The shiny white Cadillac Seville had polished wire hubcaps with red glass center caps over a gold Cadillac logo, and the driver looked like Al Pacino, circa *Serpico*. He wore a white, short-sleeved T-shirt, slicked-back, thick jet-black hair, and he was loudly singing along to Zeppelin through the rolled down driver's-side window.

"Somebody called for a ride?" Jimmy Pacela shouted over Jimmy Page's frantic guitar solo.

"Aw, Jimmy, that was fast! Dude, turn down the stereo, please! These are my friends here. Introducing Dr. Peter Hawn."

"Alright, turning down the jams. Nice to make your acquaintance," Jimmy said.

"And this here's his son, Johnny."

"Hey, kid."

"And last, but certainly not least, this is Amy Lee."

"You didn't say you had Miss America with you, Dave. Nice to meet you, Amy. I'm Jimmy Pacela, sounds like an 's' but it's spelled with a 'c.'"

"Yeah, yeah, enough with the flirtin', alright?" Dave said.

"Just trying to be friendly. So sue me."

"Yeah, whatever. Remember it's me—Dave. Alright guys, get in."

"Jimmy, you packing heat?"

"That's a stooooopid question, goomba! Of course I'm packin' heat. I got my snakes in the car. For the rest of you'ns, I'm talkin' 'bout my Pythons right here." Jimmy smiled, reached over and popped open the glove compartment. There sat two very large, very shiny revolvers in folded-up brown leather shoulder holsters.

"Colt .357 Magnums. Consecutive serial numbers and all that jazz…they pack a mean bite with the hollow points."

"Bring those guys out," Dave said.

"You wanna borrow my snakes? Dang, now I know you're serious. What's going down?"

"It's top-secret government shit. We found something

under Frick Park, something nobody wants getting around. This is CIA shit. The real deal," Dave said.

"Well, what is it? What'd you find? I'm not just givin' you my snakes for no reason. You know I never lend 'em out."

"I'll let Doc here tell you all about it. You'd think I was crazy as a shithouse rat if I told you." Dave laughed.

"This should be interesting," Amy said.

"Well, Jimmy, we found a piece of alien technology, seven stories down, under Frick Park. It has extraordinary powers, like the ability to heal broken bones, to see into the future, teleportation, and probably much more that we don't know about. Amy here, well, her grandfather is Cecil Stewart—THE Cecil Stewart—he's involved. I'm a professor of archeology at CMU, and this is my son, Johnny, who originally discovered the hole that led to the device. The Pittsburgh fire department, police department, Shafer Industries, the CIA and maybe the entire U.S. government are down at Frick Park right now trying to rescue us. What they don't know yet is that we used The Machine, as we call it, to teleport us from under the park into The Decade bar. Only Cecil Stewart and you, Jimmy, know that we've managed to escape. Mr. Stewart warned us that we're in danger; as in somebody wants us dead, so they can keep The Machine a secret. There's the crux of it. I know it's a lot to take in."

"Holy crap! You mean like Captain Kirk? Beam me up, Scotty? This teleportation stuff, it's real?"

"Yeah, mister. There's an alien machine down there, and my dad figured out how it works. He's a genius."

"You got the CIA and the army after you? Dave, we're gonna need more firepower than just a couple snakes. Why didn't you say so? Lemme go get a few more things I got stashed away, back at the house, some toys from 'Nam. You guys got yourselves in one hell of a shit storm! Dave, you outdid yourself this time. I thought the park job was gonna settle you down, keep you out of the bars and land you a nice fat pension. And here you go pissin' off the CIA and who knows who else?"

"Yeah, it's called having a bad day, Jimmy. I didn't wake up this morning and say to myself, 'Hey Dave, today would be a good day to fall down a seven-story hole, nearly die and get the government after me.' But hey, it happens.'"

"It's cool, Dave. Alright then, let's get this party started. It's just a little farther…and here we are. My pad. Hold on, I'll be right back with the goodies."

"Bring the LAWS," Dave shouted. "Bring 'em both!"

"Two M72s, coming up." Jimmy shouted.

Jimmy quickly disappeared into the front left door of a quaint red brick, duplex house.

"Your friend has M72 LAW rockets?" Peter said.

"For real, Doc! He's been saving them for an 'emergency,' as he calls it. He also has a crate of fully automatic M16s, one M14 in .308, a ton of pistols and a box of grenades. Oh, and crates and crates of armor-piercing ammo. Jimmy is connected. Know what I mean?"

"I think I get your drift."

"He's a mobster?" Amy said.

"They don't appreciate that term, okay? Jimmy's father is very connected, let's say. His family lives in Bloomfield. They own a restaurant over there, and a couple of other businesses around town. I've known Jimmy my whole life. He's basically a good guy, unless you piss him off. Then he turns…psycho."

"Well, I'm glad he's on our side," Amy said.

"He looks like Serpico," Johnny said. "I saw a commercial for it over at my friend's house. They have cable."

"Yeah, people say he looks like Al Pacino. He gets that all the time, but I think it swells his head. Believe me, Jimmy doesn't need any extra ego-boost. He's got attitude to spare. He spent four years as an army ranger in Vietnam, from 1968 to basically the end, and that only made a streetwise kid even tougher. Anyway, enough of my rambling. He'll be back in a few, and then we're off to see the wizard at Frick Park!"

60

Cecil sat in his limousine, going over the night's events, when Charles's limousine approached. It was pitch black in the upper Frick Park parking lot, the distant streetlights from Beechwood Boulevard looking like tiny pinpricks of light from Cecil's vantage point. Charles's limousine slowly pogo-jumped as it drove down the ancient cobblestone access road that transitioned into the smooth black asphalt-covered parking area.

Cecil pushed a button on the armrest in his limousine, and the wheelchair-deploying device went to work. In one smooth motion, the car door opened, a metal arm extended, and Cecil in his wheelchair was lowered gently to the ground. He reached out and gently touched the control panel on the wheelchair's right armrest. The tactile pressure indicators for the onboard nitrogen tanks read full. Now it was time to finally confront his old friend.

"Good to see you, old friend, and thank you for meeting me here. Some matters require discretion." Charles spoke firmly as he slowly approached Cecil's wheelchair.

"We do have much to discuss, and I'm hoping for a fitting end to tonight's events. After all, this place has figured prominently on your schedule over the years, hasn't it?"

Charles regarded Cecil with a disdainful look. "Tell me, how did you figure it out? I've spent considerable amounts of time and money to keep this a secret."

"I bet you have, dear friend. I took a peek inside your safe tonight. Interesting what I found. You've made yourself quite popular, and rich, with The Pulpit, haven't you?"

"Friends—of course everyone wants to know the future, Cecil. And yes, I've made billions. Did you think I was satisfied with the paltry arrangement we agreed to when we were just naïve children? The Pulpit has served me well throughout the years."

"I also know, Charles, that you have no intention of rescuing anyone tonight. Am I right?"

"Right again! It's all been an elaborate charade, at least on my part. The firefighters and the rest are just innocent bystanders."

"You know I can't let you get away with this."

"You don't have a choice, old fool." Charles reached

in his pocket and brought out the Taser as he moved a few steps closer to Cecil. "Do you know what this is?"

"I haven't the foggiest idea, but I'd bet it's something you brought back from the future."

"Well done again, Cecil. It's called a Taser. Picked it up in 2005. Look down at your chest. See that red dot? That's a red laser-targeting system. All I have to do is push this little button, and you get fifty thousand volts right to the chest. I'm not sure your aged heart can handle that kind of shock, though. If you should survive, well, then I'm going to give you a ringside seat to a devastating explosion."

"That is a neat little toy you have there, and I admire your resourcefulness, but I have a better idea." With that, Cecil deftly moved his right index finger to push a red button on the wheelchair's control panel. Instantly, several rapid bangs were heard, like small fireworks, and a multitude of tiny puffs of smoke rose from the sides of the wheelchair.

Charles felt like thirty bees had stung him all at once. His muscles locked up, and as he tried to speak, he couldn't move his jaw. His tongue felt like a wet sack of flour, too heavy to lift from the inside base of his mouth.

"The poison from a sea snake is quite deadly. You've just been injected with enough venom to put down a herd of elephants. I'm sorry, my old friend, that it had to end this way for you. I had to be sure that you were behind all of this.

I've also recorded our entire conversation on both video and audio. I like to do things the understated way, hence my innocuous-looking wheelchair. It's anything but, as you just found out." Charles fell to his knees, clutching his chest.

"The venom will soon stop your heart. It's time to say goodbye, old friend. Oh, by the way, Amy and the others were able to escape using The Pulpit. They discovered what you obviously did, that it can teleport objects. They're safe and sound, Charles. You lose, and I will ensure that Shafer Industries is exposed for the heinous criminal acts you've committed tonight. Goodbye."

Cecil heard a car door open, and turned his head to watch Charles's driver exit the car and raise a pistol-grip shotgun, pointed at Cecil.

"Mr. Shafer always had a plan B, Mr. Stewart. Now, put your hands in the air." Cecil started to raise his hands above his head, when he heard a muffled crack. The distinct report of a large caliber rifle came from the park's woods, behind Shafer's driver. The driver dropped the shotgun, clutched his chest and fell face-forward to the ground. Dead.

"Nice of you to show up, Larry. I was all out of options, as my driver is unarmed. Thank you, and nice shooting. I've seen many incredible things in my life, but never a night like this."

"Well, it's not over yet. We've got more trouble."

"The Hornets?"

"Yes, we're pretty sure there are more of them. And then there are the bombs. We'll have to disarm them."

"I think Joseph and his friend can handle that, don't you?

"I do sir, but that still leaves the question of the rescue, and then what to do with Shafer and his chauffeur?"

"The rescue is now a moot point. Amy and her friends have used The Pulpit to escape from the underground chamber. I must say, that Hawn fellow is quite ingenious —he unlocked a hidden power of The Pulpit and teleported them to safety. The four of them are safe and sound in Oakland, where I instructed them to remain. Isn't that wonderful?"

"Well, that's excellent news, sir. So what now?"

"I suggest a change of plans. We must take care of the soldiers and those government agents, but perhaps we should let Shafer's men sabotage the TBM. If you could arrange to have Charles and his driver placed at the rescue site at the time of the detonation that would be most convenient. Tell Joseph and his friend their new orders. I entrust you will get Charles and his driver to the TBM on time and inconspicuously?"

"Yes, of course. We can use our undercover team for that. I have them dressed as Pittsburgh firefighters. Right now, they're installing a portable radar system that will locate the rest of those Hornets. After they're done with that, I'll have them move Shafer and the driver. I suggest you stay in the limousine, sir, until we destroy the flying beasties. I've seen one up close, and it's a lethal device."

"I'm sure Charles brought them back from one of his expeditions into the future. He's been pirating God knows what for the past sixty-odd years, and I'd say we better be prepared for anything tonight. We've defeated the opposing army's general, but we've yet to win the war."

61

"New orders. We're supposed to recon the area, but we've been instructed to allow Schafer's men to blow up the boring machine."

"That doesn't make a whole lot of sense, does it?" Josh said.

"I don't know. We don't get to see the whole picture. That's Larry's job, and we have to trust him."

"What about the Hornets still flying around?"

"We'll take care of those as soon as Larry's got his radar system up and running. In a few minutes, we'll know their exact location, then it's just matter of target practice! Well, just don't miss, anyway."

"I wish I'd brought my pump shotgun. I've got some duck loads that'd put a hurt on those Hornets!"

"We weren't exactly expecting killer flying-robot bugs, now were we?"

"Nope."

"Using a rifle or pistol, it just makes it more of a challenge. Using a shotgun, you and I both know that would be too easy."

"At this point, I'd take the easy way. When you called me earlier tonight, I didn't know what to expect." Josh shook his head.

"Umm, hold on, my phone is buzzing. Yes, it's ready? That was fast. Excellent. I'll let him know."

"Radar's up?"

"Yes, and they're already tracking the Hornets. They're flying over the south side of the park. Let's go."

"Following you, boss," Josh said.

Peter sat in the back of the Cadillac Seville, and watched the buildings on 5th Avenue blur by. Central Catholic High School, the large synagogue Rodef Shalom, then the steel barons' mansions on the left side, farther up toward Wilkins Avenue. He figured Jimmy Pacela was doing about seventy, making the streetlights and telephone poles look like a picket fence, when Peter's thoughts ran back to Laura. I guess you know a marriage is over when death is at your doorstop, then you miraculously survive, only to dread reuniting with your spouse. Peter looked over at Amy and marveled at her strength and beauty. She looked exquisitely pretty, yet she also was intelligent, sweet and very down-to-earth. His thoughts drifted back to the dreams in the cave, and he was sure he was falling in love with Amy. It wasn't hard to imagine divorcing Laura now.

Then he thought about Darren. He was so proud of him. Just ten years old, yet he'd been so incredibly brave! When Peter was Darren's age, he had a speech impediment, which stress only seemed to exaggerate. *A young Peter Hawn would've struggled to do what Darren did tonight*, he thought. Peter smiled; he had been blessed with two incredible boys. It suddenly occurred to him that Darren would've called Laura and his father. Peter envisioned his dad taking care of Darren and Laura, and that thought comforted him. He would see them both soon.

Jimmy kept barreling down 5th Avenue, passing Mellon Park on the right, headed toward Braddock Avenue.

"You're taking the fast way, Mr. Pacela." Peter had to yell over the music. Jimmy kept bopping his head to the Zep. "I said, you don't waste any time."

"Am I driving too fast for ya?"

"No, not at all," Peter yelled.

"Good, 'cause I would've said, 'Shove it, Doc.' I got this sled with a V8 so I could fly! Hey, you handy with a rifle, Doc?"

"I'm a veteran, so if it's an M16, M14 or a 1911, I can handle it. I never shot a rocket though."

"Don't worry. You ain't shooting any LAW rockets tonight, Doc. Those are my babies!" Jimmy shouted.

"You'd think I'd get thrown in the slammer for kicking off a LAW in the city, but I have friends in the department!"

"It's all yours, Mr. Pacela," Peter shouted back.

"Call me Jimmy. All my friends do."

"Alright, Jimmy."

"That's better, Doc. Not so formal, you know? We're all friends here." Jimmy's right hand reached for the radio. "Let me turn down the jams. Ah, that's better. Hey Doc, you saved my best friend's life, so now you're *amici*."

"What's *amici*?" Johnny asked.

"It's Italian for friend," Jimmy said. "We're all friends now, including you, kid. You like Italian food?"

"I love spaghetti with meatballs, and lasagna," Johnny said.

"Good to hear, 'cause after this is all over we're gonna go over to Bloomfield and I'm gonna personally serve you the best lasagna you've ever had, and some homemade spumoni. You're gonna love it!"

"What's spumoni?" Johnny asked.

"Spumoni? Just the best ice cream you ever had. Don't worry about it. You'll be asking for seconds, I promise," Jimmy said.

"Okay," Johnny said, looking at him.

"See, that's better. We're friends now. Hey, guys, we're getting close to the park. Jeez, will you look at that!"

As Jimmy made the right onto South Braddock

Avenue from 5th Avenue, they hit the tail end of a traffic jam.

"I never seen Braddock backed up this bad," Jimmy said. "This must be because of you guys! I bet the police have the whole area blocked off. So how we gonna get to the park now?"

"Let's cut through Edgewood to the back side of Regent Square," Dave said. "Then we'll take the access road into lower Frick."

"Good idea. Edgewood it is," Jimmy said.

The white Cadillac zoomed down East End Avenue, bouncing over the frost heaves and potholes in the asphalt. Jimmy ran the stop signs, only slowing the car when they reached West Hutchinson Avenue.

"We'll never make it to the parking lot by the tennis courts, Doc. Braddock Avenue is locked up solid from this end too," Jimmy said.

"That's why we're going to take that access road I was talking about. Jeez, something wrong with your hearing?" Dave said, touching his own ear.

"I know, I know. I was just tryin' to get the Doc closer. He's gotta see his wife and his other kid. He's a family man, Dave. Think about it!"

"Going through the backside of the park is the only way in, Jimmy. We can park down there and walk up the trail to the rescue site," Dave said.

"Looks like we don't have any choice." Jimmy grimaced. "Alright you guys, hang on!"

Jimmy floored the gas pedal, propelling the Cadillac across a hole in traffic on South Braddock Avenue, down Hutchinson Street, into a neighborhood next to the park.

"I see a lot of firetrucks, Dad." Johnny yelled.

"I see them. It's a circus up there. See that, Amy?"

"I see. My grandfather must have called in the cavalry, so to speak."

"Your grandfather is really Cecil Stewart?" Dave asked. And then added, "What's it like having a grandfather who's one of the richest men in the world?"

Jimmy interrupted, "Leave her alone, you can't help what family you're born into. See, you was raised by wolves, and I've always tried to take that into consideration."

"Ha ha, funny man. Okay, well forget the question."

"No, it's okay. A lot of it has to do with the media. People see my grandfather's picture everywhere, so they're naturally curious about his life. Just be thankful you've never had to deal with paparazzi."

"What's that? A pizza?" Jimmy said.

"No, photographers—the worst kind. They'll do anything for a photograph: peek over your fence, into your bedroom window, interrupt your dinner at a restaurant, just to get a picture they can sell to the rag-mags at the supermarket. Horrible people!" Amy said.

"They'd be catching a bullet, where I come from," Jimmy said.

Dave interrupted, "See, there's nobody on this side of

the park. Most people don't even know about the lower parking lot. Hey, Jimmy, hang a ralphie on Lancaster Avenue, and the access road is about a block down. It's locked up at night, but I got a key."

"Your wish is my command, Kemosabe. Right on Lancaster it is. Of course you have a key. You're a park ranger, dude!"

"It's right up here on the left. Hey, the chain is down. That's weird. We always lock it up after sundown. Anyway, turn down there."

Jimmy began driving down the twisty road that descended into the bottom of Frick Park.

"Man, it's dark down here. You guys ever think about putting up some lights?" Jimmy said.

"Just keep going," Dave said. "It'll open up into the parking lot. Okay, we're almost there. Hey, Jimmy, kill your lights."

"It's freaking dark, man. Why would I…oh, I see what you mean."

"Yeah, look at that, there's a truck over there. Look at all those guys in white coats. What's that one guy doing? Looks like he's…what the…?" Jimmy said.

Just then, a Hornet landed on the hood of Jimmy's Cadillac.

"What is that?" Peter asked.

"It's got yellow eyes! Is it a bug?" Johnny asked.

"Look at its body, and take a look at that stinger!" Amy said.

"I don't know what it is, but it's about to die!" Jimmy yelled. He reached over into the glove compartment and scrambled to pull out his revolvers. Jimmy quickly unsnapped each holster and withdrew two gleaming Colt Python .357 Magnums.

"Bug spray!" he declared.

What happened next seemed to transpire in slow motion. Jimmy yelled, "Freaking bug!" and reached through the driver's side window, firing one gun in his left hand. Then he yelled, "Dave, take the other! Shoot it! Shoot it!"

Dave grabbed the revolver in his right hand, reached through the passenger side window and squeezed off a booming shot. The Hornet exploded into a smoking, blinding fireball, leaving behind tiny shards of metal and what looked like bits of yellow fabric.

"Bingo, Dave. Nice shot!" Jimmy yelled.

"Did you see that thing?" Dave asked.

"Yeah, crazy man. Whatever it was, you sent it to heaven," Jimmy said.

All five passengers heard the punch of 9mm bullets tearing through metal, the rapid staccato "pops" as Shafer's men opened fire on the Cadillac with fully automatic Uzi carbines.

"They're firing! They're firing on us!" Peter yelled.

"I think we hurt their feelings by killing their pet bug," Jimmy said. "They mess up my car, and I swear." Just then, a trio of bullets smashed through the top of the

Cadillac's windshield, leaving three ragged holes above the rear-view mirror, spraying Jimmy and Dave with shards of glass.

"That does it! Okay, everybody out. Time to finish this! Doc, you, Dave, and me have to get to the trunk. Dave, hand me the Python. These guys are really pissing me off! Lady, you get that kid outta here, outta the line of fire. Run to the woods behind us when I say go. I'll cover you," Jimmy said.

"Okay, Johnny, you and I are going to make a run for it," Amy said.

"Son, stay with Amy. Just hold her hand and run fast when she runs, okay? I love you."

"Okay, I can do it."

"I know you can, honey, you're tough. Get ready to run!"

"Okay, Dad!"

"Now, Amy!" Jimmy screamed as he got out of the car, raised up both guns, and started firing the revolvers in syncopation. The powerful concussion of two .357 magnums going off one after the other was deafening. Amy jumped out of the car and Johnny followed, holding her hand. They ran to the thicket of trees behind the Cadillac and jumped down into a gulley. Jimmy continued firing as he, Dave and Peter scurried to the back of the car, then Jimmy quickly opened the trunk.

"They made it!" Peter yelled. "Thank God, they made it!"

"C'mon, Doc, I'm outta ammo. We've gotta up the ante a little bit. Here, take this M16 and an extra magazine. It's ready to go with a round in. Dave, here's yours. Listen, I want you guys to pin 'em down, 'cause I'm bringing out the LAW. This is ridiculous. These sons of bitches have machine guns! I say... don't bring a machine gun to an anti-tank weapon fight!"

Jimmy had become somewhat of an expert in anti-tank weapons in Vietnam. He knew one LAW could stop a firefight quickly, and he'd proven that in the jungles of Southeast Asia. Jimmy deftly extended the cylindrical weapon, thereby activating it. He checked to see that the area behind him was clear, as the exhaust from a LAW rocket can charbroil a man. He quickly stood up, then flipped up the front aperture and centered it on the white van.

"Damn you to hell, whoever you are!" Jimmy screamed.

Whoosh! The rocket launched from the fiberglass tube, the force of it rocking Jimmy back on his heels.

The projectile's smoke trail left an acrid, pungent smell as Jimmy, Dave and Peter watched the rocket zoom across the parking lot. It exploded on impact, sending the delivery van hurtling up twenty feet in the air, engulfed in flame. A roiling black-and-orange mushroom cloud rose high in the air, like a miniature Hiroshima.

"Holy crap! Did you see that? I mean, did you SEE that?" Jimmy yelled and jumped up and pumped his fist in the air. "Game over, fellas. Game over!"

Josh and Joe moved quickly and quietly through the dark forest, taking one of the trails on the west side of the Frick Park valley. They had just passed the rescue site, when they paused to spy on the bright lights and the technicians working on the TBM. That's when they saw an incoming Hornet, approaching from the south. They watched semi-hypnotized as a yellow eye dropped down from the tree line to just above the gravel trail. It wobbled, made a slight course correction, and then it flew down the trail toward them.

"Oh no, here we go again."

"Get ready!" Joe hissed.

Joe shouldered his carbine and began lining up his sights on the Hornet, when all of a sudden it paused, mid-air.

"What the heck?" Josh said. Suddenly they saw a fire-ball rise from the south end of the park. Joe looked at Josh as they felt the concussion of the explosion ripple past them. Then, as if on cue, the Hornet dropped to the ground in front of them. It landed upside down, legs wiggling, the telltale yellow eye fading to black.

"Okay, explain that!" Josh said. "This mission is getting weirder and weirder. That was a big explosion, dude, bigger than a grenade. And look at the Hornet! It's dead!"

"I know, like someone hit the off switch. Thank God. I don't like real bugs, let alone killer-robot ones," Joe said.

"Me neither. Well, ding-dong, the witch is dead. We got some help from somewhere. I thought you said it was just you, me and Larry down here?"

"That's what I was told. But you're right, we either got some help, or Shafer screwed up big time. I say we investigate."

"I'm with you, bro, on that one. Let's go."

The Shafer technicians who'd been hiding in the southwest part of the park, waiting for orders, were sitting behind a log, nodding off, when they were awakened by the massive explosion.

One technician turned to the other. "They've been compromised. There goes our air cover. Damn!"

The other replied, "You know our orders. No matter what, at three a.m. we deliver the payload to the target. I say we suit up an hour before and then start walking. We'll use this trail here."

"Agreed. Too bad about the Hornets."

"Yeah, it's down to us now. Now we just sit and wait."

62

"Here, put him in here," Larry Siebert said as he helped lower Charles Shafer's body into the orange Porta-Potty.

"He needs to be in a seated position, with his pants pulled down," Larry said. "I'll leave that joyous undertaking to you two." The two firemen looked up and one smiled.

"Use these tie-downs to secure him to the toilet. We don't want him falling off while you make the trek down to the lower parking lot. A fitting end to this piece of…" Just as Larry was about to equate Charles Shafer with a canine's stool, he heard a loud pop and he raised his eyes to see a fireball rise above the trees.

"What the…?" Larry said.

"Sounded like artillery, sir," one of the firemen said.

"We don't have anybody down there, do we?" Larry said.

"No, sir, the radar truck is up here. I've got all our guys on the airborne devices. It wasn't our team."

"Maybe the other team fumbled the ball. We can use all the luck we can get tonight. You guys finish up here. I've got to make a call."

Larry walked into the trees, away from the lights. He removed the radio from the holster on his utility belt as he kept walking.

"Joe, come in. Did you see that?"

"Yes, we saw it. It wasn't us. We're headed over there right now."

"Good. Let me know what you find."

"Will do, boss. Oh, one more thing. We think the Hornets are done for the night. We had one about to attack us, then it shut down after the explosion."

"That's a relief. Shafer never did fight fair. But Charles Shafer won't be fighting any more battles. Not now, not ever. Let's stick to the plan, but keep me updated."

"Roger that. We're mobile, moving to the south end of the park."

Amy and Johnny came stumbling out of the forest, holding hands as they approached Peter, Dave and Jimmy. The parking lot looked like a collegiate bonfire run amok.

The delivery van was nothing but a blackened, twisted wreck of metal and melted tires, as waist-high flames licked at what remained. They heard popping sounds and then a scream, muffled and rather distant-sounding. Peter tilted his head and began walking over to the fire.

"Peter, wait!" Amy pleaded. Johnny tensed against Amy's arm.

"Dad, don't go!"

"Did you hear that? One of them is still alive," Peter said.

"She's right, Doc, just let 'em die. Sometimes dead rattlesnakes can bite for days after, just on reflex," Dave said.

"We need to know what those men were doing. They tried to kill us!" Peter shouted. "I'll be careful." He lifted up his M16 rifle. "Don't worry."

"Well, if you're going, I'm going," Jimmy said. "We can do a little interrogating if one of them crispies can still talk."

"Be careful, Peter. I love you," Amy said. Peter turned around and his eyes met Amy's. He felt a wave crash over his heart.

"I love you both. Be right back." Peter waved, and then he and Jimmy started toward the wreckage.

As they reached what was left of the burning van, they saw charred bodies lying stacked on one another. Just beyond, they saw a blackened figure crawling on the ground, looking strangely like a burnt sausage. His legs were jagged, amputated at the knees, and he moaned as he clawed at the ground with disfigured hands.

Jimmy walked over, pushed the barrel of his M16 down and flipped the crispy man over.

"What's your name?" Jimmy said.

"Steve…Steve Dobbs," the man uttered in a choked whisper.

"Dobbs, we can make this easier for you. You're not going to make it." Jimmy turned to Peter. "Just like 'Nam, huh?"

"Tell us what you were doing down here," Peter said.

"Surveillance…" Dobbs said. "Hornets…"

Dobbs's chest was rising and falling, slower now, and he stared wide-eyed at Jimmy and Peter.

"New…new…" Dobbs gasped. Then his head lolled to one side, and he was gone.

"And I was gonna put a bullet in him. Now he goes and dies on us," Jimmy said.

"We didn't get much, did we, Doc?"

"Maybe not. What was that last part? New? What does that mean? New what?" Peter said.

"Maybe something new they were trying out, like that giant flying bug. That's a new one on me!" Jimmy laughed.

"That would make sense," Peter said. "Did you hear him say 'hornet'?"

"Yeah, I heard it. That must be what they call them

bugs…hornets. Well, I hate real hornets, and now I know I hate the artificial kind even more."

"Me, too. Me too. I hope we got all the hornets, and all the bad guys. That LAW rocket was very effective."

"There's nothing left of them, Doc. My dad is gonna love this story. Wait till I tell him. Oh, and I don't know about you, but I'm starving! Dinner, or early breakfast, is on me. I'm gonna take all of youns up to my family's restaurant in Bloomfield."

"You know, that sounds pretty good right about now. I think we'll eventually take you up on that offer. But first, I need to find my son Darren, my wife and my father. Let's head up to the Braddock Avenue side of the park. They're probably waiting up there.

"Sounds good, Doc, but those people up there are gonna have a cow when you guys just stroll in."

63

Joe and Josh approached the lower Frick Park parking lot on high alert. Through the trees, they could see the burning wreckage of a large truck and five people standing around it.

"Do you see that?"

"Yeah, I see them. We got three unidentifieds carrying M16s. They're in street clothes. Interesting. There's also a blonde chick and a young boy."

"Amy?" Joe said out loud.

"What are you talking about? That can't be your cousin. You said she's trapped underground." Josh pointed to the quintet.

"That's Amy, I'm sure of it! I'd recognize her blonde mane anywhere!" Joe shouted and stood up, running down the trail, with Josh following. They emerged into the parking lot, behind Amy and the others.

"Amy!" Joe shouted. "Oh, my God. You're alive!"

"Joe? Joe, is that you?"

"Who's Joe?" Dave said.

"This is my crazy, beautiful cousin Joe and his friend Josh! Oh, my God, what are you guys doing here?" Amy said as she fell into Joe's arms. "You came for me?"

"Amy, how did you guys escape? You were buried underground. I mean, I'm so glad you're here. But how?"

"It's a long story, but right now I'm exhausted. I promise I'll tell you everything later. Where's Grandpa? Is he okay?"

"Yes, Grandpa's fine. He's been working non-stop, trying to rescue you and your friends. Josh and I have been helping him. The narcissistic playboy thing was something Grandpa invented. That's a long story as well."

Amy laughed. "I'm sure it is. You're carrying a gun. You look like a soldier."

"We can trade stories when you're feeling up to it," Joe said.

"Joe, these are my friends. Dr. Peter Hawn, his son Johnny, Dave Rondinelli, and Jimmy Pacela. Guys, this is my first cousin, Joe."

"Nice to meet you, Joe," Peter said.

"Hi, Joe," Johnny said.

"Joe," Dave said and extended his hand to shake.

"Joe, I'm Jimmy." Jimmy pursed his lips and nodded his head.

"Nice to meet you. This is Josh, my good friend… from Special Forces."

"Hi, everyone."

All the men and Johnny took turns shaking Josh's hand, then Amy gave Josh a big hug.

"Great to see you, Josh. Thanks for all your help," Amy said.

"No problem. I'm just glad you guys made it out. I can't wait to hear about it. Right now, there are about fifty Pittsburgh firemen, police, and others working on saving you, right up there." Josh pointed north.

Joe interrupted. "It's complicated, but we have to keep you all safely hidden, for now. Well everyone, except for your friend Jimmy. Grandpa has a plan, and it's close to completion. You guys will have to trust me on this."

"I believe you, but is there any way I can talk to Grandpa? I just want to hear his voice."

"Sure thing, hold on," Joe said and handed his radio to her. "Just push the button on the side."

"Grandpa, this is Amy. Do you hear me?"

"Amy, I hear you! Oh child, you are with Joseph?"

"Yes, we're safe with Joe and Josh. Are you okay, Grandpa?"

"I'm fine, child. Stay with your cousin. You and your friends must remain hidden for the meantime. We will be reunited soon. Do you understand?"

"Yes, Grandpa. I love you."

"I love you, too. Now, be careful and stay out of sight."

"Okay, bye, Grandpa."

"Hey, why do they gotta stay hidden?" Jimmy walked up to Joe, his chest puffed out.

"It's a long story….Jimmy. They just can't be seen. You're going to have to trust me. By the way, how did you guys get here? Do you have wheels?"

"Do I have wheels? We're riding in style, soldier-boy. Check out the Cadillac behind you. It needs a new windshield, but hey."

"Excellent. Nice car, Jimmy. Okay, everybody, here's the plan." Joe raised his voice. "We're all going to get in Jimmy's Cadillac, then we're going to wait here until we get the all-clear signal. It shouldn't be long now."

"Sounds okay, I guess," Peter said. "But I need to find the rest of my family. They're probably worried sick by now."

Joe interrupted. "Dr. Hawn, you'll be reunited with your family soon. I can tell you that they're all safe, and my grandfather is taking good care of them. No need to worry."

"Thank you. I believe you. Any friend of Amy's is a friend of mine."

"Listen, right now we need to take cover," Joe said. "Does everyone understand the plan?"

The group nodded their heads in agreement and turned to start walking toward Jimmy's car.

"I like your Cadillac," Josh said. "What model is it?"

"It's a brand new Seville. Just got it. It's got tinted windows and an eight-track killer stereo. You like Zeppelin?"

"I love Zeppelin. I have every record, from Led Zeppelin One up to the new one. 'Good Times, Bad Times' is my favorite song."

"Well, you're in luck tonight, my man, cause I got it on tape."

"Sounds like a fitting song for what we've been through," Peter said.

"Yeah, Doc, yeah!" Jimmy shouted. "It's been a wild ride so far. I never thought I'd be shooting a LAW rocket off in the middle of Pittsburgh! But hey, those guys had it coming. It was like kicking a real hornet's nest when we showed up. You know, pun intended."

"Sounds like we're benched for the rest of the game," Dave said to Jimmy.

"That's alright. Let 'em fight over who knows what. It's always about money, or a woman," Jimmy said.

"Hey, watch it," Amy said.

"No offense. But it's been going on since Adam and Eve," Jimmy said.

"Or Helen of Troy," Peter quipped. "A war fought over a woman, Jimmy. It destroyed a nation."

"I call shotgun!" Dave said.

"Smooth move, Dave, but we got a lot of people here, and shotgun's not going to work," Jimmy said. "Actually we can fit three up front and three in the back. The big guys go in the back. I guess that's Dave, Doc and Joe. Me, the kid and Amy sit up front. What about you, soldier?" Jimmy said, pointing to Josh.

"You guys sit tight, I'm going to take a look around, secure the perimeter. I'd hate to see the whole mission ruined by a straggler," Josh said.

"Good idea, buddy. I'll stay on the radio. Just give me a heads-up if you see anything."

"Will do. I think we're in the home stretch on this one. I bet Shafer's men were sure surprised by that rocket! I wish I could have seen the looks on their faces!"

"I like my toys, just a souvenir from time spent in East Asia," Jimmy said.

"Understatement of the year," Amy said.

"I agree. But thank heaven for crazy Jimmy!" Dave said.

"Here's to you, James!" Joe lifted his canteen to salute Jimmy.

"Only my momma calls me James, but thanks anyway, soldier-boy."

"Here's to Jimmy!" They all shouted, "Hear, hear!"

"Alright, you moolies, get in the car and shaddup, for chrissakes!" Jimmy said.

Larry picked up the radio and called, "Joe, what's your status?"

"We're sitting pretty with all the prizes, and we're sitting tight, waiting for the fireworks."

"Good, good. Tell those civilians, 'Good work.'"

"We got two ex-military here. Vietnam vets. One happened to have a LAW in his trunk. Big surprise for Shafer's chumps."

"Well, tell them good job. I don't care where they got the firepower, just thankful they were there. I've got some other fish to fry up here. Take care of our guests, and have Josh recon the perimeter. I'll give you the all-clear signal when it's over."

"Roger that."

"Good luck, Joe."

"Hey, Josh, Larry and you were thinking alike. He wants you to recon the perimeter here. Just don't be bashful if you see anything unusual. Call it in," Joe said.

"Got it. I'll keep my eyes peeled and my ears open. I'm outta here, so good night, everyone."

"Bye," Amy said. The rest of them waved and watched Josh walk off, down past the still glowing and smoldering wreckage of the white delivery truck and into the darkness beyond.

"Josh is a cool guy," Amy said. "I can see why you two are friends."

"Yeah, he's cool. If he says he's got your back, then

you can count on it. He doesn't make mistakes, and that's why he was top of our class at Ranger School."

"So the six months you spent in Europe a few years ago, that was just a ruse?" Amy asked.

"Yes, that was a cover story set up by Grandpa. I actually stayed stateside, went through basic training, A.I.T., and then on to Airborne School. That's where I met Josh. Then last year we went through a Q-course together. That's a Special Forces qualifying course. And in January, we went through Phase 1 of Special Forces training together. Grandpa wanted it all kept hush-hush, though he wouldn't tell me why. The public believes I'm just a rich playboy, and you know better than anyone that that's an easy role for me to play. I can go places that regular military can't. I suppose that makes me a valuable asset to Grandpa and the CIA. You know, I never would have met Josh if it weren't for the military, and I think we make a pretty good team."

"Thank you for coming," Amy said.

"Thank you," Peter said and shook his hand.

"Thank you, sir." Johnny shook his hand.

"Thanks, man," Dave said.

"I'm not shaking your damn hand, soldier-boy. We were doing alright before you got down here. But I guess I don't mind if you stick around for a while. Maybe I can learn something from this new military we got going on," Jimmy said.

"Sounds like you got a lot of combat experience,

Jimmy. I'm glad you were here. And you, Dr. Hawn, you were in Vietnam too, right?"

"I was, albeit just for two years, early in the war. I can shoot a rifle and a pistol okay."

"Well, thank you for your service," Joe said. "You guys made a major difference tonight. Now all we have to do is sit tight and wait it out."

"Do you know what's going on?" Amy asked.

"I do, but it's classified. I can't talk about it with anyone outside of my team. No offense, cousin."

"No, I understand. I just didn't know you were such a.... such a soldier!"

"Yeah, imagine if the rest of our family knew? Knowing them, though, they wouldn't believe it."

"You're right," Amy said. "They wouldn't."

64

Cecil Stewart watched through his Hensoldt DF 8x30 binoculars as the workmen unloaded the two Porta-Potties to the rescue site. One of the portable toilets had a piece of heavy strapping tape stretched across the door that read "Out of Order, Servicing Required." The other toilet worked just fine. Cecil thought that having two toilets delivered instead of one non-functioning one would be less suspicious. The plan seemed to be working, as one of Shafer's employees wasted no time in entering the available Porta-Potty.

Cecil watched as Larry approached the fire chief and told him the good news, a catering truck had just arrived in the upper parking lot with free gourmet food refreshments for the entire rescue crew. This was a ploy to get the innocent people away from the TBM. Cecil watched firefighters and Shafer employees alike leave and walk up the trail to the catering truck. This was the moment they'd been waiting for. Cecil saw Larry walk up to the TBM and casually drop a black backpack next to it. Larry then ran up the ridge to where Cecil was sitting. Their plan was to remotely trigger the backpack-bomb, fooling the bad guys into thinking their explosives had detonated prematurely.

Cecil looked at Larry then lifted his binoculars to scan the rescue site one last time. Cecil nodded and Larry pushed a button on a small black box he held in his hand.

The explosion was massive. The earth trembled like a California earthquake with a thundering concussion, and Cecil watched as a huge tongue of flame and a fireball rose into the Pittsburgh night sky. Trees surrounding the site were set on fire or were scattered like so many tooth-picks. Firefighters immediately started running back down the trail, scrambling to hoist their hoses over the steep terrain. Others rushed down the trail, two-by-two, carrying large red fire extinguishers, spraying the ignited forest down with fire-fighting foam. The TBM had been completely destroyed, along with all the rescuer's equip-ment and, of course, the Porta Potties.

Cecil smiled to himself at the turn of events. He'd spared innocent lives and at the same time created the perfect alibi for Charles's death. The media would predictably spin Charles Shafer into some shining martyr, and for that Cecil was strangely grateful. He thought, yes, Charles needed to be stopped, but why ruin the man's legacy in the eyes of history? Shafer Industries was a thriving company. Certainly the honest people working there shouldn't all have to pay for their namesake's greed. *History shall be again written with an opaque eye and a magician's sleight of hand*, Cecil thought.

Jimmy's Cadillac was rocked by the explosion, the car gyrating luridly on its springs like one of the kiddie rides at nearby Kennywood Amusement Park.

"Oh, my God!" Amy screamed as her head bounced off the headliner.

"Just relax, everyone. That was part of the plan. It's a long story, but I can tell you that Charles Shafer is dead," Joe said. "We should be getting the all-clear signal soon from my team leader."

"Charles Shafer was here?" Jimmy said. "THE Charles Shafer? Some say that dude's got more dough than Howard Hughes."

"He's gone to meet his maker," Joe said. "Those were his employees that you took out with that rocket."

"Those were Shafer's people? Aww, man. This is getting deep. What's going on here? How about a little explaining?"

"I'm sorry, but this is now official CIA business, and it goes all the way to the top," Joe said.

"Normally, I'd tell you to go shove it, soldier-boy. But hey, I'm gonna humor you and ride this thing out. Sounds like some kind of black-ops conspiracy! This is like 'who shot JFK.' My dad's gonna love this!"

"So what just blew up? Can you at least tell us that?" Peter said.

"Okay, I can tell you this. I was ordered to stand down while Shafer's own employees sabotaged their TBM, short for Tunnel Boring Machine. Charles Shafer brought the TBM here from North Carolina tonight to aid in your rescue. Only he wasn't ever going to begin tunneling. Follow me?" Joe said.

"I'm trying to understand this. So Shafer was the one who ordered the first explosion? I found this down in the cavern," Peter said, reaching into his pocket and removing a tiny piece of silvery metal.

"Yes, that was Shafer's attempt at permanently burying you. Whatever you found down there, he wanted to make sure you never lived to tell anybody about it. Also, the flying bugs were his, and who knows what else." Joe looked down at his rifle. "I'm sure everything that happened tonight will be classified top secret, and all of our lips will have to stay permanently sealed."

"I expected that," Peter said.

"Dad, what does 'top secret' mean?" Johnny mumbled as he leaned against Amy's arm in the front seat of the Caddie.

"It means that we'd have to make a promise to the president to never talk about what happened tonight. If we break that promise, we go to jail."

"That's pretty much it," Joe said.

"Sounds like good ol' Uncle Sam to me," Jimmy said. "He never misses a chance to stick it to you. Fortunately, I got my own uncles, and they don't take orders from nobody. Even Uncle Sam." Jimmy laughed.

"Okay, relax, everyone," Joe said. "It's early to be talking about all this. Let's wait and talk to my grandfather. He'll explain it a lot better than I can."

"I'm relaxed, soldier-boy…I'm just saying."

65

T he two men hiding in the woods watched the explosion with studied interest. That was their signal to contact Mr. Shafer over their encrypted phones— thin black devices the size of Pop-Tarts. One of the men pushed a button and waited. The phone just rang and rang. No answer.

"Something's up," said the one to the other.

"Shafer's not answering," he added.

"Well, you know the plan. We're to proceed no matter what. Is it time?"

"It's time. We're EPA, remember?"

"I know what to do."

"Let's check the Geiger counters."

"Okay, but watch the payload."

"Got it."

The two men opened the large case that they had

carried up into the woods earlier that night. Inside the large case sat two black, smaller cases, neatly sitting side-by-side, ensconced in heavy black Styrofoam. Each man removed one case and sat crouched down next to it. They looked at each other, nodded, and then simultaneously opened their respective case. Inside sat two items. The first, a Jordan Electronics Geiger counter, standard military and government-issued. The second was more exotic; designed to look like a construction worker's coffee thermos, it was actually a triple-lead-lined container made from stainless steel and forged magnesium. It could hold four ounces of liquid.

The men removed the Geiger counters and checked the batteries. Both units had a full battery charge, and they noisily clicked and popped as each man swung them over their "coffee thermos."

"Three layers of lead in there, and I'm still getting a high reading. Let's put the thermos bottles back in their cases, as the extra shielding will help."

"I know, I know. What good is two million dollars in the bank if you're too sick to enjoy it?"

"Well, I'm going to enjoy my permanent vacation after all this is over. Even if my skin starts to bubble, at least I'll be rich. Okay, it's time."

The two men went over to the large black duffel bag sitting nearby. One of them unzipped it and reached inside. "These things are heavier than they look," he said as he lifted out one of the radiation suits and let it unravel.

"Yeah, we're lucky it's cool tonight. Remember training in Arizona? Jeez!"

The two men undressed down to their underwear, then slid the radiation suits on. The suits were constructed with the boots and the suit as one piece. The only separate items were the gloves and the helmet. The helmet went on first, of course, so that they could use their unfettered hands to fasten the lock that secured it to the suit. It locked in with a loud beep. The gloves were next, and they also locked in with a beep. Then each man inspected the other's suit to see if certain tabs lined up and it was properly sealed. Finally, after dressing, they stood there in the woods looking otherworldly in their bright yellow radiation suits with "EPA" emblazoned boldly on the front and back.

"Time to go," came the muffled voice out of a small speaker in the helmet portion of the suit. "Once we get to the site, we show our credentials, then we turn on the Geigers. They'll be clicking and popping from the thermoses, and that will scare them pretty good. Then we order an evacuation, and when they're all gone, we take a 'radiation coffee break.' Seems a shame to ruin this place for the next century, though. Anyway, after that, we're out of here. We'll take the trail up to the parking lot by Beechwood Boulevard, and a van will be waiting. Got it?"

"Got it," said the other, and the two men picked up their respective briefcases and headed up the trail.

66

"It's over, alright!" Joseph shouted as he listened on his radio. "Jimmy, if you'd be so kind as to turn this car around and drive us up to Beechwood Boulevard. My grandfather and team leader are waiting for us."

"Sounds good, soldier-boy. I'm starving!"

"It's really over?" Amy said.

"Yes, it's finally over."

"What about my family?" Peter said. "Where are they?"

"They're being protected, and you will see them soon," Joe said. "That's all Grandfather told me."

"I sure hope so. We've waited long enough. I need to see them."

"I can understand that, Dr. Hawn. It won't be long now," Joe said.

"Dad, I'm so tired. I miss Mom and Darren."

"We'll see them soon, honey. Just hang on a little while longer. Close your eyes if you need to sleep."

"If Mom and Grandpa and Darren are there, can they go to the restaurant with us?"

"Sure, honey, of course. Mr. Pacela will get us all the spaghetti and ice cream we can eat. Right, Jimmy?"

"Oh yeah, kid. Don't worry. Your whole family is invited, and you're gonna love it! It won't be too long… right, soldier-boy?"

"Not too much longer. Hey, can Josh and I come along?"

"Sure, like I said, everybody's invited," Jimmy said.

"Thank you. I love Italian food!" Joe smiled.

Josh heard his radio buzz. He answered, and Larry gave him the news that the mission was over. He listened to his new orders to head due west, up to the parking lot to meet with Joe's grandfather, Larry and the others. He felt a sudden wave of relief mixed with fatigue, sweep through his body as he reached into the pocket of his combat pants. He removed the compass that Joe had given him upon their graduation from Phase 1 Special Forces training. He watched the luminescent pointer spin due north, then he turned west to walk.

Just as he was about to take his first step off the trail,

he saw something out of the peripheral vision of his right eye. Two hooded figures were slowly moving, two hundred yards away. At first Josh thought it could be a couple of kids in Halloween costumes, but then he adjusted his night-vision goggles and realized it was two men in radiation suits carrying oversized briefcases. *What the...?* he thought. Their suits had "EPA" stamped in large letters on the back. Josh let the hooded figures walk out of sight, then he got out his radio.

"Larry, come in. I got two guys in EPA suits walking due north on the trail. Each is carrying a large briefcase."

"Josh, they are not EPA. Repeat, Negatory EPA! I don't know who these jokers are, but... hold on." Joe waited. "Okay, new intel. One of our satellites just flew over and picked up two radiation signatures from inside the park, most likely your two bogeys. Immediately remove the targets, but do NOT puncture those briefcases."

"Affirmative. Remove the targets but protect the briefcases."

"Roger that."

Josh clipped the radio back on his utility belt and unslung his HK rifle. Right now he longed for his old Remington 700 heavy barrel in .308 Winchester. The added range and one-shot knockdown power of that sniper round would make this job a lot easier. Shrugging his shoulders, he inserted a fresh magazine into the HK, twenty-five rounds of 5.56 ready to go. *I'll only need two, maybe three rounds*, he thought. *Nuclear*? Josh thought. *Man, could this mission get any crazier?*

The most direct route between two points is a straight line, so Josh decided he didn't have time to sweep around and flank the two targets. No, he'd have to sneak up behind them and shoot them in the back of the head. *The chance of them hearing me approach is greater this way*, he thought, *or will their radiation suits muffle their hearing? No matter*, he thought. Larry said immediately, so it was time to take action.

Josh began stalking his targets, rifle butt on his shoulder, with the barrel pointing down. He was confident he could make the head shots from this distance, even while walking, but it would be better to close the distance.

He stripped off his utility belt, along with his .45ACP 1911 pistol and the extra magazines for the HK, and placed them gently on the ground. He muted his radio and tucked it in his pants pocket. For some reason he thought about *Batman*, the TV show, and how Adam West would look at Robin and put a finger to his lips and mouth the word "Quiet." *A soldier's utility belt is probably a lot heavier, and a lot noisier than the Caped Crusader's*, Josh thought. He resumed stalking the men, advancing rapidly but quietly. He closed the distance to his targets in a just a few minutes. Now eighty yards behind, Josh checked the wind, then dropped down on one knee. *Close enough*, he thought.

He placed the crosshair of the scope on the center of the left man's yellow hood. Josh had sighted in this particular rifle at a hundred yards, and he could place three shots inside of a quarter at that distance. He knew the first guy would go easy, but the second would have time to turn and run. He decided to send one bullet to the first guy's head, then double-tap the second target's upper torso. Since they both carried their briefcases down at arm's length, hopefully the cases would withstand the fall once he killed the men. Josh rested his finger on the trigger, took a breath, let out half, and then gently squeezed the two-pound German Match trigger.

One of the men in the radiation suits thought he heard something, and he stopped walking. As he turned to look, his partner suddenly fell to his knees, the top half of the suit's helmet torn off and along with it part of the man's skull. He screamed and started to run, taking one awkward step in the bulky suit, and then it felt like Muhammad Ali himself punched him twice in his upper back. The next impact he never felt at all as another 5.56 round from Josh's rifle entered his brain at three thousand feet per second, killing him instantly.

Josh approached the fallen men cautiously. He pulled out his pocketknife and cut a slit in each of the men's suits, near the bottom of their helmets. He reached in and placed his index and middle finger over one man's carotid artery, found no pulse, and then checked the other guy. Both dead. Josh relaxed. Grabbing the suitcases, he sat down and examined each one for bullet holes. Except for minor scratches, they looked almost new. Josh blew a sigh of relief.

J immy pulled his white Cadillac into the Frick Park parking lot from Beechwood Blvd. He saw two black limousines parked about forty feet apart. He drove closer, and the driver's door opened from the nearest car. A tall man got out, dressed in a typical chauffeur's outfit, complete with cap. He calmly walked over to Jimmy's car and stood there. Jimmy lowered his window, and the tall man leaned down to speak.

"Mr. Stewart would like all of you to join him. Please follow me. Oh, hello, Amy, good to see you, babe." The tall man winked, turned and walked away.

"Tom Daley," Amy hissed. "What a bastard. He works for my grandfather. He's been perving on me my entire life, and I've had enough."

"That guy bothering you?" Jimmy said. "Let me handle it."

The five of them got out of the Cadillac and headed over to Cecil Stewart's limousine. Tom Daley stood erect, holding the door open as each of them got into the car. Four got in, but Jimmy hesitated in front of the tall chauffeur.

Jimmy turned and spoke, "Hey, Tom, I'd appreciate it if you'd leave my friend Amy alone. I mean forever. *Capisce*?"

"Who do you think you—" Tom started to say before Jimmy's right fist slammed into his jaw. The chauffeur's eyes rolled up into his head, and he fell face-first on the asphalt.

"Yeah, I thought you'd see it my way. You really should learn to listen better," Jimmy said as he got in the car.

"My, Amy, your friend has quite a temper," Cecil said. "I suppose Tom had it coming to him, as some of us have to learn the hard way. I suppose my old friend Charles did as well. Listen, I'm so relieved that all of you are okay! You were all so very brave. Mr. Rondinelli, your family has been notified that you are safe. Dr. Hawn, your son Darren and your father are in that car over there, waiting to see you."

Peter looked out the limousine window and watched as Lou and Darren exited the other limousine.

"We'll be right back!" Peter shouted. "C'mon, Johnny," he said as he grabbed his son's hand. Peter and Johnny jumped out of the car and ran across the parking lot, pulling Lou and Darren into a giant huddle of a family hug. They all stood arm in arm, laughing, and then crying, then hugging again. Afterward, they walked back, holding hands, to Cecil's car.

"Thank you, Mr. Stewart. Thank you," Peter said, leaning into the open door on Cecil's limousine.

"Yes, thank you again, Mr. Stewart," Lou chimed in.

"My pleasure, Mr. Garvey. Dr. Hawn, your wife had a minor mishap, but she will be fine. She is in stable condition and is receiving the finest medical care at Mercy Hospital." Cecil leaned in close to Peter's ear and whispered, "Your wife swallowed some pills, but she is stable. Rest assured, she has the finest doctors looking after her. I've made sure of it."

"I can't tell you how much I appreciate that, Mr. Stewart. Thank you, thank you."

"Think nothing of it, Dr. Hawn. Joseph will drive you to the hospital after our meeting."

"Thank you one more time," Peter said.

"We're going to see Mom!" Johnny said to Darren.

"Yeah!" Darren shouted.

"I'm so glad your family is okay," Amy said. Peter and Amy's eyes met.

"Thanks, Amy. Thanks for everything."

"Listen, we've much to discuss and not much time to do it," Cecil said. "With the exception of Joseph here, and your Italian boxer friend, you four experienced what my friends and I once deemed, 'The Pulpit'."

"Grandpa, you know about The Machine?" Amy said.

"Yes, I do. Once, there were three very young and ambitious men, the closest of friends, who went through high school prep, and then through Harvard together. After college, they decided to go into business for themselves. You have to remember that this was in the year 1913, some would say the height of the Industrial Revolution, and opportunities abounded here in Pittsburgh. These young men—myself, Charles Shafer and Bill Nollem— bought controlling interests in steel mills and coal mines throughout the area. From Republic to Ambridge to McKeesport, we invested and reinvested our money into Pittsburgh. Along with the likes of Andrew Carnegie and the park's namesake, Henry Frick, we became quite wealthy from our investments.

"The general details of our lives have been recorded in the history books, but it's an incomplete history. For one day, Charles discovered something paradoxically wonderful and terrible in an exploratory coal tunnel under East Pittsburgh. He shared his secret with his two friends, and we named it The Pulpit. This mysterious machine soon became the sole focus of our lives. We hired scientists to perform tests on it, to tell us what it was. Their conclusions were banal. They concluded The Pulpit's symbols resembled the Sumerian alphabet, and that the obelisk was composed of an unearthly element. Beyond that, they were as mystified as we were. Soon, my friends and I began to have strange narcoleptic episodes, complete with fantastic dreams of the future, and other unusual physiological effects. I gather the four of you know what I speak of?" Cecil pointed to Peter and the others.

"The things we experienced were so disturbing, that eventually, we decided to destroy it. Well, we tried to anyway. We tried to burn it, cut it, move it, and nothing! The Pulpit resisted those efforts. Then we tried to blow it up! A crate of nitroglycerin, and still it stood there, glowing in its subterranean grotto. We learned that it couldn't be destroyed, not by us anyway. So we decided that if we couldn't destroy it, we'd bury it forever—to protect mankind from its devastating powers. We succeeded in sealing off the mine tunnel to the chamber, and I truly believed that was the end of it. My friends and I made a gentlemen's agreement to leave The Pulpit alone. Forever. Bill Nollem took that agreement to his grave, but Charles broke his word and proved to be my Judas."

"My dad says a man's word is the only thing he's got," Johnny said.

"Your father is wise, young man. But greed is a powerful persuader, and Charles's greed knew few bounds. When you boys went digging in Frick Park yesterday, you stumbled upon his secret access tunnel to The Pulpit."

"We were just looking for fossils, Mr. Stewart."

"It's okay, son, you didn't do anything wrong. Everything is fine now."

"That's an incredible story," Peter said.

"It's a true story, Dr. Hawn. And now, all of you are a part of it. Listen, I know you are all exhausted, starving and missing your loved ones, and here I am boring you with ancient history. I want all of you to first visit Mercy Hospital, so Dr. Hawn and his sons can see their beloved Laura. After that, why not visit your new friend's restaurant here, and get some much-needed food and refreshments?

"How do you know about my place?" Jimmy said.

"I have my sources Mr. Pacela. Anyway, please take Joseph and Josh along with you, just in case. I will stay here with Mr. Siebert, as we have a few details to clean up. After you eat, you'll return to the park, and I have it arranged that the four of you will be 'discovered' by the fire department and the other rescuers. Did you know that there is a secret underground river that flows beneath Frick Park?"

"No, I wasn't aware of that, but there was a small stream in the room with The Machine," Peter said.

"That stream runs into an underground river. Oh, yes, Charles and I discovered it years ago. Pittsburgh's fourth river! Sometime around sunrise, the press will learn that you escaped from the 'coal mine' into the underground river, devised a raft, and simply floated yourselves right out from under the park and into the Monongahela. I came up with that myself!" Cecil laughed. "The Pulpit will remain our shared secret, at least for the time being, and that order comes directly from the White House."

The car door opened, and Larry and Josh appeared, their faces a ghostly white.

"Excuse the interruption, sir," Larry said, out of breath. "There's something you should see. Sir, Mr. Shafer had one more trick up his sleeve, but we got lucky. Josh intercepted two more of Shafer's men, carrying two of these." Larry Siebert lifted up a blocky, black briefcase.

"I assume it's nuclear?" Cecil said.

"Nuclear!" Peter said.

"Nukes!" Jimmy yelled.

"Not nuclear bombs, Mr. Pacela, but instead liquid nuclear waste," Larry said. "The effects would have been just as devastating in the long run. I believe Shafer's plan involved spreading toxic transuranic plutonium waste over the rescue area. These imposter EPA workers would have contaminated the site, and then the entire park would've been quarantined. Shafer's goal was to make Frick Park uninhabitable, thus keeping his secret safe."

"Plutonium has a half-life of eighty-eight years," Peter said. "He was willing to ruin Frick Park for generations, just to hide The Machine?"

"Not only that, Dr. Hawn, but Charles was willing to sacrifice the four of you in the process," Cecil said.

"Shafer sounds like a real piece of work. Let me get my hands on him!" Jimmy said.

"No need for that, Mr. Pacela," Larry said. "Charles

Shafer has already met his demise. My men will take it from here."

"Good, 'cause Shafer was...rotten. Hey, I'm holding back the language because of the kid here," Jimmy said, smiling and pointing to Johnny.

"I'm twelve years old. I'm not a little kid, you know."

"When I was twelve, I was running numbers..."

"Everyone relax. We have the briefcases, and posthumously, Charles has been completely defeated. All of you are safe, and the park is safe. What more could we ask for? Joseph, will you do the honors of driving my limousine? Mr. Daley is...still sleeping off the effects of Mr. Pacela's artful right cross."

"Of course, Grandpa," Joe said, opening the driver's door.

"Drop Larry and me at the lower parking lot, please," Cecil said.

"I love you, Grandpa!" Amy said.

"I love you too, child. I want to say a special 'thank you,' to all of you who were so very brave tonight. Mr. Rondinelli, perhaps you would consider working for me instead of the parks department? I'm sure there's a place for you in my company."

"Yeah, thank you, sir. That's very generous. After today, I think I'm ready for a change of scenery."

"Excellent." Cecil smiled. "And Dr. Hawn, your brilliant mind saved everyone tonight. Without you, we wouldn't be here together. I'm impressed by your perseverance, your intelligence, and the fact that my grand-daughter thinks so highly of you. I would enjoy a chat with you about your future plans and about making a substantial donation to your program at Charles Masters University. We could meet for lunch at my house in Fox Chapel, say, in a few days?"

"That sounds...wonderful, Mr. Stewart. Thank you!"

"You're welcome, Peter. Call me Cecil."

THE END

ABOUT THE AUTHOR

Jon Klein is an emerging author of fiction thrillers. Jon is also a professional guitarist, songwriter, former radio reporter, business owner and motorcycle racer. Jon graduated from The University of Arizona and The Musicians Institute, and attended Berklee College of Music in Boston. Jon lives in Idaho with his son Conner, girlfriend Lisa, and dog Smokey.